G.A.B.O.S

G.A.B.O.S

Game Ain't Based on Sympathy

Tyler Gore

Library of Congress Control Number:		2013908790
ISBN:	Hardcover	978-1-4836-4095-2
	Softcover	978-1-4836-4094-5
	Ebook	978-1-4836-4096-9

This book was printed in the United States of America.

Rev. date: 05/13/2013

To order additional copies of this book, contact:
Xlibris Corporation
1-888-795-4274
www.Xlibris.com
Orders@Xlibris.com
132309

Contents

Part 1

ACKNOWLEDGMENTS

FIRST AND FOREMOST, I gotta give the one up above all the glory. First for bringing a long-lost friend by the name of Sterling Haywood back into my corner just when I was on the brink of losing all hope. He told me with God anything is possible. And that's what led me to write this book. Even though I had no idea where to begin. But the real inspiration for me sticking it out, even when I felt I had no business even trying to write a book, was my two beautiful daughters Tykia. S. A. Gore and Tazzaria J. Gore, My oldest, (Tykida) it's been a long time since I held you in my arms. The last time, but not the final, was August 11,1999. Now it's 2012, but I still remember it like it was yesterday, and, Princess, I love you more than you'll ever know. You're the reason I'm still striving to do better. My baby girl, whom I call bad to the bone. (Tazzaria) Even though I never got the chance to hold you. Just know the time is coming. It's just around the corner, and believe me, we'll travel the world together if you want to. Baby girl, you'll always be my little princess, and I thank you 'cause you always showed your love for me over the phone. And that alone helped me in so many ways. I just want you to know I love you, and no matter how old you get you'll still be my little princess!

No, Shakia, I didn't forget about you. You're the mother of my two beautiful daughters. Without you, I woulda never known real love. I just want you to know, I give you a 110% salute. 'Cause even in my absence, you did what you had to do as a woman and took care of our babies on your own. And I already know times weren't always easy, but you did your thing, and I'm proud of you. And I'll always love you! Rosa Walls, my mother, every woman could learn from you what a real queen is made of. You did this time with me, day for day, minute for minute, and hour for hour, tear for tear, worry for worry; now it's almost over. And I want you to know, if I could choose another mother in this world, it would still be you. Your love is real, and I love you. And I just hope I'm doing something that will make you proud! Last but not the least, I gotta thank my three sisters. First my oldest, Tiffany R. Gore. TP, I really don't know how you do it, but you always manage to find time for me and all you do for me. I could never repay you. Not even in a million years! You have walked in my shoes. You did 7 years, and with the letters we wrote each other while locked up. I just want to say thank you, 'cause every promise you made you kept, and there's so much more I could say, but you know how little bro feels about ya! Just keep doing your thing, and hopefully one day soon, we'll make it rain! Tia and Renee Gore, I just want y'all to know, I love y'all, even though y'all caught up in the world doing y'all own thing. I respect the fact y'all still send and show love, and that's a plus in my book. Before I bring this to a close, I gotta give all my nieces a shout-out. Trirena Anderson, my oldest and wisest niece, keep up the good work, and don't forget the things we talked about. Go to college and become that lawyer. You said you're gonna be! Tashamah, Blessing, and Bre, I love y'all and hope this book touches ya lives to never make the mistakes I made. Love those who love you my two nephews, Zell and Chris. When I come home, y'all gonna hang with me. So I can teach y'all the do's and dont's of life. To all the people who just gave up on me and left me for dead – no letters, no pictures – it's all good. That's what haters do. So I ain't mad, 'cause now I know and understand the meaning of GABOS. So holla when you C-ME.

GABOS

PROLOGUE

"DAMN, IT'S BEEN a long time coming. But it's finally here," Pokey said to no one in particular, as the day arrived for him to be released from the prison that held him hostage against his own will for the last eighteen months, day by day, as he walked out the open gates. He was blinded by the bright sun. Reaching up to cover his eyes, he heard a horn blowing. Looking around for the sound of the horn, he spotted his mother's beat-up Honda. As he watched his mother get out of the car and slowly walk toward him, Pokey had one thing in mind. "Man, I gotta make sum Major Doe," he was thinking, as his mother reached out and gave him a hug. "Thanks, Mom. Glad I didn't have to ride that stank-ass bus all the way home," he told his mother, who just smiled as she turned around and made her way back to the car, with Pokey on her heels.

"I don't know what you coming on this side for," his mother said, pushing him over to the driver's side. "You driving," she said. "I gotta get some beauty sleep," she said, sliding in the car.

On the ride home, it was quiet, with Pokey in his own thoughts. As he was listening to his mother snore lightly, he promised, "Momma, I'mma make shit happen." Being in prison, Pokey learned a lot, but he also learned that if you want something bad enough, you gotta go get it. With that in mind and the words Old School used to tell him all the time. "Young blood, you gotta be ruthless in the game of life. Sometimes you will be forced to bite the hands that feed you, so always keep in mind game ain't based on sympathy. If a motherfucker wanna get in your way, don't hesitate to roll over them, and leave them where they lay." As he was in deep thought, his mother brought him back to the here and now.

"So, boy, now that you free, what you gonna do to stay free?" his mother asked, turning in her seat to face him.

"Whatever I gotta do," Pokey said, keeping it real.

"So you gonna get a job?" his mother asked.

"Never, Mom. You know me. I ain't working no nine-to-five for no minimum wage so that working shit is dead," he said. While driving, as he looked out the corner of his eye, he saw his mother shake her head, as she closed her eyes and stopped talking. But he went back to thinking. "Damn shit crazy, when ya own momma trying to keep you down, she on some 'get a job' shit, but I'mma live and die in the streets." As he pulled up in the projects, where they stayed, he noticed nothing has changed, but changes were about to take place, if he had something to do with it. "My thing is, to be paid and get my game sharper than a motherfucking razor blade."

As he pulled up and parked, he said, "Ma, we here." Waking up, all his mother did was look at him, then exit the car. As Pokey watched his mother enter the house, he said, "This the shit I'm talking about, a nigga been gone eighteen months, leave with nothing and come home with nothing, so it's time I make something." Looking around, shaking his head at all the dirty buildings that held this project together, his last thought was, "Now I gotta get some soldiers on my team and make this picture come to life," as he looked around one more time before walking into the house. He mumbled, "GABOS, this time around, that's how it's gonna be. Niggaz showed no love, they receive none." With that being said, he walked into the house ready to take a nice long shower before he could formulate his next move, not forgetting his next move better be his best move 'cause GABOS.

CHAPTER 1

Born into a Sinful World

BEING BORN THE only boy in a home, 'cause you couldn't call the projects a house, with a mother and three sisters, who never knew the crown would fall on me to become a man so early in life. All fingers were pointed in my direction, at least that's what I thought, to be the provider for the family. The wannabe baller, the shot caller. So with no real father or father figure around to give me guidance, I guess the streets were the next best thing to teaching a boy how to be a man. Though my momma tried to raise me, I still lacked a real man to teach me how to be a man. So I felt I had to provide for my mother and three sisters any way I could. My mother couldn't find a job, so we always fell on hard times. Even though she tried, she never succeeded in doing so. I can't say we were poor 'cause we always had enough to eat, mainly thanks to the government and the food stamps they gave out every month. So food wasn't a problem. So here I am.

One Saturday morning, walking around the projects, trying to get into something that will make time go by. When outta nowhere, I hear, "Psst, psst, lil nigga, check this out." I hear a voice but see no face. "Psst, damn, lil nigga. You deaf or something?" As I turn around in the direction of where the voice is coming from, I see a kid 'bout my size, my height, and age. Walking toward me with a mean mug on his face. Me being the cautious lil kid I am, I said, "What's up," with my hands balled into two tiny fists, ready for this strange kid to say something sideways, only to hear him laughing.

"Damn, lil nigga, what you got your fists balled up for? I ain't gonna mess with you, I just came to say what's up, 'cause you look like a new face that's lost in the wrong projects," the kid said, looking me up and down first off. I start getting defensive.

"My name ain't lil nigga, it's Fatboy. Or you can call me Fats for short. Other than that, keep in mind it's not lil nigga."

"All right, damn. My bad, calm down. I got you. I'll call you Fatboy or Fats, but why you got a name like that is besides me, 'cause you skinny as a pole."

"Look, man, what is it you want?" Fatboy said, getting aggravated.

"Look, Fatboy, my name is Pokey," he said, giving me a some dap. I been seeing you walk around the projects all morning, like you done lost ya best friend," Pokey said, laughing again.

"Yeah, and we all know looks can be deceiving. But I'm good, I'm a long ways from being lost. I'm just checking things out, if that's cool with you, Mr. Officer," Fatboy said, now the one laughing as Pokey's smiles turned upside down. "Pokey, or whatever your name is, how come I been living here over a year now and I never seen you before? Answer that."

"Oh, Your Honor, I went away on a trip, and I didn't go to Hawaii either," Pokey said, laughing again.

"Okay, where you went then?"

"Damn, fam, you ask a million and one questions. Who you is, Alex Trabek or somebody? I was locked up."

"Yeah, and I can fly a plane with my eyes close, 'cause you too young to be locked up, so I know you lying," Fatboy responds.

"Man, I wish I was, but you can do me a favor and tell them crackers in them courthouses uptown I'm too young to be getting locked up," Pokey said, laughing.

"Real shit, why them crackers locked you up?" Fatboy asked.

"Oh, on some real petty shit," Poker said,

"Like what, man?"

"I tried to rob a store and got caught up," Pokey said, while looking down at the ground.

"How much time you did?"

"The first time six months in Leon County Boot Camp. This time I did eighteen months, damn near day for day. So that's why you never seen me round here, but I've been here all my life, stuck in the projects, trying to live better, but the white man won't let me. So I gotta do what I gotta do, to make ends meet. I also just came home and ain't trying to go back up the road no time soon, feel me?"

"I feel you, dog."

"Hey, Fatboy."

"Yeah, what's up?"

"I need someone on my team who can think better than I can, and I know you just met me, but you talk like you can think," Pokey said.

Just as I was about to reply, another young nigga I've seen around the projects and go to school with runs up to Pokey and gives him a hug.

"Damn, nigga, it's been a minute," Flick said.

"Yeah, dog, but now the wait is over. And this time, I promise you, shit gonna be a whole lot different. Ain't no mo' fucking off," Pokey said, giving Flick some dap, taking a step back to check his longtime friend out. "And the way you dressed, my nigga, I can tell you need the money," Pokey said, smiling.

"Man, fuck that. I'mma be good in a minute. Nigga, just wait and see," Flick said, getting angry that his own friend tried to clown him in front of this nobody nigga, with his curly-ass hair, Flick was thinking. "Anyway, nigga, when you came home, 'cause I thought you wrote and said you should be home in four months. That was six months ago," Flick said.

"Yeah, dirty. I was acting a ape in that bitch. So them crackers maxed my ass out, day for day. But fuck all that, I'm here now, and I'm ready to get this shit started," Pokey said. "I came home this morning though, 'bout two hours now," Pokey said, watching Flick look at Fatboy like they had beef or some shit.

"Nigga, what the fuck you looking at me for?" Fatboy said. "Do I look like a bitch to you, nigga?" Fatboy said, stepping into Flick's chest.

"First off, nigga, fuck you 'cause a nigga ain't watching you," Flick said, mean mugging, taking a step back, just in case this nigga wanna act stupid. As Pokey watched Flick and Fatboy about to tear shit up, his plan came into mind.

"I can use these two niggas on my team. If I can get them to be friends." Pokey was deep in thought, and a smile spread across his face. "We gonna set this bitch on fire," Pokey was thinking, when he heard a familiar voice boom throughout the projects.

"Flick, Flick! Boy, I know you hear me calling you. Bring your ass here right now, and come clean this damn room."

"Damn, nigga, you lucky," Flick said, yeasting Fatboy.

"Nigga, what you wanna do?" Fatboy said, yeasting back.

"Man, y'all chill with that guy shit!" Pokey screamed, getting tired of the back-and-forth bullshit.

"Look, Pokey, I'mma holla at you later. I gotta burn up. You know how my momma be clowning and shit. She already thinking she Bruce Lee," Flick said, as all three boys bust out laughing.

"All right, dirty, go do you and tell Mrs. Brown I said hello," Pokey said, watching Flick about to haul ass.

"Hey, Flick, before you go, this my new friend, Fatboy."

"Dog, I know who this nigga is," Flick said. "We go to school together. And can't you see we stay in the same rat-infested projects," Flick said with an attitude.

"Check me out, Flick."

"What y'all beefing or something?" Pokey asked. "'Cause if y'all is, y'all need to go 'head and bump and squash that shit 'cause we got money to make. And if y'all wanna act like lil bitches, I'll find some real niggaz who will roll with me," Pokey said, looking back and forth at both boys.

Then Fatboy said, "Man, I don't beef, unless I need to. This nigga just thinks he better than everybody else, like he ain't living in the same bricks as me. Like his family rich or some shit. Fuck that, nigga," Fatboy said.

As Flick was about to respond, Pokey cut him off. "Fatboy, my nigga, I just met you. And I'mma be honest with you. You tripping. This lil nigga right here is a soldier. Ready for war at any given time. It's good the nigga smart and shit, 'cause at the same time, what would you rather have on your team, a dumb soldier or a smart soldier?"

"Shit, easy answer, a smart soldier to go to war with, a dumb soldier to take the first bullet," Fatboy said and smiled.

"Okay then, you on point," Pokey said.

Then Flick cut in. "And I don't think I'm smarter than nobody. I just try to do better. If that's a crime, send me to the chair," Flick said.

"Real talk, Fatboy, Flick is one of the realest young nigga you'll ever meet, but you'll learn that with time. Anyways, nigga, I know you ain't that lame. You should know, never judge a book by its cover."

"All right, man."

"Damn, one more thing, in order for shit that I have planned to work, we all gotta get on the same page. Y'all feeling me?"

"Yeah," both boys said simultaneously.

"'Cause we gonna try and take over these streets. Piece by piece," Pokey said.

Flick broke into his wishful thinking. "Dog, look, I gotta run. I already told you. When I enter the crib, I know I gotta be ducking karate kicks and shit," Flick said, jogging off.

Pokey screamed, "Hey, Flick!"

"Yeah, man, what's up?"

"Damn! When you done doing, you meet us at the park. You know shit jumping, or should be since it Saturday, all right? Whatever."

Flick said, "Burner rubber."

"Come on, lil nigga. I mean Fatboy, let's roll. Hold up, check this out. How you just gonna volunteer me to be down with y'all?"

"Dog, I ain't taking orders from you or nobody else," Fatboy said.

"Dog, chill out. Either you wanna make this money with us, or go against us, and get ranned over, your choice, if you just listen. I bet you won't regret this decision. Hardheaded-ass nigga, ain't you tired of struggling?" Pokey asked.

"Hell yeah," Fatboy said.

"Then ride with us, and let's make this cheddar!" Pokey said.

"Well, in that case, count me in," Fatboy said, extending his hand for some dap.

"Listen," Pokey said. "Dog, you sure you gonna be ready for all this?"

"Man, I'm ready for anything at any given time," Fatboy responded.

"In that case, let burn up."

As they began their walk through the projects, they saw lil kids playing around, doing backflips on a used mattress, just making the most outta the shit they had. The older people were either staring off into space, wishing for better days, or just chilling, listening to some Marvin Gaye. Every now and then you heard some other old-school beats. But mostly you could count on it being Marvin Gaye. Pokey came out of his zone when he heard Tupac screaming from someone's ride.

"Damn, that shit clean," Fatboy said. "Dog, who dat?"

"Shit, from the looks of it, it look like my uncle Sico crazy ass. As a matter fact, that is him, 'cause there go his baby momma, dumping in the ride. Anywayz, like I said, that's my uncle. The nigga told me, before I got locked up, he was gonna put me on my feet, but I had to wait till my sixteenth birthday, so shit. As you can see, that time ain't come yet! And at the same time, I ain't asking for no handouts. So I'mma always make away, outta no way, feel me?" Pokey said.

"I feel you, dog," Fatboy replied, while looking back over his shoulder at the nice whip.

"Anyways, I got seven more months till I turn sixteen. What, the nigga expect me to want and just starve to death? Yeah right," Pokey said, patting his pockets empty but not for long. Pokey said, "'Cause at the same time I'm trying to get up, out the projects."

"I'm feeling that. 'Cause I ain't trying to be staying in these small-ass buildings all my life either. These shits too small for me, my momma and three sisters to be resting our head," Fatboy said. "My goal is to get my family out the hood. Even if I die trying."

"Now you talking," hollered Pokey.

"What's up, though? We been walking like twenty minutes now, and, nigga, it's hotter than a bitch out here, and we still ain't made it nowhere," Fatboy said, wiping sweat from his face.

"Chill, we almost there," Pokey said.

"Almost there. Man, a nigga 'bout to pass out, and all you screaming is we almost there. What we trying to do, walk to the end of the world?" Fatboy said, smiling.

"While looking up at the sun, just be patient, 'cause when we get to where we going, and you see all the finer things in life we can have, you won't be complaining," Pokey said, with a serious look on his face. "We almost there, though."

About ten more minutes of walking, the niggas started smelling BBQ and all types of other shit black people were cooking.

"Damn, that shit smell good. It's been eighteen months since a nigga had some real food," Pokey said, rubbing his stomach.

"Where we going though? 'Cause to me, it smell like we going to a cookout 'n' all, dog."

"We headed to the park. Before I left to do that lil time, this shit used to be jumping on Saturdays and Sundays, where all the ballers and major dope dealers hang out and show out. You ever heard the saying show up and show out? Well, if not, you'll soon see what I mean."

"So what brings us here?" Fatboy asked. "'Cause we broker than a motherfucker," he said laughing.

"Yeah, we is light now, but I promise we won't be for long," Pokey said. "Look," pulling his shirt up to reveal an all-black 8 mm. "Listen, lil dog. The way to make money is to be around those who got money. It's a few things you gotta learn in this game we about to jump in. If a nigga don't wanna help you make money, number one it's because he don't owe you shit. So number two, sit back and come up with a scheme and just take his shit."

"Easy work, if you got a plan, but that's how the business goes."

Pokey replied, "Dirty, you crazy as fuck."

"But I'm 'bout that shit," Fatboy said.

"We here, dog," Pokey said, tapping Fatboy on the shoulder. As Fatboy looks up, he sees fine-ass bitches everywhere, dressed in tight skirts or barely nothing at all.

"Damn, this shit got a nigga wanna some pussy, badder than a motherfucker," Pokey said, looking over at all the shit that was going on. As he was about to say something else, they hear a female screaming.

"Pokey, hey! Pokey, come 'ere," this red chick screams, while signaling us to come over with her finger.

"Damn, what she want," Pokey said. "Come on, dog." And the two friends walk over to this chick.

She starts screaming, "What you doing here, and when you came home?"

"Look, Kecia, I came home this morning, but why you so concern now? You ain't write a nigga or send a nigga one cent, so why be worried now?"

"For one I asked 'cause ain't nothing but grown-up here, that's why. Your lil ass should be somewhere playing with some toys or something," Kecia said, showing she was angry.

"Kecia, fuck you and that bullshit you talking. The same reason you here, me and my lil homie here."

"Ain't that right, dirty."

"Hell yeah," both boys said at the same time. "To make some money, baby!"

"Boy, look, with your ugly self, I just ask you a question."

"And I gave you an answer. So what's the problem?"

"Ooh!" Kecia screamed and started to walk off.

But before she could, Pokey said, "The truth hurts, doesn't it?" Sticking his middle finger up, and Kecia turned back around and stormed off.

"Damn, dog. Who was that you snapped on?" Fatboy asked.

"Oh, that's my sister. She be acting like she be so worried 'bout a nigga when they home. But when a nigga doing time, it's a different story. Look, the bitch ain't even tell me she was glad I made it home safe."

"Dog, ya sister fine as fuck, looking like Halle Berry. She should be a model," Fatboy said.

"That's what everybody says. But she love being a hoe. So fuck it. It is what it is," Pokey said. "Come on, dog."

Just as we were about to walk off, we see Flick coming through, breathing hard, and shit, like he was running from Popo or somebody.

"What's up y'all?" Flick screams.

While holding his chest, "Nigga, what's up? You okay?" Pokey asked.

"Yeah, yeah, I'm cool. I just ran all the way here. Trying to get ready for the track meet next month, that's all!"

"Shit, for a minute, we thought Jason was chasing your ass with his machete or something," Pokey said. And all three boys start to laugh.

"All right now that you here, let's handle business," Pokey says, as they start walking round the park. They are in a trance state of mind. Walking 'round, looking at all these bad bitches, nice-ass whips, and all this money being thrown in the air by niggas betting on the crap games, basketball games, and whatever else there is to make a dollar out of! One thing in particular though that caught all their attention was the two twin Mercedes sitting on dubs with three of the baddest hitches a nigga will ever lay eyes on.

"Damn, these niggas balling," Fatboy said.

"I told you, dog. You would see what I was talking about. I had to let you see for yourself the things we can have if we play our cards right," Pokey said. "Listen, it's only a matter of time before we be riding around flossing and shit," Pokey said. "It's just a matter of time. Y'all, listen, when I was doing them eighteen months, an old-school cat name Tony Black said in order to do it big, you gotta do big thing, and in order to do all that, you gotta be around the niggas whose already doing it big and decipher all the game you can and learn from there mistakes. And once we are strong enough, we can knock him out the boy and sit on the throne," Pokey said, smiling at the remembrance of the game TB gave him. Now him to his friends. "Look, like I said, I been gone a minute, and in that time I know a lotta shit, done changed 'round this bitch. Once I get back in tune, to who's who and who's doing what, that's when my plan will come into affect. Until then we just gonna scope shit out, 'cause I just got out, and I can't let these crackers catch me slipping like before behind some petty, chump change. 'Cause I already know next go round, these crackers gonna be playing for keeps. They already got more niggas locked down than a bitch can count," Pokey said, thinking of the time he spent behind them razor-wire fences. Interrupting him from his train of thought was Flick speaking out.

"Dog, you act like you just did a million and one years," Flick said, laughing. But Pokey didn't see the humor in the lil jokes. "Besides, dog, I kept you up-to-date about everything containing to the streets. Every time I wrote you a letter," Flick said.

"Yeah, you did that. You held a nigga down, but like I said, a lot of shit can change without you even knowing it," Pokey said. "The streets gonna only talk so much, that's why I ask you to keep ya ears on the streets at all time. But you couldn't, and lil dog, I ain't mad at cha, 'cause now I'm home, and I'mma run these streets before long." Pokey said. "Anyway, Flick, who that is?"

"Who?" Flick asked, looking around.

"Over there, the nigga who just pulled up, in the all-black Rolls-Royce, with the gold grill on."

"That's, that's – shit, I don't know," Flick said in defeat.

"That's what I thought," Pokey said, playfully slapping Flick up side the head.

"Shit, I can't know every damn baby," Flick said, laughing.

"It don't matter though, 'cause one way or the other I'mma find out," Pokey said, walking off then stopping and turning around. "Y'all coming or what," Pokey said.

"Oh yeah, dog, we coming," his two friends said, falling in step.

About three minutes of looking around, Fatboy said, "Damn, nigga, who we looking for?"

"Just chill, I know he 'round here somewhere. That nigga always be here. Ever since I can remember," Pokey said to himself, but at the same time scanning his surrounding, looking for this particular person.

"Oh, nigga. You must be looking for Double D basing ass," Flick said.

"You know it," Pokey said, looking back at Flick.

"Look," Flick said, pointing in front of them, "here he comes now."

"What this nigga riding?" Pokey asked, busting out laughing.

Fatboy said, "A motherfucking pink Beach Cruiser with a plasma screen TV on the handle bars. This nigga gotta be tripping," Fatboy mumbled under his breath, as they all watched.

Double D rolls up to the nigga in the Rolls-Royce and jumps off his bike with TV in hand and asks the nigga do he wanna buy it. At first the nigga was looking all crazy, then a smile slowly appears on his face, when Double D starts shaking.

"Man, you wanna buy this brand-new heavy-ass TV or what?" Double D asked, looking around for another potential buyer, just in case this fool didn't want the TV.

"Nigga, what you trying to get for that shit?" Mr. Big, a.k.a. Sterling, asked.

"Oh, not too much. Just give me five dimes and three hundred dollars in cash," Double D said, showing a mouth full of rotten teeth, "That's chump change to you," Double D said, stroking Mr. Big's ego to get what he wants. To Double D's surprise, Mr. Big just turned around and started vibing on his cell phone, like Double D didn't just ask him a question.

"Oh well," Double D said. "Fuck you too, nigga," Double D mumbled under his breath, as he scooped up the TV from off the ground, as he was placing the TV back on his handle bars. He felt a tap on his shoulder. Scared to turn around thinking it was Mr. Big, he said what's up, without turning around. At the sound of a female's voice, Double D turned around, to be standing in front of one of the finest females he ever saw, with his mouth hanging open. Double D looked this sexy red bitch up and down, and as he was about to say something, she cut him off.

"Nigga, you trying to sell this TV or what?" the chick said.

"Oh yeah, yeah," Double D stuttered.

"Well, here you go. Five dimes and three hundred. Petty-ass dollars," she said, throwing the money at him.

"Damn, it's like that?" Double asked.

"Just like that," she said and put the TV over there by the car. "We'll handle it from there," she said.

"All right, no problem," Double D said, carrying the TV over to the car. With a big-ass ole smile on his face, turning and heading back toward his bike. Double D said, "All in a day's work." Pokey watched Double D hop on his bike.

He said, "Damn, I need to holla at that nigga, but I already know it's gonna be hard to catch that nigga, now that he got him something to smoke." Just when Pokey was about to say fuck it and turn around, Double D yells out, "Young blood, young blood, what's up? I see you don't let them crackers lock your ass up again, and this time, you was gone, what five years?"

"Hell naw, I ain't do no five years, nigga," Pokey said.

"Well, it seems like it to me," Double D says. "Boy, I done told your ass. You ain't got but one life to live. If you trying to spend it behind bars, keep fucking with them crackers shit, your ass gonna catch a zillion years."

"Man, basing-ass nigga, how you gonna tell me something, and your ass done been to prison, what, seven times," Pokey said.

"Yeah, and I ain't did no more than three years all seven times either. 'Cause I don't rob and all that dumb shit. Y'all young niggas do, that will get you a life sentence. I do the petty stuff, that's why I'm out now."

"All right, nigga, damn. I hear you. You preaching to a nigga like you all high and mighty," Pokey said.

"Boy, I'm just trying to tell you, life is a gift. So you better watch how you use it. 'Cause these crackers don't mind taking it away from you." Even though Pokey was tired of hearing Double D preach to him, he knew if he fucked up, those same words would one day haunt him, so he kept in mind, "This time I gotta get shit right."

He was thinking, when he heard Fatboy say, "Yo, Double D, if life is so good and one to be treasured, why you keep tearing your temple down smoking that shit," Fatboy said, watching his new friends laugh, but really wanted to know the answer.

"Look, lil nigga, for one you don't know what you talking about. I see them crackers got you believing the Holy Bible too," Double D said, laughing, at the same time reaching in his pocket and pulling out the crack. "Young blood, for your information, this right here, is what keeps me in heaven all-day long."

"Yeah, and I bet your basing-ass go through hell to get it too," Flick said, as they all laughed, including Double D who started looking all stupid, when he heard someone say, "Nigga, you gonna always be a baser."

Looking at Fatboy like he said it, Double D snaps, "Lil young-ass nigga, you can call me baser, crackhead, old junky, smoker, whatever you want. But I bet you can't call me broke!" Double D yells and pulls out the money he made for the TV and pushes the money in each boyz's faces and says, "Smell them dead bodies. I bet these motherfucker don't stank in ya pockets now!" Double D says, sticking out his tongue, "How you like that, call me baser. At Double D's last remark, we all bust out laughing.

Then Pokey gets serious. "Hey, Double D, all jokes aside I need to holla at you, it's business!" Pokey says.

"Well, in that case what's up?" Double D said, hoping to make a quick come-up.

"Look, I need to ask you a favor," Pokey said.

"Boy, you been knowing me all your life, and you know how I rock. Ain't nothing in life for free. So before you ask your favor, let me ask you a question, do you have some money to pay me for my services? I ain't got a pot to pee in."

Pokey said, "But I'll be straight in a minute."

"In a minute!" Double D yells, "Man, boy, I can die today, then I'll die broke all cuz I let you owe me. Oh hell na'll, I can't go out like that!" Double D screams. "I'll tell you what though, when you get ya paper right, holla at me. Until then, I can't do shit for ya, that's my rules, and I ain't breaking 'em for you or nobody else. I hope ain't no ill feelings, and before I go, when you get ya shit together and start making money like ya ole boy? I mean these balling-ass niggas out here. I got something to stress at you about, till then be E-Z, you know where to find me."

"Yeah, in a crackhouse," Flick said.

At first Pokey was thrown by the last comment Double D made but remembered his mother said his father died when he was just a baby. So he chalked it up as nothing and told his friends, "Well, I guess we won't get the info we need until we get our cheddar right. But maybe, just maybe, we'll hear something sooner than we think."

CHAPTER 2

Still Trying

"DAMN, I'LL BE glad when we get back to the projects, 'cause it's hot and a nigga feet on fire," Flick said, looking over at Pokey. "Hey Pokey, you all right? 'Cause you ain't said shit the whole walk back."

"Oh, I'm good, dirty. I'm just thinking about a lot of shit. It's so much a nigga gotta do. The shit have me zoned out sometimes, that's all," Pokey said, looking Flick dead in his eyes.

"All right, dog," Flick said, feeling bad for his long-time friend. "Just know, my nigga, if it's ever too much on your plate, you can pass the dish to me, and I'll help you handle whatever it is," Flick said.

"I know you will. I just don't understand a lot of shit, 'cause a lot of things ain't adding up."

"Man, fuck that. We'll stress about this shit some other time. Right now, let's roll over to my momma's crib."

"Right quick," Pokey said, as they enter the projects, looking around. Pokey was thinking, "Man, I'm tired of this shit, tired of being broke, tired of watching my momma struggle. Shit gonna change." As he looked at all the dirty buildings he was passing by, he said, "I'mma make shit happen."

Sooner than later, as he was thinking, a kid 'bout twelve years old ran up to him, yelling, "Hey Pokey. Pokey, you got a dollar?" the young kid said.

"Na'll, lil man. I'm fucked up."

"Oh, all right," lil man said, walking away with his head down.

"See, this the shit I'm talking about!" Pokey yelled. "A nigga can't even help a young nigga out. I ain't even got a dollar, that's bad," Pokey said. His two friends just looked at him.

"In a minute shit gonna happen for us, watch and see, if not, it's on and popping," Pokey said, pulling his shirt up, exposing the gun he had tucked in his pants.

"Look, y'all, let me go holla at ma dukes right quick," Flick said, running to his building.

"I'mma do the same," Fatboy said, with thoughts running 'round in his head. "Shit, I'm tired of living like this too. So it's whatever," he said, entering his building.

As Pokey watched his two friends go their separate ways, he was saying, "One day, we gonna get up out this hood. I'mma just need y'all to trust me," he was thinking as he walked in the door, looking around the house. He sees his mother asleep on the couch, slowly making his way over to the sofa, he places a soft kiss on her cheek.

As she slowly opens her eyes, she says, "Boy, you better stay out them streets, 'cause you never know when you PB officers will call or come around. You know them people don't give a damn about you and trying to give your behind a lotta of time if you mess up again."

"I know that, Ma, but I ain't doing shit. I mean nothing, so I ain't worried 'bout them crackers messing with me," Pokey said.

"A hard head makes a soft behind," his mother said, closing her eyes.

"Hey, Ma. What you got in here to eat? I'm hungry as a baby bear."

"Look in the microwave, it's a plate in there," she said, rolling over.

"Thanks, Mom."

"Hey, Pokey, what's up? When you leave again, make sure you lock the door for me, 'cause I'm going back to sleep," his mother said, yawning. "And did you run across your sister yet?"

"Yeah, I seen her at the park, she tried to clown on me though."

"I bet she did," his mother said. "You know she mess with that old-ass man Walter, right?"

"Na'll I didn't know that," Pokey said.

"Damn, she tripping. That's what I told her. But that's hers, what's between her legs," his mom said.

"So she gonna do what she want, Ma. If you want me to fall back and chill with you, I will."

"Baby, hush that fuss. Go have some fun. I know you just came home from prison. And I ain't trying to lock you down," she said, smiling at her only son. "I just want you to be careful and stay outta trouble."

"I will, Mom, and I love you," he said, heading toward the kitchen to get his grub on. Removing the plate from the microwave and taking a seat at the table, he ponders his next move. He knows it's a couple months before his birthday, and that's when his Uncle Sico is supposed to help him get on his feet. But in the back of his mind, he knows that's a ways away. And a nigga can't be broke all that time. "So I wonder who that nigga was at the park in the Rolls-Royce." As he takes his last bite of fried chicken, he gets up, and walks toward the phone, dialing his uncle's number. After the third ring, a voice yells, "Speak, who this?"

"Uncle Sico, it's me, Pokey."

"Boy, when you came home?" his uncle asked.

"On this morning."

"Well, what's up, 'cause I'm in the middle of something very important," his Uncle Sico said, looking back at the dime piece, who had her legs wide open. Playing in her pussy with two fingers while motioning for Sico to get off the phone. "What's up nephew? Damn, boy, you call at a bad time."

"Oh, Unc, I just need a lil favor, that's all."

"Boy, you know I said. When you turn –"

"Unc," Pokey said, cutting him off. "I ain't even talking 'bout that. I just need a lil money, some money."

"For what?" his uncle asked.

"'Cause I just got home from doing eighteen months, and I ain't got shit, you know, momma shooting bad. So she really can't help."

"All right, boy. Damn, but if you wasn't family, you'll be ass out," Sico said, looking back at the chick, who by now done closed her legs and rolled over on her side. "Oh well," Sico said. "Look, nephew, I'mma get dressed right quick, then I'll roll through."

"No'll, Unc, don't do that. Just meet me at the 7-Eleven. You know how momma be tripping on you."

"Boy, you dead right. I'll be there in no less than forty-five minutes," Sico said, hanging up.

"Damn, its 'bout time. Now a nigga might be able to move 'round a lil bit," Pokey was thinking. As he hung up the phone and started walking toward the door, he saw Fatboy and Flick about to knock on the door. Taking off running and jumping over the table that sat in the middle of the floor, he ran and snatched the door open before his dogs had a chance to knock and wake his momma up. "Shh, my momma sleep," Pokey whispered, as he looks at his mother asleep, he starts thinking, "One of these days, I'mma buy you a house with AL in it, just trust me," he was thinking.

Then he asked his dogs, "What's up?"

"Nothing," they both replied. "Look, y'all, I gotta go meet my uncle at the 7-Eleven right quick. Y'all gonna roll with me."

"Let's ride," they both said.

"That's what's up," Pokey said.

"What you got to meet him for?" Flick asked.

"Oh, nothing major. He finna hit me off with a lil chance, that's all," Pokey said.

"Well, let's burn up then, 'cause it's hot as hell standing in this sun," Fatboy said.

Flick throws in, "It's hotter than cooking grease you mean. I hope your uncle got enough money to buy some ice creams, since he the reason we walking in this hot-ass sun."

"Don't worry about that, nigga. I got us," Pokey says, giving his friends some dap, and they started toward their destination and the walkup to the 7-Eleven.

"It's was jam-packed. Damn, they act like this the block or something," Flick said, looking at all the people come and go.

Looking around, Pokey said, "Damn, outta all these peoples. I ain't see my uncle yet. Y'all, let's sit down and wait on this nigga," Pokey said. After about ten more minutes of waiting, they look up to hear the sounds of Tupac, "Picture me rolling, coming from this brand-new candy apple red box Chevy, sitting on datons."

"Here goes the nigga right there," Pokey said, standing up.

"I can't wait till we be rolling like that," Flick said, standing up, beside his dog, as they looking at this shinning-ass car.

Sico rolls the window down and yells, "Nigga, tighten your ass up. I got other things to do than to sit out here in this hot-ass sun waiting on you."

Pokey slowly started making his way toward his uncle's side of the whip. All he can do is smile as he sees the bills his uncle is counting, "Huh, nephew, here you go. That should do you a lil justice," he said, handing Pokey five hundred dollars.

"Boy, two hundred of them dollars for your momma, make sure she get it. Just don't tell her it's from me, 'cause she'll trip," Sico said, laughing. "Tell her you found it or something."

"I got you, Unc, and good looking," Pokey said, walking back toward his friends, stuffing the money in his pockets. As he walked up to his friends, Flick yelled out.

"Shit, I guess ice cream on you, right?" Flick asked.

"Nigga, chill out with your greedy ass. I told you I got y'all," Pokey said, watching his uncle exit the parking lot. "All right, he gone," Pokey said, "so check this out. I told y'all we in this together. So look at this as our first come up together," Pokey said, reaching in his pockets and pulling the money out. Dividing the money, he gave Fatboy and Flick both a hundred dollars, which they gladly accepted.

"Now that y'all got y'all own money, y'all can buy y'all own ice cream," Pokey said, giving them dap. "Tighten up. It's getting late," Pokey said as they started making their way back to the projects with ice cream in hand. The thought of the money Flick and Fatboy just received had them both thinking about the big picture. Money makes the world go round, but one thought invaded their mind, would the money solve the problem in the end, or would it make shit worse? Only one way to find out though, make the money and see.

"So what y'all gonna buy with the rest of the money," Pokey asked, not really caring what they did with it 'cause it's theirs now.

"Shit, I don't know, dog, I might invest for a rainy day, feel me?" Fatboy said.

"Yeah, I'm feeling that. What about you, Flick?"

"Oh, I might cop me some new track shoes or start saving too."

"Well, y'all know I'm on the come-up, so I'mma take what I got and try to flip it," Pokey said, as they enter the projects. "Now that we home and it's almost dark, what y'all wanna do, sit out here and chill, or what?" Pokey asked.

"Shit, I'm 'bout to head to the crib and take a shower, get some of this funk off me," Fatboy said.

"Yeah, I'mma call it a night too, 'cause I gotta catch up on this homework," Flick says. "But before I go, y'all wanna hit the mall or something in the morning?" Flick asked.

"Yeah, dirty, we might do that, but you know it's a party tomorrow in Sutton Place, and they talking like that bitch gonna be off the chain," Pokey said. "So we'll hit the mall, then swing through the party," Pokey said.

"I'mma get up with y'all then," Flick said, walking off.

"I'mma holla at you later, dog, Fatboy said, leaving. As Pokey watched both his friends leave, he sees Double D coming on a different bike and runs back down the stairs.

"Hey Double D, Double D!"

"Boy, what you want?" Double D yells. "You scared the shit outta me. Now I gotta check my pants to see if I shitted on myself, smelling like shit, for real. Now what you want, young blood?"

"Man, just tell me, who that nigga was at the park?" Pokey asked.

"Young blood, it was over a hundred niggas at the park, and you talking 'bout tell you who that nigga was. What nigga?" Double D asked.

"The nigga you sold the TV to, stupid," Pokey said.

"You got some money?"

"Yeah," but then thinks about the come-up. "He's on, no, I don't, not yet anyways,

"Then you know the rules," Double D says, jumping back on his bike, peeling off, waving.

"Well, at least I tried," Pokey says. "I guess it's time to call it a day," as he walks back upstairs. "Momma, I'm home."

"Baby, I'm in the tub right now," his mother yells.

"Okay, I was just making sure you was all right. I'm about to watch some TV."

"All right, baby," his mother yells.

As Pokey begins watching juice for the millionth time, he dozes off on the couch, not realizing the money hanging out his right pocket. After drying off and slipping into her nightclothes, Mrs. Queen goes into the living room to find her son asleep on the sofa. As she walks over to give him a kiss on the cheek, she notices the money sticking out his pocket, ready to snap, she pauses, and takes a deep breath, "Lord, I hope this boy ain't out here being stupid again. I done told him, them people gonna end up giving him a life sentence in prison," she cries. "Lord, whatever he is doing, please let it be the right thing," she says, heading to her room. She knows one day she will get another call, telling her, her son is in jail, or worse, dead. But she knows she can't do nothing but pray, as she walks over to her bed and slowly falls to her knees, she begins reciting the 23 Psalms, "The Lord is my shepherd, there is nothing I lack. In green pastures, you let me grace. To soft waters, you lead me. You restore my strength, you guide me along the right paths. For the sake of your name, even when I walk through the valley of shadow and death, you protect me." As she finishes her prayer, in her mind she can only hope faith is enough to keep her son from the street life.

"Momma, you all right?" Pokey says on the other side of the door.

"Yeah, I'm all right," his mother says back.

"Okay, Mom. I love you," he says, sliding two one hundred dollar bills under her door. Before she has a chance to say anything, she hears his door being closed. And she tells herself, "I'll let him sleep right now," bending over to pick up the money. "But in the morning we gotta talk," she said, getting in her bed.

CHAPTER 3

Tomorrow

"MOMMA, WILL YOU drop me and my friends off at the mall on your way to work?"

"Boy, how you gonna get back home? You know I don't get off till eleven o'clock tonight," Mrs. Brown told her son.

"Mom, I know. But if we have to, we'll walk back. It's not like we never did it before. It's nothing but four or five miles, and I can run that far," Flick said with a smile.

"All right, boy, that's on y'all, but what you going to the mall for anyways, to window-shop?" his mom said, laughing to herself.

"No, Mom. We just going to hang out and talk to a few females, that's all," Flick responded back.

"Boy, you ain't got no game to be talking to no girls," she says, playing.

"Momma, if you only knew," he says, poking his chest out like he's the man.

"All right, boy. You better tell ya lil friends to be ready, 'cause I'm leaving in a hour."

"Okay, Momma, I got you. Let me go call Fatboy and Pokey and tell them to tighten up."

"Oh, here you go," his mom replies, trying to give him twenty dollars, which he turns down. Being that his mom worked hard to make sure he had all he needed. He couldn't see himself taking money from his momma when he still had close to a hundred dollars in his pockets already that she knew nothing about but probably could use.

"Nah, Momma, I'm good. I don't need no money. We just going to hang out and chill, but thank you anyway," Flick told his mom. Looking at her son like he was crazy, all Mrs. Brown could say was, "Okay, baby."

Now over at Pokey's crib. His mother was still thirty-eight degrees hot going off and snapping about the two hundred dollars he gave her.

"Boy, where you get this money from?" Mrs. Rolle asked.

"Mom, I know you think I did something crazy to get this money but I didn't. I found it. Maybe it was a gift from God. Who knows?"

"Boy, don't bring God in your foolishness, you hear me?" Mrs. Rolle said.

"Yes, ma'am. Mom, look, I really didn't do nothing. I found the money and thought you could use it. That's not a crime, is it?"

As she looked at her son, all she could hope was he was being honest. 'Cause in her heart she knew she could use the money.

"Mom, I gotta go," he said, breaking her thoughts. "Mrs. Brown is dropping us off at the mall today on her way to work."

"How y'all getting back home?" she asked.

"We'll probably walk."

"Here, boy." She handed him the money back, but when she turned around and walked into the kitchen, he placed the money on the coffee table.

In his mind all he could say was, "You need the money more than I do. She musta forgot what she used to tell me and my sister, that God blesses a child that can hold his own!" And with that thought in mind he walked out the door. Fatboy telephoned boy.

"Who is it, who this is?" asked Tiffany, his oldest sister.

"This Flick."

"Hold on, boy. It's ya lil friend Flick."

"Okay, I'm coming. I got it. Yeah, dog, what's up?"

"Nothing," Flick says. "I just called to see if you was ready."

"Ready for what?"

"The mall, nigga. You forgot?"

"Yeah, dog, I did," Fats says.

"Hey, I called Pokey and next thing I know I heard him and his mom fussing so I don't know if he coming," Flick said, sounding sad.

"He'll be there, dog. Now I gotta see what's up? TP what? Where Momma at? In her room sleep why? Dang, girl, touch ya nose," I told my sister, smiling.

"Well, since you wanna be so smart next time, don't ask me," Tiffany said, full of anger as she walked off toward her room.

"She mad, dog."

"Who?" Flick asked.

"My sister."

"Oh," Flick says.

"Hold on, dog. I'm finna ask my mom can I roll with y'all."

Knock, knock.

"What?"

"Momma?"

"What, boy?" Mrs. Walls asked, sleepy-eyed.

"Mom, Mrs. Brown gonna drop us off at the mall this morning. Is it all right if I go?"

"I don't care as long as you did your chores."

"I already did that, Momma."

"Okay, you can go then you need some change. I got 'bout twenty dollars in my purse."

"Na'll, Mom, I'm good. I'll do without in order to see you with."

"Boy, get outta my room trying to sweet-talk me," she says, smiling. She loved her only son more than her own life and just hoped she was doing the right thing by giving him his freedom so young in life.

"Okay, Mom, I'm out."

"Before you leave tell Tia to come here, all right?"

"Tia, Tia!" Fatboy said, screaming.

"Boy, shut up. If I wanted you to wake the whole hood up, I woulda yelled myself."

"Oh, my bad, Momma. I'll go get here." On the way to his sister's room, Tia was already headed to Mom's room. As she passes me, she pushes me in to the wall and takes off running.

"That's for calling my name like you stupid," she says, sticking her middle finger up as she enters Mom's room. When she enters Mom's room and closes the door, I run to my room, grab my shoes and the money outta my shoe box. Just as I'm putting the money in my pockets, my little sister walks in the room.

"Ooh, where you get all that money? I'mma tell Mom."

"Look, girl, here goes five dollars. So don't tell Momma and I'll give you five more later." But I know I can't trust my lil sister, even though she talking 'bout bet. So I push her in the room and take off running. I had just enough time to escape before my momma is calling my name in the doorway.

"Fatboy, bring your behind here."

But I'm already gone.

"Lord, please protect my baby and please keep him butta trouble. Please, Lord, don't let him be but there doing nothing illegal." She prayed while tears fell to the floor in front of her.

"It's about time you got here, boy," Mrs. Brown tells Fatboy. "One more minute and you woulda got left."

"I'm sorry, Mrs. Brown, that's my bad. I had to do my lil chores before I left."

"That's understandable," Mrs. Brown says, looking in her rearview mirror, letting Fats know it's okay.

"Momma, turn the radio on," Flick asked.

"Boy, y'all already know if it's not the oldie goldies, we ain't listening to nothing," all three boys said while laughing. We also knew Mrs. Brown was dead-ass for real. So nobody bothered asking 'bout the radio the whole ride to the mall. About fifteen minutes later we pull up in front of the Paddock Mall, and you knew if the parking lot was on swoll the mall had to be overflowing with people as we exited the car.

Mrs. Brown says, "Y'all be careful and stay outta trouble," looking directly at Pokey.

"Mrs. Brown, thanks for the ride," Pokey and Fats said.

"Damn, everybody think I'm a thug," Pokey said, referring to the look Mrs. Brown gave him.

"Man, you know sometimes my momma be bugging!" Flick says. "Don't let it bother you though, all right, man? We here now. What, we gonna stand out here all day or go in? Let's ride." As all three boys enter the mall, it's crowded with people. After about an hour of walking around, they all take a break on a bench.

"Hey look, I bet y'all before we leave the mall I'll have more numbers than y'all," Fatboy said.

"All right, that's a bet," his two friends say.

"What we betting though, fat mouth?"

"We'll bet a light five dollars," Fat says.

That's a deal, they say, giving one another dap. After 'bout five more minutes of clowning around, they get up and head to Foot Locker. Before they make it there, Fats sees a shortie that done caught his attention.

"Damn, shortie fine as Halle Berry," Fats says looking in the Carl's direction. I might make shortie my baby momma."

"Yeah, we hear you. And yeah, she bad but you can't do nothing by just standing here," Pokey said, laughing.

"She look young as hell," Flick says.

"Chill, I got this." As I stroll over to shortie, she 'bout 5'2", 135 pounds, light-skinned with long silky hair and a fat round butt, with the prettiest face I ever seen in my life, I guess it is a thing called love at first sight.

"Man, forget all the daydreaming. Go holla at shortie, she keep looking over here anyways," Pokey says.

"Man, chill, watch this hello. Hey, my name is Fatboy."

Before he could finish the girl cut him off by saying, "I thought you were scared or something to come holla at me. I was about to come holla at you."

"Word."

"Anyways, my name is Shakia. But my friends call me Kiki."

"So that means I can call you Kiki then."

"Well, really you still a stranger, but since you so cute. Yeah, you can call me Kiki."

"Where you from? 'cause I never seen you round here before," Fats asked.

"Oh, I'm from Invernest, Florida. I'm only here to help my grandma sell these vitamins. My granddad pasted, and now she doing all she can to help other people."

"That's cool. Damn, you stay a lil minute away. Listen, before I go, 'cause my friends all in my business, can I get ya number?"

"Hold up." As she looks in her purse and grabs a pen and a piece of paper, she writes the number down asking, "I'm I gonna call?"

"Yeah, shortie, I'mma hit you up tonight sometime."

"All right, I'll be home 'round nine o'clock," she replies.

"All right, I'mma holla at you tonight then."

"Okay, bye bye," she throws in.

Walking back over to my friends all smiles, "I say, niggaz, I ain't been in the mall over a hour, and I got the baddest shortie already," showing them the number. As I was showing them the number, Pokey taps Flick on the shoulder.

"Hey, Flick, ain't that's the chick you go to school with, the one you said be throwing everybody shade."

"Yeah, that's her," Flick says.

"Shortie fine, I think she mix of something," Flick says. "I had my eye on shortie for a minute now. I heard people calling her Rosa. Rosy or something like that," Flick tells his dog.

"Man, go holla at the girl," Fatboy says.

"Man, y'all so impatient," Flick says with his trademark grin. "Man, everybody in school done shot bullets at shortie only to empty they gun, and shortie still standing, sending niggas on 'bout they business. I ain't trying to waste no bullets. So my first shot gonna be aim at her chest," Flicks says.

"Dog, we all know kill the brain the body dies," Pokey said.

"Yeah, catch her heart and she'll do anything for you," Flick shoots back.

As his boys clap talking 'bout go, Romeo, go, "Okay we feeling that, but just talking ain't gonna get you nowhere."

"Dog, here she comes now. Okay, watch a smooth operator in action. Hey, excuse me. Could I speak with you for just a moment?"

"Well, you done stopped me already, so you might as well," the female voiced with attitude.

"Look, Ma. I ain't trying to stop you from doing you. I just like what I see, and if I'm wrong for that, then kill me and I know I'll see you in heaven," Flicks shoots back.

"That's nice, and first my name isn't Ma, it's Rosie. And yours is?"

"Everybody calls me Flick."

"I know your alias name, boy. I know you run track and play basketball too. I'm talking 'bout your real name."

"Oh, my bad. It's Javair, and I'mma be honest with you. I've seen you around school too, dissing niggaz left and right."

"Yeah, it's only one thing y'all want," Rosie says. "And I shouldn't have to tell you what," she replies.

"Listen, Rosie, everybody ain't the same. So don't let others give me a blackout without first putting up a fight," Flick says.

"Okay, you is a little cute and you seem to have yourself together –"

Before she could finish, Flick cuts her off. "Excuse me, Rosie, I'mma holla at you later," Flicks sets and peels off, leaving Rosie standing there in awe, 'cause never has a dude just left her standing; it's always vice versa.

"No, this nigga didn't. He didn't even write my number down or ask for it," she said, watching him walk off in the other direction.

"Damn, Romeo, what you told that girl that had her drooling out the mouth?" His two friends asked.

Flick just looks at his two friends and says life is not always a matter of holding good cards, but sometimes playing a poor hand well.

"All I did was reverse the game!"

"And how you did that?" his friends asked.

"I left her before she could leave me."

"Okay, we feeling that, but where the number at?"

"Trust me, dog. She'll find me before she leave."

"And how can you be so sure?" Pokey asked.

"Just trust me on this one, dog. Oh, by the way, look over there," Flick told Pokey, pointing in the direction this girl was standing, looking thinner than LisaRaye.

"Oh hell, yeah, that's the bit. I mean girl I was gonna holla at before I got locked up. Well, look like luck is with us, 'cause here she comes walking this," Pokey remarks.

"Watch a real player handle business," he said as he started walking in the same direction the girl was coming from. As she gets close enough, Pokey bumps her just a little bit, enough to throw her off balance, but not enough to make her fall. Just the right touch to get her attention.

"Dang, boy, can't you see where you going?" she replies.

"Oh my bad, but to be honest with you, Miss, I was blinded by your beauty so really this is all your fault," Pokey says. "Listen though, my name is Pokey, and yours is?"

"Oh, my name is Amanda."

"Well, Amanda, it's nice to meet you. Maybe we can become friends or something."

"We'll see," Amanda said, trying not to blush. "Well, look, Pokey, I gotta go before my mom's come. She see me talking to you, she gonna have a fit."

"Before you bounce, can I get your number?"

"Oh sure, it's 352-629-0803. Please don't call me till after eight. My mom will be at work," she said, then turning to leave. Before she took a step further, she said, "Pokey, don't you go to Vanguard High School?"

"Yeah, I do," he said.

"Well, I'll see you at school too then."

"All right, I'mma get at cha," Pokey says, heading back toward his friends with the number in hand, waving it in the air at his dogs.

"Dog, you did that," his two friends say, giving him dap.

"Well, I got me a number," Pokey says.

"Shot, I got one too," Fats responds.

"So, Flick, since you the lone lost ranger without a number, you owe us 2.50 apiece. Give me my money," they both say, laughing.

"Y'all got that," Flick said, reaching in his pocket to pay his friends. The Carl's Rosie runs up to him with a piece of paper in her hand. Placing it in his hands, she whispered in his ear, "Make sure you call me, and I'll see you at school," she says, placing a kiss on his cheek, and she turns to walk the other way.

"Well well well, Mr. Lover Man, it seems you got the bigger prize," Pokey said. You got a last-minute phone number and a little kiss," Pokey said.

"I guess that makes us all even, right?"

"Yeah, we good even though I got a kiss with my number," Flick says.

"Look y'all, let's go hit the Foot Locker right quick before the mall close," Pokey said, taking off. "Man, I'm about to cope these Nike Airs," Pokey said. "They straight as hell, and they ain't nothing but seventy-five dollars," Pokey said, placing the shoes in front of him. While Pokey was talking to Fats, Flick was looking at some shoes and walks up with a pair of Puma track shoes.

"I'mma get these," Flick says, showing us the shoes.

"Fats, what you gonna cope?"

"Man, I'm good on shoes right now. All right, let us go pay for these shoes then we gonna slide up outta here. The mall about to close in a hour or so, and we got some walking to do before we get back to the projects," Pokey says. As they exited the mall all smiles, feeling good about the number they all caught and the brand-new shoes, all three friends have the same thought in mind, "Damn, I can't wait to get home to see what shortie really about." About an hour or so later they make it back to the projects, and all go separate ways to their own building, ready to put the calls in.

CHAPTER 4

Mrs. Walls "Momma Tripping"

"I SEE YOU finally made it home, and before you do anything, I need to talk to you."

"Momma I just walked four miles from the mall to get home, and I'm tired, sweaty, and need a shower. Can we talk after I get out the shower?"

"No, right now," Mrs. Walls responded with anger in her voice and worry writing all over her face. In his mind he knew what this was all about, his lil sister and her big mouth. "Snitching on me about the lil money I got. Now I gotta explain something that's really nothing," he was thinking.

"Okay, Mom, what's up?"

"You need to be telling me what's up. You the one running 'round here with a pocket full of money. And Lord knows what you did to get it."

"Mom, it ain't nothing but a few."

"Boy, shut up till I get finish talking. It ain't nothing but a few dollars you was about to say. Right. Okay, if that's the case why you kept running when I called you, and don't say you ain't hear me 'cause you ain't that fast. You only got two less not four."

"Mom, look, Pokey Uncle's Sico give him some money the other day, and Pokey just looked out for me and Flick. That's where the money came from, I swear."

"Boy, what I told you 'bout swearing in my house?"

"I know, but I don't want you to think I'm lying," Fats says.

"Boy, I really don't know what to believe. All I know is I love you, you my only son, and I know you just wanna have fun. But every day I'm seeing less and less of you."

"But I still ain't doing nothing. I just chill with my two friends, that all."

"Baby, look, I know Flick a good kid, but your friend policy Pokey gonna be your downfall. I just hope I can save enough money and move from 'round here before that happen. Lord knows I ain't trying to come visit my only son behind bars or six feet deep."

"Momma, stop stressing yourself 'bout nothing. You know I ain't stupid."

"I know, baby."

"Mom, won't you let me help? I can get a job or something."

"Baby, I wish you could. But you only fifteen, and you gotta finish school. Besides where you gonna get a job at, and I can't even find one."

"Mom, I'll be sixteen in eight more months though."

"Baby, just do this for me, stay in school. And stay outta trouble."

"All right, Momma, I got you." But little do she know that in a minute Fatboy will have more money than they know what to do with it.

"Come 'ere, baby," she says, giving him a hug, something she usually don't do.

"Hey, Ma. Here you go," Fatboy says, reaching in his pockets to remove the money. He hands his mother the money. She looks at him like he crazy.

"Baby, you just left the mall. Why you ain't buy nothing?"

"'Cause I felt you needed it more than I did so I kept it."

"Boy, get your money back."

"Nah, Mom, keep it. Just pay it with the money you saving up for us to move."

"Baby, you sure?" his mother asked.

"Yes, ma'am, I'm sure."

"If you need this money, baby, just tell me and I'll give it right back."

"All right, Mom, let me go take a shower right quick."

"Okay, baby go 'head," his mother says, feeling a lot better and knowing in her heart her son gonna be okay.

After about fifteen minutes I step out the shower feeling good and clean. I grab the one phone and bring it to my room. Good thing my sister then ain't here right now, or I woulda never got the phone. "Damn, it's early. It's only 9:20, and I'm about to call shortie. Where the number at? Oh here it go, 325-21629-0803," I say out loud. As I dialed the number, after two rings an older female answers the phone.

"Hello, may I speak to Shakia please?"

"Hold on just a moment. Shakia, baby, the telephone. And don't stay on too long you know you got school in the morning."

"I got you, Grandma. Hello, oh hey, what's up?"

"Nothing."

"I didn't think you were going to call."

About twenty-five minutes of talking, we hook up and I end the call by saying, "I'mma call you tomorrow, all right?"

"All right," the girl says and hangs up.

Let me call my dogs before I go to sleep. I'mma call Pokey first. After about the fourth ring, I hear Pokey's voice.

"Yeah, what's up man?"

"What took you so long to answer the phone?"

"Oh, I'm on the other line, talking to Amanda."

"By the way, what's up? Pokey asked.

"Na'll, I just called to tell you me and the shortie from the mall hooked up."

"That's good, nigga. Now let me put my bid in," Pokey says.

"I'll holla at you tomorrow, all right. I'm out."

Last but not least I gotta hit Flick up. After the first ring Flick picks up with a sleepy voice.

"Hello, man. What's up, dog?"

"Oh nothing, man I was almost asleep."

"Man, it's only 10:23."

"Yeah, I got school in the morning too," Flicks says. "Oh, did you holla at the girl from the mall?" Flick asked.

"Yeah, dog, we good. Yeah, I talked to Rosie 'bout a hour till the conversation cast boring, and we both said well see each other at school tomorrow."

"Dog, look, I'm 'bout to catch some Zs. You know I got a track meet tomorrow."

"All right, dog, I'll see you tomorrow!" Fats says, hanging up the phone.

CHAPTER 5

Going Hard

WHEN WE MADE our way off the bus at Vanguard High School, all eyes were on us. Not too many people expected to see us three together, so I guess it's something people better get used to. As we started walking to our classes, four niggaz by the name of Turtle, Wacko, Rachet, and Tim approached us, speaking to Pokey first.

"Pokey, what's up, dog? I see you made it home in one piece," Rachet said, being funny. As Pokey looked at the boy like he was ready to kill, all he said was, "Yeah, dog, I did my time. Now I'm back trying to do the right thing, if people let me, and if not, sorry for that person," Pokey said also being funny, but dead ass for real.

"Whatever, nigga," Rachet said. "Anyways, what's up, Fatboy? When you started hanging with lames?"

"Man, look these my niggaz, and we gonna ride or die together, respect it or check it."

"Man, forget all that," Turtle said. "We just came to holla at ya boy Flick, but since all three of y'all a team, it goes for all y'all then."

"What's that?" Fatboy asked, ready for whatever.

"Listen, I got a 150 dollars on my dog Tim that he'll beat ya boy Flick racing."

"In my mind I had my doubts," Fatboy was thinking, "'Cause everybody know Tim is supposed to be the fastest at school. I know my dog Flick can run and he fast, but this kid Tim is fast as lighting."

Just as I was about to say we good, the skinny nigga named Wacko started saying, "You niggas scared? Y'all ain't got no confidence in ya dog, or y'all ain't got no confidence in ya money?"

Just as I was about to call the bet outta pride, Pokey pulls Flick over to the side and starts talking to him, "Flick, you think you can beat this nigga or not?"

"Man, I don't know the nigga running."

"Man, so what? You running too. You gotta have confidence in yourself, before anybody in life will have confidence in you. Now what I'mma do is call this bet, and what you gonna do is win the race," Pokey said, giving Flick some dap. "Hey Turtle, that's a bet, but if we lose I'll pay you tomorrow, 'cause I ain't bring no bread with me," Pokey said, knowing if Flick lost he was gonna buck anyway.

"Say no more then," Turtle said.

"It's a bet. After school is over we'll all stay after and watch the track meet. Then when it's all said and done, we'll ask Coach to let y'all two race," Pokey said.

"Man, we'll be there," Turtle said, with his dog Rachet putting in his say.

"So in, y'all niggas might as well not even show up, 'cause y'all know Fick isn't gonna beat Tim."

"All right, dog, you said enough. We'll be there. Just bring your running shoes 'cause you gonna need them fucking with my dog," Fatboy says.

"Man, we'll see."

As they started walking off, Rachet started yelling, "No show bet still go, and you lose you gonna pay that money. That's the rules."

"Same go for y'all too. Don't get it twisted," Pokey said back.

"Damn, the bell just ringed. Let me get to this classroom before Mrs. Hope start tripping," Flick says.

"Yeah, I'mma see y'all at lunch," Pokey said, heading toward his class. Fatboy watched as both his friends disappeared down the halls in different directions before he turned around and walked to his class.

As he steps in the door Mr. Cracker looks at him and tells him, "You're five minutes late. I know you heard the bell ring. But since I know you don't care, I want you to know the next time you will get detention."

"I got you, man. That's my bad I'm late," Fatboy remarks back with a scowl on his face. Just as Fatboy finished talking, a white kid walks in, and all the teacher told him was, "Have a sit, son," instead of making a smart comment. All Fats did was laugh to himself, which caught the teacher's attention and made him turn red in the face.

"Damn these some racists-ass teachers," Fatboy was still thinking as the bell rang for the kids to switch classes. "Damn, time flew by" was all Fatboy could say as he walked out the door, glad to be out that class.

As Flick was walking down the hall, he sees Rosie, walking toward him with her arms out, like she reaching for a hug.

"Boy, what's up?" Rosie says. "I've been looking for you all morning. I even waited out front 'bout five minutes, but I didn't see you, so I just went to class."

"Oh baby, my bad. I was out front though, you probably just didn't see me 'cause me and my dogs was going back and forth with these niggaz about me and they dog racing. It's supposed to go down after school though," Flick said.

"Boy, you must be talking about Tim and his dogs," Rosie says. "You know they say he the fastest at school."

"Yeah, I heard that, but it's somebody for everybody," Flick says. "I'm saying thou, you gonna be able to stay after school and watch the race, or you gotta go home, baby, I don't know."

Rosie said, "I gotta call my mom during lunch break, and see if she can pick me up, but I'll let you know, okay?"

Rosie said, "All right, baby, the bell just rang, so let me get to my class. I'mma holla at you later," she said, as she peeled off all smiles.

On the way to his other class, Fatboy sees Pokey walking with Amanda, all smiles. In his mind all he could say was, "It's good to see my dirty smiling."

About thirty more seconds went by, and Fatboy calls Pokey, "Hey Pokey! Damn, nigga, you don't see ya dog now."

"Na'll, dog, I was just vibed out," Pokey said. "What's up though? Hold on, Fats. Hey Amanda, I'm holla at you at lunch all right?"

"All right," Amanda says and starts walking to her class.

"Look, Fatboy, I need to holla at cha."

"What's up?" Fatboy said, watching the smile that was just plastered on his face disappear and turn to a frown.

"Look," Pokey said, "this school shit ain't for me. Every time I go in these crackers' classrooms, they be looking at a nigga all funny and shit. This morning I went in class with positive thinking, trying to actually learn something. I ask this cracker for help, he just laughed at me and started walking off, talking 'bout I'll figure it out and went straight over to another kid and begin helping him. Tell me that ain't fucked up," Pokey said.

"Dog, you right, that is fucked up. But remember, a winner never quits, and a quitter never wins."

"I hear all that, but you don't understand how frustrated that shit gets me," Pokey said.

"I feel you, dog, but listen to what I heard a long time ago from one of my mother's friends. He said unless a man undertakes more than he possibly can, he will never do all he can. So just keep that lil saying in your mind, dirty. It will help you, when it seems like the walls are crumbling down."

"I'm feeling that," Pokey said, giving his friend some dap, before turning around to head to his class, with a little more bounce in his step.

As Fatboy walks the other way headed to his class, he says a lil prayer. Something he usually don't do, but just this once he decided it was worth it,

"Lord, keep my friends strong, and help us all to stay postive," he said as he walked in the door to start his second class of the day.

An hour later, the bell rings, letting the students know it was lunchtime.

"Damn, time is flying," Fatboy said. "Just as I was getting off into this math, they wanna ring the bell. Well, time to go," he said, heading but the door to meet his friends for lunch. And then he runs into a old friend by the name of Maurice Jenkins.

"Man, what's up?" Fatboy asked.

"Oh nothing, dog. You know me, I just be trying to chill," Maurice said.

"Where you being, man? I haven't seen you around in about two months. I thought you moved or something," Fatboy said.

"Nope, try again," Maurice said laughing. "Na'll, for real. I had got into a little BS with the law, and them crackers drop the charges 'cause they didn't have shit on me but hearsay, so here I am, live and in the flesh."

"Dog, you still out there robbing people? You better leave that shit alone and keep playing B-ball," Fatboy advised his friend.

"Man, basketball is my sport, I love playing it, but that shit don't feed me when I'm hungry or put clothes on my back," Maurice said.

"I understand that, dog, but before you started all that dumb-ass shit, you used to be the best ball player here, and it woulda been only a matter of time before ever college in the world new bout you then off to the pros, where basketball woulda been feeding your ass and putting silk on ya ass," Fats told his friend.

"I hear all that, but I gotta do what I gotta do, I can't go years without eating, waiting on the pros, nigga. I'll starve to death," Maurice said.

"Yeah, and you the same nigga who told me in middle school, strong people surmount obstacles, struggles against adversity and survive, right? What happen to that?"

"Man, I gotta eat, but since it's you, I'mma try and chill and get back into basketball, but I can't make no promises," Maurice said.

"All right, dog. I'mma take you up on that, and I'mma holla at you later," Fatboy said, walking toward the lunchroom. When he enters the lunchroom, he sees Pokey and Amanda with Flick and Rosie, seated in the corner, the sight of them together made him think about his shortie shaking. But the thought vanished just as quick, as he studies his surrounding. Before walking toward his friends, he sees all the niggaz Turtle, Wacko, Tim, and Rachet looking in the direction as his friends are in, pointing and saying something he couldn't quite hear. So he chalked it up as nothing major, nothing to be concerned about, until he walked passed them, and Turtle said, "Y'all got about three more hours till school's out. Tell ya friend Pokey he can cope out now, and I won't tax him but half the money."

Everybody in school knew, even the teachers, that Turtle and his crew was making money, they just didn't know how. The thing was, all four of them niggaz stayed fresh with the latest wear, and they all kept money to flaunt at all times, but everyone knew their downfall would be they liked to be seen too much by everyone, especially Rachet.

Fatboy was thinking as he found a seat next to his friends, "Damn y'all, couldn't wait on me."

"Dog, chill out, we just got here 'bout five minutes ago. You act like we ate all the pizza," Pokey said, trying to stuff a piece in his dog mouth. Just as Fats took the pizza from Pokey, Pokey began to choke.

"Ha ha! Nigga, didn't Mrs. Queen tell you about talking with ya mouth full?" Fatboy said laughing, while Amanda patted Pokey on his back.

"Flick, boy, what's up? You ready to win this money?" Fatboy asked.

"Ready as I'll ever be," Flick said, while looking at Rosie.

"Man, let's finish the rest of this pizza so we can slide. We got 'bout twenty more minutes before they ring the damn bell again."

"All right," they all said. As everyone grabbed slices of the pizza when everybody was done, Rosie said, "Flick, I'mma go call my mom's real quick, and see if she'll pick me up after school," Rosie said, leaving the table. As Fatboy, Flick, Pokey, and Amanda were leaving, this fat kid named Rico runs up to them, talking 'bout he got fifty dollars on Tim, and his friends wanna bet too. Before he could get any further, Pokey cut him off.

"Rico, man take ya fat ass on somewhere. You know ain't nobody finna bet you."

"Why," Rico said, "my money ain't no good?"

"Ain't nobody say that, dog. Nigga, just ain't about to go through the drama with you, that's all."

"All right, fuck it. You niggas just scared," Rico said.

"Yeah, we scared, scared of what we may have to do to your ass," Pokey said.

"Damn, these niggas done told everybody about one lil race, now everybody gonna stay after school just to see this shit," Fatboy said. "Well, Flick, you about to get the spotlight if you win," Fatboy said.

As they begin to walk off, they see Rosie on the phone, talking to her mom.

"Mom, can I stay after school to watch the track meet?" she asked.

"I guess, girl," her mom said. "What time will it be over?"

"I guess about 6:30."

"All right, I'll pick you up then," her mom said, hanging the phone up. When she hung up, Flick was right there.

"What she said?" Flick asked.

"She said yes, I can stay." As soon as she said yes, the bell rang, and everybody started going back to their classes.

Pokey and Amanda took off together in one direction, screaming, "We'll see y'all after school is over," Flick told Rosie. "Baby, I'mma catch up with you later."

"All right," Rosie said, taking off to class.

"Fatboy, yeah dog, you all right?" Flick asked.

"Yeah, man. I'm just chilling, thinking about a lot of things," Fatboy said.

"All right, dog. I was just checking, 'cause you been kinda quiet, that's all," Flick said.

"Man, I'm all right though, just going through the motions."

"All right then, I'mma go ahead to class," Flick said and walked off. While Fatboy just stood there for a moment in La La Land, thinking about where his life was headed, until the sound of the last bell rang for those who didn't make it to class yet to get there. About two hours later, the bell rang to let students know school was now over. As everybody ran out the classes filling the hallways, waiting to get on buses, talking to friends, and just clowning around, Turtle and his crew were already headed toward the track, playing around and talking shit about how Tim was gonna leave Flick in the dust. But little did they know it would be the other way around.

As Fatboy, Pokey, and Flick exited the school building and started walking toward the track, Amanda and Rosie ran up beside them, smiling, and talking shit.

"Damn, y'all too good to wait on us," Amanda said.

"Baby, you knew where we was going so why wait?" Pokey asked.

"'Cause I'm your girlfriend, and it's not gonna kill you to wait on me sometimes."

"All right, next time I'll wait. You happy now," Pokey said, more concentrated on this race than anything else. 'Cause he knew if Flick lost, he was bucking the payment. He also knew bucking would cause unwanted bullshit with Turtle and his friends, so he was hoping Flick would pull it off. But at the same time, "It is what it is," he said to himself. As they reached the track, watching all the people running, stretching, and everything else that goes on at a track meet.

"Coach Thomas, what's up?" Flick asked.

"Nothing, you ready?" Coach Thomas asked.

"Yes, ma'am."

"All right. Let's time you in the 220-yard dash first, then the 100 and 50," she said. Then Flick started changing from his school shoes into his track shoes, jumping up, jogging in place.

As he headed to the starting line before he ran for the 220, Pokey ran up beside him and advised him, "Dog run fast, just not your fastest, 'cause you know these niggas gonna be checking you out."

"All right, dog. I got you," Flick said, ready to run. "Coach, I'm ready, when you ready."

"Remember this is just tryouts."

"I know, Coach."

"All right then. Get set, ready, go!"

Flick took off like Carl Lewis back in his days and did the 220 in no time.

"Coach, how I look?"

"Boy, you fast, but Tim still got the record." Little did she know, Flick wasn't even running at top speed. "All right, catch ya breath, than we'll do the 100."

"All right, Coach," Flick said. About five minutes later, Flick said, "Coach, I'm ready."

"All right, let's go!" she yelled. "You ready? Yeah, all right, ready, set, go." He took off again but slowed down when he saw Turtle and his crew on the sideline, watching. And he ran the 50-yard dash with the same speed but slowed down at the end. As Coach went and timed other kids, Fatboy, Flick, and Pokey, and the girls, stood on the sidelines, watching Tim and all the other people run. As they vibed out and were laughing, 'cause they knew a secret no one else knew, beside them, that Flick was just playing around when he ran for his times. As they watched Tim take off, all they could say was that nigga, moving, that nigga fast as hell. Pokey broke everybody's thoughts. by telling Flick, "Dog, you can't play around with that nigga."

"I got you, dog. Trust me, it's no sweat," Flick said with confidence.

When Tim finished running, Turtle called him over and started telling him, "Man, let's go 'head and get this shit over with, so we can get back to the PS's."

"All right, dog, I'm ready," Tim said. "Hey Coach, you gonna ref this race for us?" Tim asked. "That kid thinks he can beat me."

"Who?" she asked.

And Tim started pointing at Flick, "Him right there." As Flick stepped up, Coach looked at Flick like he was crazy. He just watched Tim blow his time way.

"Coach, what's up? You gonna call the race or what?" Flick asked.

"Oh yeah, I got y'all," she said coming outta her lil daze. "What y'all? Running," she asked.

"The 100-yard dash," Tim said.

Flick said, "It don't matter, whatever he wanna run."

"All right then, y'all head to the starting line, and let me know when y'all ready."

"Coach, we ready!" Tim screamed.

"All right, ready, set, go!"

Both boys took off, and Tim was the first out the gate. But just as quick as he took off was just as quick as he got caught. Now Flick was running side by side and stride for stride, with him talking, "Dog, come on, I know you faster than that." As they crossed the finish line at the exact same time.

"A tie!" Coach screamed. And she really couldn't believe it, but it was a tie. She yelled again, all excited and shit, running up to Flick, talking 'bout, "Boy, I didn't know you was that fast. If the both of y'all run together, we can win everything."

"Na'll, Coach. Do it again," Tim said, breaking her excitement for the moment. "I tripped," Tim lied.

"Okay, that's all right with you, Flick?" Coach asked.

"I don't care." As Flick looked over at Pokey, he was all smiles, 'cause Flick just let him know he could beat him.

So Pokey walked over to Turtle who was saying, "I can't believe this shit."

"Hey Turtle."

"What's up, nigga," Turtle said, heated.

"Them niggas 'bout to race again, you wanna double the bet?"

Before Turtle could say anything, the skinny kid named Wacko said, "Bet them niggas double, dog. That's more money for us." With Rachet in his other ear screaming, "Man, bet that shit!"

"It's a bet," Turtle said with a little doubt in his voice. If he lost the bet, the money wasn't a problem. Turtle knew he could pay that with ease, it was just the thought of his dog losing the race to a nobody is what bothered him the most.

"Y'all ready?" Coach screamed.

"Yeah," they both said.

"All right, ready, set, go!"

They took off again, but this time Flick came out first, and that's how it was, all the way to the finish line. Flick won.

"Baby, you beat that nigga," Rosie said all happy.

Then Flick watched his two friends give each other dap and walked off to collect the money from Turtle and his crew. When Turtle paid the money, he said, "Look, we gonna do this shit again next week."

"Ya boy just had a lucky day," he said and walked off, hating the fact he lost his money to some lames.

"All right," Pokey said, walking toward Flick with a big ass smile on his face. "Dog, you did that," Pokey said, giving Flick half the money they just won.

"Back that up," Flick said.

"Damn, Pokey, you said that nigga was fast, but I didn't know dog was moving like that," Fatboy said, happy for his dog.

As Pokey gave Fatboy half the money he had left, "Thank you, dog," Fatboy said, giving Pokey dap. As they turned to start walking home, let's roll, they said.

Just as the three boys were leaving, Rosie's mom pulls up.

"Hey Rosie, ask ya mom will she drop us off at the projects," Flick asked.

"Mom, will you drop my friends off home for me?"

"You better tell them come on," she said.

"Come on," Rosie screamed all excited, as they all climbed in the car. About five minutes later, they were getting outta the car. Thanks, they all said. As Rosie said bye, and her mom pulled off, "Damn, that woman be driving like she crazy or something," Fatboy said.

"Tell me about it," Flick said. "I didn't think we was gonna make it back to the projects, the way she was in and out of traffic. Man. I ain't never been scared in my life, but that was one time I was scared as fuck. I even told God to please forgive me for my sins, 'cause here I come." Then they all laughed at how scared they were as they began walking to their buildings.

"I'mma holla at y'all later," Flick said, rushing home to tell his mom he holds the crown in racing now.

"Well, today was a good day," Fatboy said, "so I'mma go call my shortie. I'll see you in the morning, dog."

"All right," Pokey said, walking off.

CHAPTER 6

Two Weeks Later: The Come-up

AS ALL THREE boys exited their buildings to meet up, Fatboy had a funny feeling about something, but he couldn't quite put his hands on what it was, until he reached his friends.

And Pokey said, "Fatboy, did you catch the news this morning?

"Noll, I got up too late, but why?"

"What happen now, dog, ya boy Maurice got fucked up last night over in the shores."

"Doing what?" Fatboy asked, knowing now where the funny feeling came from.

"They said he tried to break into this cracker's house, and while he was in there, cleaning the place out, the cracker came home and seen the door ajar. So they say the cracker got his gun outta the glove compartment, and that's when he seen ya boy, trying to sneak out the window on the low-low. With a handful of jewelry and some money and said the cracker ran up to him. As soon as he hit the ground, and the man just opened fire on ya boy, like it was the Fourth of July."

"Man, y'all playing right. I just talked to this nigga two weeks ago about that dumb shit," Fatboy said. "Damn!"

"Listen though, Fatboy. They said ya boy got hit six times in the upper body and one time in the neck. He on life support as we speak. They said he may not make it, and if he do, he'll never be the same again."

"Damn, that's some fucked-up shit, but I can't do shit about it but send up a prayer for my nigga. I don't know if it's best he pull through or just give up the fight, throw in the towel, 'cause any way you look at it, dog, he gonna be messed up. And I would rather be dead than living a life behind bars," Fatboy said.

"Dog, understand something. Sometimes that's the chance people take when you fucking with other people stuff," Pokey said. "Y'all know how the game goes, and I'm pretty sure ya dog knew the chances he was taking as well. We all know LGO. Life goes on. We also know if Maurice dies, it's a sad story with tragic ending, that but was raw at basketball, Fatboy."

"I understand all that," Pokey said. "But people gotta eat to survive. And that's all ya boy understood, live by, die by. Anyways, all we can do is hope for the best. 'Cause it's better to be alive any day than dead and gone," Pokey said, making the sign of the cross while looking up at the sky.

"Hey dog, you gonna be all right?" Flick asked his dog outta love.

"Yeah, dirty, I'mma be all right. I losted a friend, but someone else may have lost a son, brother, father that they can never get back," Fatboy said, thinking 'bout his dog Maurice. "Damn, I'mma miss watching that nigga do them 360 dunks with ease though," Fatboy said, thinking back to the days his friend was just clowning and having a good ole time. Now all that is in the hands of God either way. He gonna either be carry by six or judge by twelve unless God does a miracle.

"Y'all think I can go see my dog?" Fatboy asked.

"Really, dog, it's no use, 'cause if he lives, you know them stanking-ass crackers gone be waiting at the door to take ya boy end, so you might as well just fall back and see what happens," Pokey said.

"Hey dog, to clear ya mind a little, 'cause I know the pain is deep, let's walk over to the park and see what's going on over there," Pokey said. "Let's roll, 'cause ain't nothing popping in the projects this morning."

Seems like everybody either sleep or just stuck in the house but us three. As we made our way to the park, everyone was in total silence, thinking, "How quick one minute you here, the next minute you gone. It's funny how the sun shines on the good and bad. I guess that's how fucked up the world is."

When they enter the park, it was crowded to be so early, you seen people already dancing, playing card, horse shoes, and even basketball. Like every Saturday, the park was crunk and the place to be. As we just walked around, the first person to catch our attention was Pokey's uncle, Uncle Sico.

"Man, what's up with you?"

"What you talking 'bout, nephew?"

"Unc, you look like you done lost some weight."

"Na'll, nephew, I been stressing," his uncle told him, knowing he was lying. "Anyways, boy, a few more months you'll be ready to make this bread like ya uncle," Sico said, changing the subject.

"Yeah, Unc, I can't wait. A nigga tired of being broke."

"I got you, nephew. I'mma show you all the ropes when ya time comes."

"All right, Unc," Pokey said, giving his uncle some dap. Then his uncle turned and walked off toward his ride, jumping in, and leaving the park early.

"Damn, ya uncle leaving already."

"I guess he is," Pokey said.

"He gone, ain't he, Pokey."

"Look at Double D ask."

"Where, oh, over there, I see – that fool, clowning, dancing with that fine-ass red bone, let that fool do him," Pokey said. As they started walking around the park, looking for no one in particular until they happened to notice Mr. Big, sitting on the hood of his ride, with the same three fine ladies he had with him the last time, bringing him food, beer, and whatever else he may have wanted.

"This nigga living like a king, ain't he?" Pokey asked his friends.

"Hell yeah," they both said.

"Look, let's go holla at this nigga!" Pokey said.

"For what? The nigga ain't gonna do shit for us," Fatboy said.

"Yeah, and as long as I been living, I know a close mouth ain't never got fed."

As Pokey started walking toward Mr. Big, he stopped and said, "Y'all niggas coming or what?"

"Yeah, we coming." Catching up with Pokey as they reached Mr. Big, he pulled up his shirt, exposing something that looked like a nine, like they was supposed to be scared or something.

"Man, nigga, what you showing us that shit for? We ain't trying to rob you," Pokey said.

"Well, what y'all young ass niggas want then?" Mr. Big asked.

"Man, shit, we want to be eating like you," Pokey shot back.

Mr. Big just laughed, "Y'all hear this shit, ladies? These young-ass niggaz said they wanna be eating just like me but don't know the shit I went through to make it on top and the shit I go through to stay on top. That shit funny, ain't it?" Mr. Big said, looking at the ladies. "Let me ask y'all a question," Mr. Big said.

"What's that?" they asked.

"What's y'all name?"

"My name is Fatboy."

"And mine is Flick."

"And you?" he said, pointing at Pokey.

"My name is Pokey." When Pokey said his name, Mr. Big looked at him again, like he seen a ghost.

"You said your name is Pokey?"

"Yeah," Pokey said.

"And what's your momma name?" Mr. Big ask.

"Mrs. Queen. Why, you the feds or something?"

"Just asking," Mr. Big said, knowing why he was really asking. "Sico told me this lil nigga look just like me, and the way he talking seems as though he got his heart from me too," Mr. Big was thinking. Back in the day, Mr. Big and Mrs. Queen used to mess around and ended up falling in love. The sad thing was, Mrs. Queen wanted Mr. Big to love her only, so they could be a family. But Mr. Big loved the street life more than anything, so after a few months of trying to convince him to leave the streets alone, she gave up and just left him alone and tried to keep it a secret that she was having his baby boy. But Sico knew the whole time. Even though Mrs. Queen told her son his father died a long time, when he was just a baby, she always knew one day he would find out that she lied to him because she didn't want him to follow in his father's footsteps.

"Listen," Mr. Big asked, "y'all young cats know anything about the streets and the street life?"

"We know enough," Pokey said, speaking for them all.

"Okay, since you know so much, hip me to game," Mr. Big said.

"We know if we live by the gun, there's a 90 percent chance we'll die by the gun, and to never ever get high off ya own supply," Pokey said, remembering what his uncle told him. "And last but not the least, keep ya friends close, 'cause you'll always know how to deal with ya enemies," Pokey said.

"I see y'all know a little something, but who told you that?"

"Never expose the one who put you up on game, game is to be sold, not told," Pokey said, laughing at Mr. Big looking all stupid now.

"I know Sico told him that," Mr. Big was thinking. And the reason why he knew it was his baby brother Sico, 'cause it's the same thing he told him when he put him in the game.

"One thing y'all jits forgot," Mr. Big said.

"What's that, old school?"

"Now I'm old school."

"Yeah, shit, you called us jits, we called you old school."

"Young buck, I like ya sway, but always remember it's two things to preserve in life, your health, followed by your freedom. You lose one, you lose both, y'all got that?"

"Yeah, we got that. But what's up, you talking like you 'bout to put us on."

"Look, young bucks, always remember patience is a must. I didn't get here overnight," Mr. Big said. "Now this what I'mma do for y'all, and this on the strength I see the same thing in y'all I had in me, what's that, determination, so I'mma give y'all a pound of weed and see how y'all handled business. You don't owe me nothing, but when something is free, you should always be able to come up," Mr. Big said.

In the back of Pokey's mind, he was thinking, "This nigga think we lame, ain't nothing in this world free but the air we breathing. So like I was told, always pay your dues," Pokey was thinking.

"Hey baby, bring a pound of that good good out the stash box for me." As the girl did what she was told, Mr. Big was thinking, "Is this young nigga my son, and do I really want my own son in the game? If it is, fuck it. If I don't, somebody else will." Just as he was finished thinking, the girl came with a black book bag and handed it to Mr. Big. Mr. Big took the bag, opened it, and looked in it, then said, "Here y'all go," handing the bag to Pokey. "This what I want y'all to do. In two weeks meet me back here, and let me know how things went, all right?" Mr. Big said, leaving his presence and walking back to the PJ's. But instead of leaving empty-handed, this time they had something that could put them on, just as soon as they hit the project grounds, Pokey said, "Damn, I hope Uncle Sico don't find out and be tripping and shit."

"Dog, all we gotta do is keep the shit on the low-low," Fatboy said.

"What he don't know won't hurt him, right? All right, where we gonna keep this shit at?" Flick asked.

"Look, I'll just keep it in my room," Pokey said. "And we'll see what we can get off in the projects and the rest at school."

"Word," Fatboy said. "All right, take some of that shit out and let's roll a blunt."

"Man, look, y'all know Mr. Big said we can't get high off our own supply, as bad as I wanna burn, we gotta make this bread. Keep in mind this nigga could be our meal ticket out the hood if we handle this right. So what we gonna do is go to Mrs. Jones's house and see if she will sell us some baggies and bag this shit up in dimes, 'cause we'll make more money that way, then selling quarters and ounces," Pokey said.

About two hours later, everything was done and ready to go.

"Now that we finish with that, let's see what we can sell before it gets too late."

"So how we gonna do that?" Fatboy asked.

"We don't know too many people 'round here who gonna cope from us, 'cause they all straight with Mrs. Jones," Flick said.

"You right 'bout that," Fatboy said. "I guess it's our luck though, here comes ya boy Double D on that beat-up ass bike. He know everybody that knows somebody."

"All right, let me holla at him. Double D, hey Double D!"

"What, young blood? What you calling my name all out loud, like I'm the damn president or somebody? What you want? I can't even sneak in the projects without you telling a motherfucker I'm here. Now what you want, young blood?" Double D says.

"I need you to do something for me."

"What's that, young blood? I ain't killing nobody, and I ain't robbing no banks."

"Man, shut up. We ain't talking 'bout no shit like that." All three boys laugh.

"Oh, 'cause I ain't doing no time for nobody."

"All right, man. Damn." Pokey said. "I just need you to let people know we in business on the weed tip."

"That ain't my drug of choice, but I'mma see what I can do for you. Where y'all gonna be posted at, man?"

"We just gonna be out back, right behind the projects."

"All right, I got y'all," Double D said. "Just remember my services ain't for free. For every person I send, I want a dollar in return."

"All right, bet, we got you. Just go spread the word on. And, Double D, don't let my Uncle Sico know about this all right?"

"Boy, do I look like a snitch? I thought so," Double D said, hopping on his bike and peeling off.

Not even an hour later, we had people coming and coping from us, left and right, like we the only ones who had weed.

"Dog, let's close this shit down for the day," Pokey said.

"Why, dog, we on fire right now."

"'Cause we ain't trying to make this spot too hot. You know how niggas is in the hood, they see something, they want in. Plus we ain't trying to get caught. With all these people coming behind the projects, a bitch gonna know something going on. Anyways, we done sold half the shit already, so that's good for the day."

"At least we know we in business," they said walking off.

"Dat shit go fast as fuck too. Just think if we had plenty of this shit, we'll be balling in no time."

"Yeah, I know," Pokey said, "But one thing at a time, y'all already know when my birthday come, we gonna move up from this petty shit to the big boy shit that these niggas will sell they own momma for."

"Yeah, but ya b-day four months away," Fatboy said.

"That's nothing, dog. As long as that nigga keep giving us this shit, we gonna be good. Feel me?" Pokey said.

"That's what's up," his two friends said, turning around, to hear Double D yelling.

"Hey Pokey, boy, where my money? And don't say you ain't got none, I seen all these people come back there, like y'all was selling crack instead of weed. Y'all ain't got no crack, do y'all?"

"Hell no, but here go your money. I know you thought we was gonna shit on you, but you did your part, now we gotta do our part," Pokey said, removing forty dollars from the book bag and handing it to Double D.

"All right, that's what I'm talking 'bout. If you niggas had some hard, I woulda let y'all make y'all money back, but since y'all don't, I gotta be moving," Double D said, jumping on his bike and speeding off, like he trying to win a race.

"Pokey, ain't that your uncle over there in the car sleep?"

"It looks like it. Let's go see, 'cause if it is, I know he seen all the shit going on." When they reached the car, Pokey's uncle was knocked out.

"Uncle Sico, man, what's up? You all right?"

"Huh? Oh yeah, nephew, I'm good. Just taking a lil nap, that's all."

But little did he know, Pokey finally realized the reason for his uncle losing so much weight. "This nigga was getting high off the same shit," he said. And Pokey woulda never believe it if he wouldn't have saw the pipe his uncle tried to cover up on the sly. Filled with anger and disgust, all Pokey could do was tell his uncle, "I'mma holla at you later," while looking at him with hate in his eyes, instead of the love he used to have for his uncle. They say it's a thin line between love and hate.

"Let's roll y'all," Pokey said. "Look, I'mma tell y'all something, and this stays between us, 'cause out here in these streets, we all the family we got."

Fatboy and Flick looked kinda thrown by the sudden change in Pokey's attitude, but they listened anyways.

"If we ever come up big in this game, and either one of us gets hooked on anything but money, it's over, life must end. So let's stay true. We in this for money and to try and help our families up out the hood, nothing more, nothing less," Pokey said.

"Dog, we hear you, but where all this shit coming from?" Fatboy asked.

"The heart, dog. As of now, we all bleed the same blood, we in whatever together, and my reason for saying this is because my Uncle Sico told me he'll never let the same game he running be his downfall or take him under. And if it did, he told me to promise I'll put a bullet in his head, 'cause he'll be better off dead 'cause a junkie ain't shit. And since I'm a man of my word, when the time comes, I'mma do just that."

They never thought Pokey was talking about killing his own uncle, but seeing him use that shit really fucked Pokey up, and he would rather see him dead than lose his crown or his freedom behind some stupid shit like that. So our saying is fuck with nothing that will cause you death, and all three boys gave each other dap.

"Dog, we gonna take this shit to another level, and we gonna have to turn our hearts cold in the process. If we wanna make it to the top, that's what's up," they said, walking off, feeling different already. "The beast is in every man. I do not understand what I do, for what I want to do, I do not do, but what I hate to do . . . As it is, it is no longer I myself who do it, but it is the beast living in me." With that thought in mind, they knew in order to win this game, they couldn't fear anything and had to always remember GABOS. Game ain't based on sympathy. Ain't no love in the streets, so why should we show it? It's every man against us. The first to make it to the top and stays there wins.

"And if we handle business right, we'll be looking down at all our haters," Fatboy said, smiling.

That's how it is.

GABOS, they all said. And it doesn't mean "God, angels, bless our streets," 'cause if we have to, we'll turn these streets BLOODRED. They said this, walking off! With one thing in common taking over.

CHAPTER 7

Time for a Change

"MAN, WHAT THE fuck is all that noise?" Fatboy said. Getting up, looking out the window. "Damn, this bitch swarming with polkes, I wonder what the hell done popped off now," he said to himself, putting his shoes on, getting ready to head out the door.

"But where you going with ya noise ass?" his sister Tiffany asked.

"Man, I'm going on outside to get some fresh air," Fatboy said.

"Yeah, I bet your noise butt, just going outside to see what done happen, that's all."

"Whatever, tip. I'mma holla," Fatboy said, as he opened the door and jumped the stairs, two at a time. When he hit the ground, he saw Pokey and Flick, coming in his direction. "What's up y'all?" Fatboy asked.

"Nothing, dog, we was just coming to get you," Flick said.

"Dog, what the hell happen out here? Why all these crackers swarming the projects like this?"

"Oh, you ain't heard? They kicked Mrs. Jones's door in."

"Na'll, man. For real?"

"Yeah, dog. But the thing is Mrs. Jones acted like she knew they was coming. They said she went out with a bang, busting her gun."

"What the fuck she do that for? She ain't have nothing but some weed."

"Na'll, dog. They found all kinds of shits in her house. Kilos of crack, scales, money, and guns. I guess Mrs. Jones was doing her thing on the low-low."

"Man, damn, I can't believe this shit," Fatboy said. "So where she at now?"

"Bro, the only way y'all ever see Mrs. Jones again is if you attend her funeral. When she just open fire on them crackers, they started shooting back. Said she died instantly. She got hit like twelve or thirteen times. People are saying, damn, another life."

"Gone down the drain," Fatboy said.

"So I guess you did see the news this morning then?" Pokey said.

"Man, I ain't watched no news. I was asleep till I heard all the shooting going down," Fatboy said, "Why?"

"What happened now, ya boy Maurice gone!"

"What you mean gone?"

"Oh, his momma snatch the plug on him. 'Cause they say the doctors told her it's a 25 percent chance he'll make it. But if he do, he won't remember nothing."

"He'll have to start all over, so she just snatched the plug?" Fatboy asked.

"Yeah, dog. Said she know her son loved life too much to live it as a vegetable, so she pulled the plug, killed her own son," Pokey said.

"They supposed to have his funeral sometime this week, said the services will be held at the church of God on Martin L. King Boulevard. You going?" Flick asked Fatboy.

"I really don't know, dog. Sometimes I feel it's best to remember people alive than dead," Fatboy said.

"Look, if you decide to go, I'll roll with you," Flick said, feeling sorry for his friend.

"I'll let you know, but as of now, I'mma fall back."

"Look, they putting Mrs. Jones's body in the hearse now!" Pokey screamed. "Then niggas over there look like they 'bout to go ham out this bitch. Y'all see them two niggas over there, they twins, them her two sons, and them niggas stay in some shit. They be locked up more than anything," Pokey said. "But one thing for sure, them young niggas gonna keep it all the way live, Pokey said.

"Who you talking 'bout?" asked Flick. "Shine and Boo Boo?"

"Yeah, that's them. Anyways, what's up, what we gonna do, first off? Check this out right quick. Of half the weed we sold yesterday, we made three hundred and sixty dollars, so that's one twenty apiece," Pokey said, splitting the money up. "And once we sell the rest, we'll make 'bout the same thing on a lil more. So between the three of us, we'll have close to 250 apiece. A good lil come-up for free! Well, we know we can't do shit today. With what just went down, we know them crackers gonna be here all day and night. So we gotta find something else to get into."

"Like what?" Flick asked.

"Shit, I don't know."

As they started walking away, they seen Mr. Big's BMW pull up, and out goes Mr. Big, looking around at what just went down.

"Let's go holla at him," Pokey said. "Mr. Big, what's up?"

"What's up, lil nigga? What happen 'round here?"

"Oh, the crackers ran down on Mrs. Jones and shot and killed her."

"Damn," Mr. Big said, as he put his head down. And when he looked back up, he had hatred in his eyes, and I knew this was a man nobody wanted to see or be fucked with.

"You all right, man?"

"Yeah, shortie, I'm good. You just don't know how bad I wanna call my goons and kill all these crackers. But I gotta think," Mr. Big said. In an angry tone, "Look, what y'all about to get into?" Mr. Big asked.

"Nothing. Why, what's up?"

"Come on, take a ride with me," Mr. Big said.

"All right, where we going?" Pokey asked.

As they climbed into the car, he said, "First I gotta make a run right quick. Then to ease a lil stress off my mind, I'mma take you young niggaz shopping and get y'all fresh to death."

"Man, we ain't got no money like that," Flick said.

"Boy, I said I'mma take y'all shopping. So that means it's on me, all right?"

"Shit, that's cool with us!" Pokey said. "You wanna blow your money on us?"

"We 'bout that, boy. I got more money than you'll ever be able to count and probably will see in your whole lifetime," Mr. Big said. "Hey, y'all chill out for a moment while I think about a few important things," Mr. Big asked them.

About thirty-five minutes later, we pulled up to some shit that looked like an abandoned building, probably was a storage room.

"Y'all just chill, I'll be back in a second." What seem like seconds turned into about twenty minutes, as chilling, so long.

Pokey turned around, telling his friends, "I told y'all, we was gonna come up fucking who this nigga."

"We gonna see," Fatboy said.

"Damn, this bitch cleaner in the inside than it is on the outside," Flick said.

"Sho is," they all said, looking around for the first time. "This nigga gotta be caked up, to be rolling in this shit."

As soon as they finished talking 'bout the whip, Mr. Big came strolling back with a briefcase in hand, as he opened the trunk, he slid the briefcase in and slowly made his way back inside the ride. "Y'all ready to ride?"

"Yeah, man, we ready."

"Y'all young niggaz smoke green?"

"Hell yeah," they said. "Roll it up, and we'll make it disappear," they said, laughing.

"Look in the glove box, in the cigar box, it's some joints in there. They already rolled up so just light it. Anyways," Mr. Big said, "what y'all do with that weed I gave y'all?"

"Oh, we sold half of it already, and I got cha bread," Pokey said.

"Young nigga, I like your style, a man who don't want or take nothing for free. Will always make it to the top, but keep the money. I gave that to y'all as a present."

"Bet that up," they said.

"Y'all listening, first my name ain't Mr. Big, it's Sterling. But y'all can keep calling me Mr. Big, 'cause I like the way it sounds," he said, laughing.

"We cool with that," they said.

"Damn, you ain't fire the joint up yet?" Mr. Big asked.

"We ain't got no fire."

"Damn, nigga. You scared to ask for a lighter, huh, man?" Mr. Big said, passing the lighter to Pokey. As they began to puff, puff, pass, all you could hear was *sooooosh* then coughing, followed by "damn, this shit the bomb."

"Na'll, you niggas just ain't no real smokers," Mr. Big said, turning on Misktal, still smoking. As the weed started to take effect, everybody started to chill and bob to the beat. As Mr. Big watched all three boys, he saw something in each one of them, which was the heart of a lion and loyalty till the death toward one another, which made his plan so much better. The thing was, could he trust these kids to hold a fort down that most grown-ups couldn't? "I'll talk to them later on," he was thinking, as they pulled up in the mall parking lot.

"Damn, y'all gonna be all right? Y'all look like y'all about to puss out," Mr. Big said, laughing as he looked at the kids.

"Look. when y'all get in here, y'all get whatever y'all want. But make sure y'all can carry that shit, 'cause I ain't helping y'all carry nothing."

"Okay, we got you," they said taking off, running, then remembered who they were with and slowed down.

"Man, we tripping, we can't be acting all lame and shit in front of Mr. Big," Fatboy said.

"You right, dog," they said, looking at Mr. Big.

"Man, do y'all. Y'all good, don't worry 'bout me," Mr. Big said, talking on his cell phone as they made their way around the stores. Within two hours they got everything they thought was fly. Good thing Mr. Big called his girls on the cell phone, 'cause it was no way we woulda got all this in the car.

"Meet us back at the projects," Mr. Big told the girls, as we loaded all our shit in the rides.

"All right, Daddy," they said, taking off. When Mr. Big got back in the car, he had a serious look on his face, like he was thinking extra hard about something.

"You good, Mr. Big?" Flick asked.

"Yeah, shortie, I'm good. I was just thinking 'bout something, that's all. Look, I wanna holla at y'all both something, but it's gotta stay between us. What I just did today I usually don't do, but I wanted to show y'all how shit can go, if y'all keep it real."

"I also did this for another reason. I want make known at this time," he thought, looking at Pokey.

"I just did what I felt needed to be done." They never knew Mr. Big was talking 'bout being a father to his son Pokey.

"Always y'all like spending money, huh?"

"Shit, who don't, but we'll rather be spending our own cheddar, instead of living off another nigga cheese like a lil rat," Fatboy said.

"Back to business, look y'all knew Mrs. Jones?"

"Yeah, who didn't and don't know Mrs. Jones? She be living in the projects her whole life, and she cool as fuck," they said.

"Yeah, I know," Mr. Big said. "And very loyal, I shouldn't be telling y'all this, but I am. She died today 'cause of me."

"What you mean 'cause of you?" Pokey asked, confused.

"Look, she was doing shit for me," Mr. Big said, getting all mushy and shit. "She damn near raised me, she was the only mother I knew. When I started making real paper, I tried to buy her a house. Anywhere she wanted, but she loved the hood. Said this where she was born, and this is where she would die, she kept her promise. She always preached to me about keeping it real. That's why I am who I am today, but listen, enough of that, I need some solid niggas on my team. Who can hold a fort down in the PJ's till I can find someone trustworthy enough to do the right things. Y'all know anybody I can trust?" Mr. Big asked.

"Yeah, you can trust us."

"That said, it's a lot of work that has to be done, but I'mma try y'all out and see how y'all handled things."

"So you gonna put us on?"

"Nope, y'all gone put y'all self on. I'mma just supply the work."

"Word. So what we gotta do?"

"Listen, Mrs. Jones got two sons. One is Boo Boo, the other is Shine, ever heard of them?"

"Yeah, we know them," they said.

"Well, them two niggas like my lil brothers, but they hotheads. What I'mma do is talk to them. Since they might still be stating in the momma apartment, I figure I could use them too. I'll just let them know, the same shit goes, business still gotta get done one way or another. I'll let them know about you three how y'all gonna be in and out as needed," Mr. Big told them.

"So what we gonna be selling?" Pokey asked.

"Look," Mr. Big said, "whatever they want, it will be there. I kinda figure y'all didn't know too much 'bout dope, so I'mma let Shine and Boo Boo teach y'all the ropes, till y'all can handle things on y'all own. Listen, y'all ever use that fire before?"

"No, but I will if I have to!" Pokey shouted,

"Look, I'mma get y'all right, 'cause in this line of work, you may need one. And always keep in mind, you pull it, you use it."

"What about when we in school?" Flick asked. "'Cause I still gotta go."

"Look, I still want y'all to go to school. Shine and Boo Boo can handle things while y'all gone."

"Hey, Mr. Big, what about my Uncle Sico?

"Not to reveal too much," Mr. Big said. "He'll be cool, but if he ask you anything, tell him I said come holla at me, or hit me up at the crib."

"All right, Mr. Big."

"Now that y'all got all them damn clothes and shoes, I know y'all momma gonna ask questions and probably trip. So just tell them Sterling took ya on a trip. They all know me, so it should be cool," he said, pulling up in the PJ's and parking his car. "Damn, this shit hotter than a motherfucker," Mr. Big said, looking at all the police walking back and forth. When he looked over to his right, he seen Shine and Boo Boo, looking lost and ready to snap. "Yo, Shine, and Boo Boo, come here," Mr. Big said, giving them a hug and wiping a lone tear from his eye.

"Dog, they killed Momma."

"Yeah, I know," Mr. Big said.

"What we gonna do?" Shine asked. "Let's shoot this bitch up," he said.

"Listen, y'all know back in my day, I woulda did just that. But in this game, you gotta learn to think. Listen, Momma gone, but we all know going to war with these crackers is a losing battle, and Momma wouldn't be too happy seeing us in heaven so soon," Mr. Big said. "Now look, I know Momma just got killed, but we gotta keep things in order. That's how she would want it. Listen, I need y'all to run shit in the PJ's for me, these three niggaz here my sons, they gone help y'all. I need y'all to teach them everything y'all can."

"We got you, bro," Shine and Boo Boo said, still wanting to flip some shit as they looked over at Pokey, Fatboy, and Flick.

"When we starting?" they asked.

"Give it 'bout three weeks," Mr. Big said. "We gotta wait till things cool down, right now let's concentrate on making Momma funeral the best ever!"

"Word," Shine, and Boo Boo said.

"Bro, I'm holla at y'all then, but I need y'all to stay outta trouble for real," Mr. Big told Shine and Boo.

"We got you," they said, walking off.

"Hey, y'all. I'm finna get up outta here," Mr. Big said.

"Y'all B-E-Z, all right, Mr. Big, and thank for the stuff," they said.

"No sweat," Mr. Big said, hopping in his ride and leaving the same way he came.

"Damn, Momma gonna trip when she see all this stuff. I know she is, but it's free, so I ain't giving it back," Flick said.

"Look y'all, let's go put all this shit up before these police-ass crackers come fucking with us," Pokey said.

"Yeah, dog, we feeling that," they said, picking up some of their stuff and carrying it upstairs till it was all put up.

"Pokey, bring your behind here right now, boy!"

"All right, Momma. I'm coming right now."

"I wanna know where in the hell did you steal or get the money from to buy all that stuff you just brought in my house?"

"Oh, Momma, Mr. B, I mean Sterling, brought it for me." At the mention of Sterling's name, she almost passed out.

"You said Sterling brought you all that stuff?"

"Yeah, Mom, why?"

"Oh nothing, baby. I just asked to make sure you ain't out there doing nothing wrong, that's all," she said. "Damn, this boy done got with his daddy. I just hope his daddy got enough since to keep out the street life," she was thinking.

"Flick, boy, hold up, son. Come here," Mr. Brown said, with a crazy look on his face. "Now where in the hell did you get all that stuff from?"

"Oh, Dad. Mr., I mean, Sterling took us shopping and brought us all the things we wanted."

"Sterling."

"Yeah, Dad, Sterling."

"Damn, I hope this nigga don't corrupt my son's mind."

"Look, boy, go put that stuff up before your momma come home, 'cause you know she'll have a fit, and I ain't trying to get cussed out 'cause of you. So hurry up, gone 'head, boy, and put that stuff up."

"All right, Dad, I got you."

"Whatever, boy!"

"Fatboy, damn lil bro, you done hit the lottery or something? I know you got something in there for me," his sister Tia asked.

"Man, I ain't got nothing. Somebody brought this for me."

"Or you done stole it one. Wait till Momma see all that stuff, she gonna trip. What you gonna tell her now?" Tia said, "But I am," his lil sister said. "Momma, hey, Momma, come look at this."

"What, girl?"

"Look at all this stuff Fatboy got."

"Boy, where in the hell you get all this shit from?"

"Momma, you always tripping 'bout nothing. Sterling bought it, he say call him if you don't believe it."

"What the hell he buying you shit for?"

"Momma, I don't know. He just did, all right."

"You better not be lying, cuz I'mma call his ass too."

"All right, Momma. You always feel like I be lying to you when I'm always honest with you."

"Whatever, boy. I'mma still call his ass, 'cause I ain't about to just watch Sterling fuck your life up."

"Mom, how he messing my life up if he helping me and telling us to stay in school?"

"He told y'all boys that?"

"Yeah, Mom."

"Well, I still, boy. All right, finish putting that stuff up."

"I got you, Mom."

"When you done your food in the microwave."

"All right, Mom, thanks!"

As he finished putting his things away, all he could think about was, "How she was gonna really act when I really start making money and be running around in new shit every day and driving all these difference cars? Momma gonna have a fit," he said, laughing to himself, as he went to the kitchen to eat his food. With thoughts of his shortie on his mind, "Yeah, I'mma call shortie when I'm done fucking this food up," he was thinking, as he began to get his grub on.

CHAPTER 8

Shed So Many TEARS

"FATBOY, BABY, GET your behind up and get dress."

"For what, Momma?"

"'Cause it's your friend and Mrs. Jones's funeral today."

"So, Mom, why I gotta go see the dead? Why I can't just keep right on, remembering them alive?"

"Look, boy, 'cause that was your friend, and you should at least pay your respect, even if you don't stay to the end."

"All right, Momma. Dang, but can my friends roll with me?"

"Boy, I don't care. That's on them."

"All right, let me call them right quick." *Ring, ring.* "Hello, hello, Mrs. Queen. Can I speak to Pokey?"

"Hold on, baby. Pokey, Pokey, your friend on the phone."

"All right, Ma, I'm coming." 'bout one minute later, Pokey comes to the phone.

"What's up, dog? My bad, I kept you waiting, I was using the bathroom."

"Look, dog, my momma making me go to my friend funeral and Mrs. Jones. You gonna roll with me?" Fatboy asked.

"Yeah, dog, I'll roll with you. What you wearing?"

"You already know, all black with the shade game."

"All right, dog. I'mma do the same."

"All right, dog. Look, I'll be over there in about twenty minutes."

"All right, I'll see you then. Flick going?" Pokey asked.

"I'm finna call him right now."

"All right then, handle that. I'm out," Pokey said.

"Hello, may I speak to Flick?"

"Who this is?" Mrs. Brown asked.

"It's Fatboy."

"Oh, hold on, baby. I think he sleep, but I'll get him. Flick, your friend wants you on the phone," his momma said.

"Momma, ask him what he wants."

"Baby, he said what's up?"

"Oh, ask him is he gonna ride with me to the funeral?"

"Hold on. He said you gonna ride with him to the funeral? Hold on, here he go."

"What's up, dog?" Flick asked.

"Man, you gonna roll or what?"

"Yeah, dog. What made you change your mind?" Flick asked.

"My momma," Fatboy said.

"When y'all leaving?"

"In about forty-five minutes."

"All right, what you wearing?"

"Me and Pokey wearing all black with the dark boys on."

"All right, I'm feeling that. Let me go hop in the shower right quick, then I'll be over there."

"All right, dog. I'll see you when you get here," Fatboy said, hanging up the phone.

About twenty-five minutes later, Pokey and Flick made their way to Fatboy's house clean as a whistle, decked in all black from head to toe with dark shades on, looking more like they were going on a business meeting than a funeral. As Fatboy opened the door, all he could say was, "Damn, y'all niggaz clean. Shit, you clean yourself. Look at cha, with the black on black."

"Dog, you rocking that shit," Pokey said. Lifting his shades up to look at his dog Fatboy. "Y'all ready to go?"

"Yes, ma'am, we ready," he said. As his mother stepped out in an all-black dress that hugged her body, "Damn, oh my bad, Mrs. Walls. Fatboy, your momma fine as hell," Flick said, giggling.

"Dog, don't make me beat your ass 'bout my momma," Fatboy said, play-punching his friend.

"I heard that too," Mrs. Walls told Flick. "Thanks for the compliment. Y'all ain't looking too bad y'all self," she said, smiling, playing with them, and they began to blush.

"Momma, you tripping," Fatboy said.

"Boy, shut up," she said smiling. "I'm just having fun, you know your lil friends too young for me," she said as they got in the car. As she began to drive, it slowly started raining, and when they reached the church, it was jam-packed. And instead of a light rain, it was now pouring.

"Dang, it's raining hard. I guess God really loved this nigga, to be doing all this crying," Pokey said.

"Boy, see that's what's wrong with y'all. Y'all don't know nothing bout God. God loves y'all," she was about to say.

"Momma, please don't start preaching, we already at church," Fatboy said.

"Boy, listen I just hope one day I ain't gotta be leaning over your coffin, crying and yelling, 'cause you done got yourself killed being stupid. A mother's kids is supposed to bury her, not the other way around."

"Momma, I hear you, and I ain't gonna do nothing stupid to leave this world early. It's too much stuff I haven't done that I gotta do," he said, with his friends saying, "We amen to that."

And all his mom did was smile, "Come on y'all, let go."

Why the rain done slacked up when they entered the church it was so many people there to see the dead, they felt like they were zombies, until they saw Maurice's mother and sisters, sitting on the front bench, shedding tears. As a lady sang "Walk Around Heaven All Day," more people began to shed tears. Even as I looked at my mom, I noticed she was crying too. As everybody started crying, me, Flick, and Pokey, put our dark boyz on and just listened to another lady start singing "The Angels in Heaven Done Signed My Name." After the song was over, the preacher by the name of Reverend T, a.k.a. Tony, began to speak today.

"Ladies and gentlemen, we have two people who are leaving this earth to go be with the father. Mrs. Jones and lil Maurice, they both died a tragic death, all in the hands of another person. We all know Mrs. Jones was a fine lady, who did and gave to everybody. She was born in the projects, and that's where she died. But we all know if she could talk to us now, she would tell us she is okay, she home, and would want us to keep living life to the fullest."

As he was speaking, the door opened and the preacher stopped talking and locked eyes with Mr. Big, a.k.a. Sterling. As Sterling made his way up front to his mother's coffin, he began to cry, and the preacher went on.

"Mrs. Jones was loved by everyone. She did all she could for the kids, even gave her last meal to see them eat. And today she is leaving us, but not forever. One day will see her again in a better life, a better world, one day, one day," Reverend T said.

As a guy began to sing a song by Boyz II Men, "It's So Hard to Say Goodbye to Yesterday" – I don't know where this road / is going to lead / all I know is where we've been / and what we've been through.

With that, Mr. Big got up off the coffin, with tears still streaming down his face and walked outta the church, filled with hurt and overcome with sadness that the only mother he ever had was now gone. He knew for him life would never be the same. As he beat his hands on the steering wheel, all he could do was yell, "God, why not me instead of her? She was only doing what I ask her to do, so it was my sin, not hers," as he began to shed his last tear.

As Shine and Boo Boo walked up to see their mother, for what they believed was the last time, they were filled with so much pain and hurt. But they refused to cry 'cause one day they realized, they too would be lying in a casket with people crying for them, but the only tears they could cry was tears of blood as their hearts began to break.

"Momma, I'mma miss you. I miss you already, and I regret always getting locked up and not spending time with you," Shine said. "I love you, Momma," he said and walked away.

"Momma, I know I was hardheaded, but you loved me regardless. And, Momma, I really can't believe you are gone. But when the reality hits, that's this is you in this casket. I really don't know what to do or how I'mma make it in this world without you. I know you would want me to be strong, and for you, momma, I'm reach the skies. I love you," he said, kissing the top of his mother's casket, turning and walking off.

As everybody began to pay their respects to a woman who was loved for who she was, they started singing "See You When I Get There." As everybody finished paying respects, some people left, most stayed to pay respects to a lil kid.

Reverend T began, "Today Maurice is leaving us too, and he will be truly miss. This was a fine young man who loved life more than anything. He loved to play basketball, he was in school, doing all the right things."

"Look, why this nigga up here lying on my dog," Fatboy said.

"That's what they get paid for," Pokey said.

As Reverend T kept going, his momma and sisters walked up to his casket.

"Baby, I'm sorry," his mother said. "I love you so much, and I know in my heart you was doing all you can for me and your sisters. And even though it was wrong, I appreciate all the things you did, 'cause I know if it wasn't for you, we wouldn't have a thing to eat. I'm sorry you lost your life, trying to save ours, but I want you to know I've always been proud of you, and I love you, baby, and I'mma miss you dearly. I know things are going to be rough, but I'mma make it, 'cause I'll always have memories of you," she said, while tears fell on his face, and she moved over to let his sisters say their good-bye.

"It's a sad story when a mother has to bend over her child," Pokey said, as he watched all his friend's sisters say their good-byes to their only brother. As everybody began to pay respects, Fatboy and his friends were the last one, even though Pokey didn't vibe with Maurice, he was doing this for his dog, as they made their way to the casket.

Pokey said, "Real G's don't cry." Pokey looked down at Maurice and said, "Dog, sorry life was taking from you so early. I guess that's the way the game goes, but you kept it G with ya people, you made sure they got fed. And for that, if I ever make it big, I'mma look out for ya peoples, that's my word," Pokey said, making the sign of the cross, lifting his glass up and looking at Maurice for the last time. "I hope heaven's got a ghetto for niggas like you and me," he said, walking off.

As Flick looked down at a lifeless body, all he could say was, "Damn, dog, this coulda been anyone of us, but it's not, it's you. And I hope, dog, you finally at peace, you can take a break, and just look over ya family from the skies up above. I know you gonna be up there balling and dunking on everybody," Flick said, smiling. "Dog, look, if I ever make it running, I'll never forget you," pulling up his glasses. Looking at his friend for the last time, he said, "Save a place up in heaven for me," Flick said, walking off.

As Fatboy moved his glasses from his face, he stared at his friend for a minute, "Lil, homey, look, I know you can hear me. I just want you to know I'mma miss you. I wish you woulda listen and stayed outta trouble, but I understand now why you did what you did, and, man, I ain't mad at cha 'cause I ain't no saint. So I'm asking why you up in heaven, look down on me and try to keep me outta trouble. Look, dog, I love ya, and I'mma miss you, but I know in my heart I'll see you again 'cause it's a heaven just for G's. I love you," Fatboy said, walking off. With no tears in sight, him and his two friends realized this was a good place to turn ya heart cold and to remember the saying GABOS. As they walked outside, they seen people talking, getting into cars, and leaving, but they also noticed . . . Mr. Big was still there, bent over the steering wheel.

CHAPTER 9

Everything Happens for a Reason

"LOOK, MR. BIG still here," Pokey said. "Let's make sure he all right, let's roll." *Knock, knock*, they tapped on his window, watching as Mr. Big rolled his window down.

"You all right, Mr. Big?"

"Yeah, son, I'm all right. Just a lil broken up, that's all."

"Why you still out here?" they asked.

"To be honest, I was waiting on y'all."

"For what?"

"Come on, get in, and ride with me."

"Hold up, I gotta go ask my momma," Fatboy said, running off. "Momma, it's all right if I roll with Mr. Big? He said he'll bring us home."

"I guess so, go 'head."

"All right, Momma. I'll see you later."

"Uh-huh," his momma said, watching him walk back the other way.

"Let's ride, she said it's cool."

"All right, hop in," Mr. Big said.

"Dang, Pokey, why you always gotta hop in the front seat?"

"'Cause I'm the oldest," he said, laughing.

As Mr. Big turned on the radio, all you heard was "Life Goes On" by Tupac blaring from the speakers – Two in the morning and we still high assed out. The part that caught everyone though and had us remembering we just left a funeral was when he said, Have a party at my funeral / Let every rapper rock it / Let all the hoes that I used to know from way before / Kiss me from my head to my toe / Give me a paper and pen / So I can write about my life of sin / A couple bottles of gin in case I don't get in

"Damn, I can't believe my momma gone, just like that," Mr. Big said. "I gotta find out who gave them crackers the ups on my momma, and when I do, it's gonna be a slow death for whoever," Mr. Big said, looking dead ass for real, like he could kill at any given moment.

"Mr. Big, where we going? We been riding around now over a hour," Pokey said.

"We'll be there any moment, and what I told y'all 'bout patience?" Mr. Big asked.

"You right," Pokey said.

"Look, light the joint up," Mr. Big said. "It will help you learn some patients," he said.

"Now you talking," Fatboy said. "Fire that shit up. I need something to ease my mind anyways." As Pokey sparked the bunt, you could smell the scent of weed all in the car.

"Damn, we got this shit smoked out," Pokey said, rolling down the window, watching the smoke slowly disappear right along with the joint. They pulled up to this big ole house surrounded by trees and different cars parked everywhere.

"Damn, Mr. Big, you got us way out here in the country. You ain't gonna kill us, is you?" Pokey asked, laughing as his two friends started laughing too.

"Lil nigga, you a trip. This one of my cribs. I use this shit when I need to get away and just think. Out here it's quiet as a motherfucker, and it's nice so just chill. I ain't gonna kill you, fools," he said, breaking a half smile, still feeling the pain that his momma is gone. "Maybe it's true, you lose someone you love, someone else will come," he was thinking, if looking at his son.

"Well, what we gonna do, sit in the car all day?" Flick asked.

"Oh, na'll come on," Mr. Big said, getting out the car and walking toward the house with the three boys right behind him, laughing and giggling from the joint they just smoked.

"Y'all higher than a kite, 'cause y'all laughing y'all ass off," Mr. Big said, being met at the door by this fine-ass woman who was thinner than Buffy.

"Hey, baby, you all right?"

"Yeah, baby, I'm good. I'mma be all right," Mr. Big said.

"Look, baby, this here is Pokey, and this Fatboy and Flick."

"How y'all doing?" she asked.

"Fine," they all said.

"Y'all this my wife Tina."

"Damn, old school, you married?"

"What I just told you?"

"Shit, I can't blame him," Fatboy said, laughing.

"All right, look, y'all make y'all self comfortable while I go talk to her. Y'all can just chill out or walk around. I know y'all probably hungry, so the kitchen is down the hall on the left," Mr. Big said.

"All right, we got cha," they said, looking over the place.

"Damn, this shit nice. This nigga got this bitch laid out," they said, walking around, touching shit they never seen before.

"This nigga got that paper for real," Pokey said. As they made their way into the kitchen, they were startled by a female voice.

"What y'all want? I got y'all, my daddy told me to fix y'all something to eat if y'all hungry," the girl said.

"Damn, Mr. Big got a daughter."

"Yep," she said, "his only child. But anyways, my name is Trirena,"

"Oh, mines is Pokey, Fatboy, Flick."

"All right, y'all want anything?"

"Yeah, y'all got some pizza?"

"Yeah, I got y'all," the girl said, digging in the freezer looking for pizza.

"Damn, this girl fine ass, the woman who answer the door," Flick thought. "And she must be sixteen or seventeen," he was thinking.

"Y'all can put it in the microwave y'all self."

"All right," they said, as she walked off, not looking back.

"Shortie cool as fuck, ain't she?" Flick asked.

"Yeah, she all right," Fatboy said.

"Man, what y'all think this nigga got planned now?"

"Shit, I don't know," Pokey said. "But it's gotta be good, he done brought us to where he lay his head." As the beep sounded to let them know the pizza was done, they grabbed it and began to eat. About five minutes later, another older chick walks in with a case in hands. As we watched her set the case on the counter and opened it, she said, "Hey y'all, my name is Blessing, and I'm about to bless y'all," she said, opening the case. "Y'all check this out," she said. As we got up and walked over, this lil ass case was loaded with guns. "Look, Sterling told me to let y'all pick whatever y'all felt comfortable with."

"Shit," Pokey said, as he looked then decided on a chrome .38 special. Fatboy looked around and grabbed a Glock 9 all black, while Flick grabbed a .22 with a clip.

"Man, that shit weak," Pokey said.

"Nigga, you tripping. Up close this bitch will fuck you up. I say up close, 'cause if I ever have to use it, *pow*, one shot to the head and he dead. Kill the head, the body dies, right?"

"I'm feeling that dog, here y'all go," Blessing said, passing each boy the bullets they would need for the guns they just picked. "All right y'all, I'm out," Blessing said, looking like she was thugged out.

"Y'all good?" Mr. Big said, walking in the kitchen.

"Hell yeah!" Pokey said.

"All right then, that's what I'm talking about."

"Mr. Big, what's up with the gats? Why you giving us guns?" Flick asked.

"Young blood, remember I told you in this game, you never know who may be plotting to take ya life, so you gotta be ready at all times. This a dirty game, and I've told y'all, in order to reach the top, you gotta be ready and willing to die to get there," Mr. Big said, tapping the top of Flick's head.

"I hear you," Flick said. "But where I'mma keep this, and what if my momma finds its then what?"

"Come on, lil nigga, I know you sharper than a knife, so use ya head. Hide it somewhere, only you know where it's at, or just keep it on you like I do at all times," Mr. Big said, pulling up his shirt, exposing the gun, "'Cause you never know when you may need it," Mr. Big said. "Look, I'mma go back in the room with wifey. When y'all ready to go, just let me know, okay?"

"Okay," they said, as Mr. Big walked off. Pokey pulled his gat and started talking all crazy.

"I wish a bitch would try me, if I don't put a bullet in his ass. My daddy ain't dead."

"Man, put that shit up, for you shoot a nigga on accidence," Fatboy said, watching his friend act a fool. "This nigga gonna be hard to deal with. They say a gun will make the weakest nigga feel like a killer. I guess that shit is true," he was thinking.

"Come on, y'all, let's walk around this shit some more before we bounce."

"Damn, look at this big-ass fish tank. Man, what the fuck is that?"

"Shit, I don't know, but it ain't no fish. This nigga got some crazy shit in here."

"Now this what I'm talking about," Flick said, walking in the game room, where there was a pool table and all kinds of games. "This nigga got every game there is." And they began to play. About two hours later, they were worn-out, full, and ready to get back to the hood.

"What's up? Y'all ready to go?" Pokey asked. "Whenever y'all ready, I'm ready." While the boys where getting ready to call Mr. Big he was in the room telling his wife that Pokey was his son from back in the day. But she knew the minute she saw him, "Shit, they look just alike, if you look hard enough," she was thinking.

"Baby, it's cool. I'm just glad you told me. Now I gotta tell Trirena she got a brother, she'll be cool about it. Mr. Big, and why they call you Mr. Big?" she said, laughing.

"Oh, that's a name they give me when I first met them."

"Oh, so you ain't tell the kid you was his father yet?"

"No, baby, I don't know how to. I'm trying to catch up on the years I missed by doing shit for him."

"Baby, you'll never catch up for the years you missed. All you can do now is enjoy the ones that to come."

"All right, baby, I got you," Mr. Big said, getting up off the bed and walking out the room.

"Yo, Mr. Big, we ready to roll."

"All right, let me put my shoes on, then we out. Y'all got everything y'all need, right?"

"Yeah, we good. Hey Mr. Big, when you gone bring us out here again to chill?" Pokey said.

"Any time y'all wanna come, just let me know and I got cha."

"All right, that's what's up," they said, heading out the door. Remembering the fire they had tucked in their waist.

"Well, let's roll."

As they entered the car, Mr. Big started to tell Pokey he was his father but changed his mind, just as quick and just got in the car. With thoughts on his mind, "Is it my fault his mother ain't tell me I had a son?" But just as quick he erased the thought, remembering his brother Sico told him from day one Mrs. Queen was having his baby. So maybe it was his fault he wasn't in his son's life.

CHAPTER 10

Two Weeks Later: Making That Money!

"DAMN! SHINE AND Boo Boo got this bitch booming," Pokey said, walking up to the building where Mrs. Jones used to live. *Knock, knock.*

"Yeah, who dat?" Shine hollered.

"It's me, Pokey."

"Oh, come in, lil nigga. The door open," Shine said.

As Pokey walked in the house, he touched his side making sure the .38 was in place.

"Damn, y'all got this bitch jumping," Pokey said.

"Yeah, dog, we just trying to make that money anyway possible."

"I feel that," Pokey said, looking at all the weed and drugs sitting on the table, while Boo Boo was bagging everything up.

"Dog, look, where ya two lil dogs at?" Shine asked.

"We need them niggas to handle something. Oh, they'll be here in a minute," Pokey said.

"All right, Pok. Check this out, all y'all gone be doing is selling weed. That's what Mr. Big told us, to let y'all handle that."

"That's cool," Pokey said.

"But look, he said as soon as y'all learn the ropes, he'll move y'all up in the game."

"All right, that's what's up," Pokey said.

Not really knowing Mr. Big told Shine and Boo Boo that he was his son, and to make sure nothing fucked up happen to him, so that's why Shine told him to just sell the weed 'cause he know how Mr. Big is about blood and friends.

"The nigga will straight snap if something happens to this lil nigga," Shine was thinking, when outta the back room comes this fine-ass chick named April, half naked, walking up to Shine.

"Daddy, everything in place. You ready to make it happen and go drop this pack off or what?"

Bam! Shine slapped the shit outta April, "Bitch, what I told you 'bout your big-ass mouth, talking all crazy and shit in front of people?"

"My bad," the girl said with her head down. "I wasn't thinking," she said.

"I know you wasn't," Shine said. "Now let's roll," he said, walking behind her.

In Pokey's mind, all he was thinking was, "If that was my sister that nigga hit like that, he woulda been dead and stinking. But since it's not, oh well," was all he was thinking, when Shine turned around, before heading out the door.

"Look, when your homeboyz get here, tell them what's up, and y'all only serving the people who want weed. Anything else Boo Boo will handle," he said, walking off.

"Whatever, nigga," Pokey was thinking. "They wanna make all the money but watch us make nickels and dimes. Bullshit!" Pokey was thinking. "I'mma sit back for a minute, but I can promise you when the smoke clears, I'mma be the man," Pokey was thinking, when he heard a knock on the door. *Boom, boom!*

"Hey Pokey, see who that is for me," Boo Boo said.

"Who is it?"

"It's us, nigga, open the door," Fatboy and Flick said, walking in.

"Where y'all niggaz been? I been waiting on y'all," Pokey said.

"Man, we was just chilling, but we here now, so what's up?"

"Man, look, they want us to sell all the weed, while they handle the big stuff. But that's cool for now, so learn all y'all can by watching, and when we find out what's what, we'll deal with things differently. But for now, we'll listen to these niggas Shine and Boo Boo," Pokey said.

"Whatever, man, you know we with you, so it's whatever."

"All right, man. Boo Boo almost finish doing what he do, and once he done shop back open, so let's sit back and chill for now," Pokey said.

"Man, it's colder than a polar bear toenail in this bitch," Fatboy said. "These nigga tripping."

"Nah, they keep it cool for a reason."

"All right, whatever, but next time I'm wearing my jacket. I don't give a damn," Fatboy said, as his two friends began to laugh.

"Yo, Pokey, check this out," Boo Boo said.

"What's up?"

"Look, this a lot of weed. It's all dimes and twenties, so when whoever want something, it's easy to handle. In about thirty minutes shop will be open, and y'all know how this bitch be flooded, so stay alert 'cause you never know who's who," Boo Boo said. "Feel me?"

"Yeah, I'm feeling that, but I can handle myself," Pokey said, showing him the .38 by pulling up his shirt.

"I'm sure you can with that," Boo Boo said. "Just make sure you bust the right person," Boo Boo said.

"Oh, I ain't gonna pull it, unless I'mma use it," Pokey said.

"That's what's up," Boo Boo said. "What about ya two lil dogs, them niggas carrying that fire too?"

"Yeah, they strapped and ready for whatever. Mr. Big made sure we got straight two weeks ago."

"I coulda figure that, that's the same nigga who gave me this," he said lifting up his shirt.

"Damn, what's that?" Pokey asked.

"Oh, this here ain't nothing special, but it will put a hole in a nigga ass so big you'll see through him," Boo Boo, said. "It's a .44 though, he gave me this shit 'bout three weeks ago, right before momma got killed. I wish I was here when the shit went down. I woulda set this bitch on fire with my old G. I still can't believe she gone," Boo Boo said, thinking back. "But you know that old junky nigga they call Double D?" he said. "He gonna find out what really happen for us. Anywayz, y'all, let's get this shit started. Everybody know 'round 3:30 shop's back open just as quick." As Boo Boo finished his sentence, there was a knock on the door.

"Dog, y'all might as well keep that bitch open, 'cause when its starts raining, its begans to pour."

"Boo Boo, this one for you. She holling she want that white stuff, that powder."

"Ask her what she want."

"What you want?"

"I just want a twenty," the lady said, showing Pokey the money.

"She said a twenty."

"Cash up front. All right, huh, Boo Boo?" as he threw the lil baggie to him. "Here you go," he told the lady, and she grabbed the bag and started walking off.

For the next two and a half hours, shit was booming. But when night fell, everything got crazy. People you never expected to see were either there buying weed, crack, or powder, but who cares who's doing what, as long as the money right. Around eight o'clock, Pokey, Fatboy, and Flick told Boo Boo they were calling it a night, 'cause they had school tomorrow.

"All right then, dog, I'll take it from here," Boo Boo said, placing his gun on the table. "Before y'all go, check this out, we made a killing today. And Sterling, a.k.a. Mr. Big, said make sure y'all straight every time y'all leave here. So here's five hundred dollars apiece, small money to a gaints. Anyway, y'all B-E-Z, and stay out them crackers' way," Boo Boo said, giving the three niggas dap.

"Bet that up," they all said, smiling as they exited the door.

"Damn, dog, we getting paid for nothing. All we do is hand out bags and take the money. This shit sweet," Flick said.

"Yeah, and just imagine when we up the ladder. If they giving us five hundred, what will we make then. Dog, I told y'all this nigga was our meal ticket out the projects!" Pokey screamed, all happy.

"Look, we got school tomorrow, so leave ya gun home. We won't need them at school anyways," Fatboy said.

"Word," Flick said.

"Pokey, you heard dog?"

"Yeah, whatever," Pokey said. "Look, I'mma catch y'all in the morning," Pokey said, turning back around, headed in the same direction he just came to go back and chill with Boo Boo. In his mind, he had to learn all he could, and the only way to do that was to be around what was going on.

"Look, Flick, Pokey going right back over there. I hope our boy don't start to acting funny and stuff. They say money is the root of all evil, but we'll soon find out, Fatboy," said.

"All right, lil homey, I'll see you tomorrow."

"All right," Flick said, jogging home. And Fatboy went in the house.

CHAPTER 11

Keeping It Real

BACK IN SCHOOL the following morning, we had shit jumping left and right once everybody realized we had that real fire-ass weed, they stopped copping from Turtle and his lil friends and started messing with us! Something we learned to love, and would always be used to, anything green we loved and lived for. The saying is money makes the world go round. And if we had anything to do with the world spinning, it would never stop, 'cause we were trying to get all the money we could. The bad thing is we knew sooner rather than later it would bring the haters and with the haters' unnecessary beef. We already had a bad feeling 'bout Turtle and his friends all because Flick beat his boy at running. Now us taking over on the weed tip, shit was about to get hectic. But we were prepared for any and everything 'cause we live by the saying GABOS, so we expected none in return.

Fatboy said, "What's up, Jay?"

"Nothing, you got something on you?" Jay asked.

"Yeah, dog, what you trying to get?"

"Let me get a twenty," he said, handing the money to Fatboy.

"All right, dog, here you go," giving the kid a twenty, but you would think it was a fifty as fat as it was. "See this the thing that had us jumping so fast. We gave you what you paid for. Turtle was selling all right weed, and the sacks was skimpy, so it was easy to take over! Ever since we stepped foot on school grounds, I've been having a bad feeling, like something wasn't right," Fatboy was thinking, touching his side. But remember he told his friends last night to leave the fire home, not knowing Pokey didn't.

"Dog, look, y'all be on point, I got a bad vibe about something," Fatboy told his two friends, who just nodded their heads. "Look, the bell just rang so I'mma catch y'all at lunch, all right!"

"All right," they said, giving one another dap.

"Hey y'all, for real stay on point," Fatboy said.

"Dog, we got you. We know you got them superpowers," Flick said, laughing.

"We got you," Pokey said, walking off.

Two hours later it was time for lunch, and this is when people be wanting to get their smoke on. As I exited the classroom and met up with Pokey and Flick, we began our journey to the lunchroom, only to be stopped by a few people. Ready to visit the angels, we did our thing.

"Sold a nick acre, a dime there, and a twenty every few steps! Damn, we got this shit on fire," Pokey said, smiling.

"Listen y'all, let's go head to the lunchroom and get something to eat so we can chill awhile." When we entered the lunchroom, something didn't quite feel right. When we looked 'round, we saw Turtle and his crew, looking at us all crazy and shit.

"Y'all be on point, in case these niggaz got some tricks up they sleeves," Fatboy said, making sure his friends was ready, just in case.

"Man, fuck them niggas," Pokey said. "Whatever them niggas wanna do, I'm 'bout that."

"Man, look, we all know it's whatever with all us, but we ain't trying to stop the world from spinning. We got plenty more money to make," Flick said.

"Man, look, let's go ask these niggas what's up," Pokey said, walking off. With his two friends beside him, ready for whatever, in Fatboy's mind all he was thinking was, "One minute you down, next minute you up. That's the way the game is. Whoever got the best and most, always win." He was thinking when he heard Turtle say, "What y'all niggas want?"

"I came to ask you the same thing, since y'all seem to be eyeing a nigga. What's up with y'all?" Pokey said. "Y'all gotta problem with us 'cause if so, we can go 'head and solve this shit right now," Pokey said, heated.

"Nigga, what you mean?" the kid named Wacko asked.

"Just what I said, lil nigga. If you niggas want some problem or got a problem with us, let's handle this shit now," Pokey said.

"Look, nigga. Don't go to feeling like you Rambo or Bruce Lee 'cause you ain't," Turtle said. "If we had a problem with y'all, trust me we would address it. So don't feel like a nigga scared of you or running from y'all 'cause we ain't."

"We just don't have time to be rapping with you fools, that's all! Niggas like us got bigger and better things to do."

"Let's ride, Pok. These niggas don't want no problem," Fatboy said.

As they turned to walk off, the nigga named Rachet hollered at Pokey, "You better watch your back," and started laughing, which made Pokey lift up his shirt and expose the gun, which we never knew he had on him.

"Dog, to be so skinny ya got a big-ass mouth, 'cause for one, I don't take kindly to threats," he said, walking toward the nigga.

"Hold up, Pok. Just a sec. Hey, Flick, dirty, get up outta here, in case this shit gets ugly. You the only one in our crew got something going for himself, and I don't wanna see you mess that up," Fatboy told his dog.

"Look, dog, you must forgot when we all became friends. We made a truce that we all family and bleed the same blood, so I ain't about to bounce on y'all. Remember GABOS so have none for me, 'cause blood is always thicker than water," Flick said.

"All right, my nigga. You dead ass right," Fatboy said. "Pok, what's up? What you wanna do? Man, ya just chill."

"I'mma whoop this nigga ass. Hun, hold this," he said, passing Fatboy the gun. As soon as he gave the gun to Fatboy, Pok hit the nigga Rachet with a three-piece, which caught him off guard and dropped him dead on his back, "Seen his dog get knocked out? They tried to get at my dog," only to hear the sound of thunder, as Fatboy let two go.

"If I was you niggaz, I wouldn't think about it," Fatboy said. "Look, these bullets ain't got y'all name on them. But I can promise if you niggas touch my dog, they'll have y'all blood on them."

"Man, you tripping," Flick said. "Put that shit up! Them crackers coming. You in here shooting in the lunchroom. You know these hating-ass niggas gonna tell on ya."

"Man, fuck these niggas," Fatboy said, heated but at the same time tucking the burning .38 back in his side. When he saw them crackers coming by, it was too late. Students began yelling and pointing, "He got a gun," pointing at Fatboy. "Damn, these some snitching-ass bitches," he was thinking, as he was bombrushed by all these crackers that were supposed to be guards or some shit. "Damn y'all, gonna break his arm, cracker. Y'all already got him down," Pokey said, wanting to do something but not knowing what to do.

Flick was so mad, he couldn't even talk. All he was thinking, "If this nigga Pokey woulda left like we said, dog wouldn't be on the ground. Probably on his way to jail, and I know this nigga heard dog say don't bring no fire to school. Good thing he sold all the weed he had on him before we came in this bitch," Flick was thinking, as they picked Fatboy up and started escorting him out the school and in to a waiting police car.

"Hey Pokey, let my old girl know what happen, all right?"

"All right, dirty, I got you," Pokey said.

"Hey Flick. Keep that nigga outta trouble."

"I got you, dog."

If Pokey wasn't already on papers, in his mind he knew he woulda never let his friend go out like that. As the police car pulled off with his dog in the backseat, all he could say was, "Man, fuck this school shit. I'm done with this bullshit," and began to walk home.

When Fatboy reached the county jail, he learned he was being charged with possession of a firearm by a minor and causing a scene while on school property. His bond was set at fifteen thousand dollars; with the 10 percent it would cost him fifteen hundred dollars to get out. After all the fingerprinting and photo taking was done, he got his one chance to make a free phone call. The first person came to mind was Mr. Big but remembered he didn't have his number, so he called his mom's.

"Hello," Kecia answered the phone.

"Kecia, where momma at?" he asked.

"She sleep. Why? Where you at?"

"I'm at the county jail."

"Boy, you in jail? What the hell you did?"

"Man, where Momma at?"

"Boy, Momma gonna have a fit. Momma, Momma!" Kecia yelled. "Your son on the phone, and he calling from the jailhouse."

"Hello, boy, where you at?"

"I'm in jail, Momma."

"For what?" she asked.

"Something happen at school earlier and I got cased up."

"Doing what, boy?"

"I had a gun, but it wasn't mines."

"Whose was it then?" In her mind she already knew none other than Pokey.

"Momma, look, I only got 'bout two more minutes before this phone hangs up. I need you to call Mr. Big, I mean Sterling, and have him bond me out."

"How much is your bond?" his mother asked, all concerned,

"Fifteen thousand. With the 10 percent, fifteen hundred."

"I'll be there in a minute, boy. Bye," she said, hanging the phone up in his ear.

"Damn, she hot," he was thinking."

"Kecia?"

"What's up, Ma?"

"Look, I'm about to go get ya brother. Make sure when Tia and Renee get home, tell them I said clean that kitchen up."

"All right, Momma, I heard you," Kecia said, watching her mother count the money she was saving to move out the hood.

"Now go to getting her brother outta jail. Momma love that stupid behind boy," Kecia was thinking as her mother left the house.

On her way to the bondsman she found herself saying a prayer, "Lord, please keep this boy outta trouble, and just help him make the right decision in life. If not he gonna get in some trouble he can't get out of. Please, Lord," she said, as she pulled up to James Bondsmen.

Jumping out her car and jogging to the door, she rushed in, "Look, my baby is in jail, and I need to bond him out."

"Slow down, ma'am please. First, who is your son?"

"Oh, Tyler Gore. They picked him up for a gun charge."

"Hold on, let me look at this cumpter. Okay, here it goes. His bond is fifteen thousand dollars, 10 percent, fifteen hundred dollars. How will you pay?"

"In cash," she said, handing him the money.

"All right. Just fill out these papers right quick, then you can go get him," the man said.

"All right, thank you," she said, filling out the proper paper work. Fifteen minutes later, Fatboy heard his name being called.

"Gore, your bond's been posted. Pack up all your stuff and come to the front."

"Damn, that was quick. Momma musta flew here," he was thinking as he was getting dressed. A few seconds later, he walked out the county jail a free man. Looking over the parking lot to see where his momma was, he saw her sitting in her car like she just got through crying. All he could do was say, "Momma I'm sorry, and thanks for coming to get me."

"Listen, boy. You my only son, and I love you, but you gotta start making better choices with your life. Unless you want me to come visit you in places like these," she said, catching a tear before it fell.

"I got you, Momma. I'mma do better!" he said as his mother began the drive home.

"Now you wanna explain to me what happen today at school?" his mother asked. "And the truth."

"Momma, look, we was about to get into it with some other dudes when my friend handed me the gun and asked me to hold it while he fight this one kid. When he knocked buddy out, his dogs acted like they were about to jump my friend, so I shot in the air. That's all, Momma. And when I turned around, them crackers was knocking me behind to the ground," he said.

"So I guess you suspended from school too," his momma said.

"More like expelled, Momma. But I'mma still try and go back. If not I'll get my GED," he said, looking at his momma. "Momma, you all right?"

"Yeah, I'm okay. Just thinking, that's all." After all the talking was over, Fatboy had time to think to himself. He knew when he went to court the most they would do was send him to a program, but he was hoping for probation or something that would keep him free. When they pulled up in front of their building, his mother cut the car off and went in the house, not looking back at her son or even saying anything else to him.

"Damn, Momma hot," he was thinking. As he walked in the house, his sisters started saying, "Jailbird home, jailbird home!"

"Trying to be funny, kiss my –" Fatboy was about to say, until he heard his momma say, "Boy, I wish you would tell somebody to kiss your dirty ass. And y'all leave that boy alone, he in enough trouble already," she said, turning walking in her room and slamming the door.

"Dang, stupid boy, now you got Momma hot at all us with your stupid butt," his sister Tia said.

"She should be," Kecia said. "She just paid all the money she was saving up to get your ass out the hood. Now she had to end up using it to get you outta jail."

"Damn, I fucked up," Fatboy was thinking. "But Momma gonna have more than enough money when I'm done!" he was thinking.

"Man, if Momma come back out, tell her I'm outside getting some air."

Not even fifteen minutes later, he sees Pokey walking up.

"What's up, dog?" Pokey asked. "I see them crackers let you go."

"Na'll, dog. My momma paid her last to get me out. But what's up with you?"

"Listen, Fatboy, I know you mad at me for bringing the piece to school. If I wouldn't have brought it like you said last night, we wouldn't be having this conversation."

"Dog, I ain't mad at cha," Fatboy said.

"Also," Pokey said, "I quit school."

"Why?" Fatboy asked.

"'Cause it's not for me, I gotta make this money. Them crackers don't give a fuck about me, they ain't trying to help me, so fuck that school shit. The streets is all I know anyways!" Pokey said, venting "What they talking 'bout with you?"

"Oh, you know, I'm expelled."

"Not that, nigga, the case."

"Oh, I don't know yet. I got a court date in twenty-one days."

"How much was ya bond?"

"Fifteen thousand dollars, but you know with the 10 percent it was only fifteen hundred dollars. My old girl came up with the money," Fatboy.

"Dog, I'm sorry about what happen."

"No sweat, dog, for real."

"Listen, give this to your momma," he said, passing Fatboy the eight hundred and twenty dollars he had in his pockets. "Tell her I'll get the rest up real soon."

"Dog, thanks, man. She may take it, she may not. But I'mma see what's up."

"That's what's up, dirty. I would handle that now."

"But shit, she thirty-eight degrees hot, so I'mma give her a few days to cool down."

"Word," Pokey said. "Dog, you know they might give you sometime for that gun," Pokey said.

"It is what it is," Fatboy said.

"I know that, but if you want me to stand up, dog, 'cause it was my gun, I will," Pokey said.

"Dead ass! Na'll, dog. It's cool, I got it. If I let you take it, that means I'll take a even bigger loss, 'cause I'll be losing a friend to the system," Fatboy said, giving his dog dap. "I'm not worried 'bout the time anyways. It's my momma, dog. I hurt her bad with this bullshit."

"I understand that, dog, and trust me, woody, I feel ya pain. But in a minute, dog, we gonna be running these streets then you'll be able to give her all the things she wants," Pokey said.

"Word, dog. But let me get back inside before she trip."

"All right, dog."

"One love, my nigga."

"Hey Fatboy, before you go, I wanna say thanks for keeping it real. Always, my nigga."

"Always," Fatboy said, walking in the house.

The biggest troublemaker you'll ever face watches you from the mirror every day.

CHAPTER 12

Hustlin' Hard

LIFE IS TOO short to wake up with regrets. Love those who treat you right and forget the ones who don't!

"Dog, this shit been gravvy, the last two weeks we done made over five grand, doing nothing."

"Yeah, dog. Shit, been popping since we, well, since I left school, and you got expelled." Pokey said.

"Hell yeah, dog, we been on the grind heavy. Everything seems to be falling in place like a puzzle," Fatboy said.

"We making money, and business is booming. At least that's what Mr. Big is telling us being that we been opening and closing, while Boo Boo and Shine make runs look like we got what we want," Pokey said.

"What's that, dog?" Fatboy asked.

"Our own trap house."

"Yeah, we doing us. But you forgot I got court today. And if them crackers lock my ass up you know you on your own, till Flick come home from school," Fatboy said.

"Yeah, dog, I'm praying for the best but imagining the worst. Feel me? 'Cause without you shit want to be the same. Damn, I hope these crackers spare you." Pokey said.

"Yeah, me too."

"Dog, we gotta start being extra careful. If them crackers lock you up, when you jump, we gotta have a plan. Remember what Mr. Big's told us?"

"Yeah, I remember," Fatboy said. "It's two things you got to preserve in life: your health, followed by your freedom. You lose one, you lose both."

"Yeah, but life's challenges shouldn't paralyze you. They're to help you discover who you really are," Fatboy said. "If they lock me up, dog, it's just a setback that I'll use to make me stronger here," he said, tapping the side of his head.

"Word," Pokey said.

"Ay," Fatboy.

"Yeah, dirty. Did they tell you what judge you had?"

"Some cracker name Futch," Fatboy said.

"Damn, they giving you the meanest judge on the bench."

"It is what it is," Fatboy said.

"The cracker nasty-ass fuck, that's the someone who gave me them eighteen months," Pokey said.

"Yeah, an' this your what five or six time in trouble. The cracker can't be too bad! Anyways, dog, I'mma let go and let God. Feel me?" Fatboy asked.

"Hold up, nigga, when you became all religious?"

"Oh, I ain't religious. I just believe in a higher power, that's all," Fatboy said.

"Look, let's go get our hustle on till it's time to roll over to the courthouse. Let's ride then you know how we do. I bet them niggas Boo Boo and Shine in here knocked out."

"Probably is. Shit, I would be sleep too if I didn't have to open up shop with your ass," Fatboy, said laughing.

"Nigga, if them crackers look your ass up today, trust me you'll get more than enough sleep," Pokey said, playing with his dog. As he took out his key and opened the door, "Damn, this bitch stink-ass fuck," Pokey said as he opened the door.

"Yeah, dog, leave the door open and let this bitch air out," Fatboy said, taking a whiff of the foul-smelling odor. Looking 'round the room he saw where the smell was coming from Double D.

"Nigga, get your azz up and get outta here."

"Damn, nigga, you done shitted on yourself."

"What? Huh? Oh, what's up, jitty bugs?" Double D said.

"Nigga, fuck all that," Pokey said, touching his side. "What the hell you doing in here? And where the fuck Shine and Boo Boo at?"

"Man, y'all chill out. Y'all act like a nigga done rob y'all or some shit. Them niggas Shine and Boo Boo told me I could chill here till this morning 'cause the police was looking for me."

"Look like ya ass was high off crack to me," Pokey said. "Man, let's find out if this nigga telling the truth. Ay yo, Shine, Boo Boo, man, y'all check this out."

"What's up? What the fuck you yelling a nigga name all loud and shit for? A nigga trying to sleep and y'all acting like the police coming or some shit," Boo Boo said, wiping sleep from his eyes with Shine looking crazy as a motherfucker, holding his pistol.

"Look y'all told this nigga he could crash here."

"Oh yeah, we did that. The nigga said he was running from the police, so I told him he could chill till this morning. Why, what's up?" Shine asked. "What he did?"

"For one he shitted on his self, and two the nigga is a baser," Fatboy said, looking at Double D wiping his nose with the back of his hands.

"Man, he a friend of my momma, so he a friend of ours," Boo Boo said, feeling sorry for Double D.

"Whatever, man," Pokey said. "All right, Double D, get your ass up and get outta here."

"Ay, Double D, I hope it's no hard feelings, old school," Fatboy said.

"Na'll, dog, we cool," Double D said, walking out the door.

"Hey, Pok, give me a pack," Fatboy said.

"For what, dog?"

"Man, just give me a fifty pack. I'll pay for it."

"Huh then," Pokey said, tossing his dog a fifty, watching Fatboy run to the door.

"Ay, Double D, here you go, old school," Fatboy said, tossing Double D the pack. "No hard feelings, right?" Fatboy asked.

"I told you, jit, we were cool, but thanks anyway," Double D, said shooting a bird and running off like a kid on Christmas day.

"Dog, why you gave that nigga that?" Pokey asked.

"To keep the nigga on our team. I said some flaw shit to the man, and you never know how people take words," Fatboy said. "Dog, remember life is too short to wake up with regrets. Love those who treat you right and fuck the ones who don't."

"My bad, dog, you dead-ass right. That was a slick ass move," Pokey said.

As Boo Boo and Shine watched with pride, "How these young nigga just handled that!"

"Look, let's get this shit started," Pokey said, "'Cause I won't be here too long, 'round 12:30 we out. Fatboy got court today, and I gotta see what these crackers trying to do with my dirty," Pokey said.

"Ay, Pokey, you got a custy at the door nigga Bright and Earle."

"What's up, old school? You trying to catch the worm?"

"Na'll youngin, I'm trying to get high, but I got like five dollars, and a nick ain't gonna do shit for me. So can I get a dime and I'll pay you tomorrow or the next time?" the fiend said. Scratching his head, almost feeling sorry for this nigga, but not sorry enough to take money out his pockets to supply another nigga habits.

"Hell no, you know how it goes. You get what you pay for, old school. You know, GABOS," Pokey said. "We trying to eat just like you, we ain't hustling for nothing. Now what you got?"

"I got four dollars and thirty-five cents, that's all I got, man. Please help a brother out. My dick is in the dirt," the baser cried.

"Give me the money," Pokey said. As the fiend slid the money to Pokey, Pokey snatched the money and said huh, giving the man a nickel. "Now got the hell on somewhere."

"Damn, Pokey, that's fucked up. We just talked about this shit," Fatboy said, getting heated. "We all know GABOS, but at the same time, you gotta start thinking, dog. If you treat a nigga right, put a lil food in his belly, he'll be ya best friend. You gotta learn sometimes it's good to tilt ya hand a little and let the crumbs hit the ground, 'cause you never know who you may be blessing. All you had to do, homie, was give the basing-ass nigga the dime, and tell him next time come correct with the loot. Always remember what Sterling, a.k.a Mr. Big, told us, 'It's the customers that make us, not the drugs'," Fatboy was telling his dog Pokey.

"Ay, dog. You dead ass right," Pokey said. "I'mma keep that in mind," as he began to think, "We came a longs ways, and our journey is not at its end."

He was thinking as Fatboy said, "Yeah, dirty, you gotta remember how I said life is too short to wake up with regrets, so we gotta treat these niggas and bitches like they our friends, then they'll always be in our corner! If not then when someone else comes along pushing shit just as good, they'll forget us and move on to the next man. All because we ain't treating them right," Fatboy said, trying to explain to his friends.

"All right, dog. Damn, please don't start preaching to me 'cause I said I heard cha," Pokey said. "Look, here comes these two dirty-ass niggas, and I bet they ain't got more than ten dollars." Pokey said.

"Well, let's see," Fatboy said, just to see how his friend would handle things. As the two fiends walked up, they started yelling, "What's up, y'all? What's up, y'all?

Until Pokey said, "Man, hold that shit down. What you want anyways?"

"Man, can we get a twenty? We got fourteen dollars to our name."

Pokey gave Fatboy a look, like nigga what I told you. As Fatboy just shrugged his shoulder, like do you.

"Hold up," Pokey said to the crackheads, "let me see what I can do for y'all, huh, man," he said, giving them a twenty rock. "Look, y'all, next time be on point with the money. I'mma bless y'all this time, but don't look for blessings from me all the time 'cause I ain't God. All right, man?"

"Thank you," the two fiends said. Bending the corner.

"Dog, that's what's up!" Fatboy said. "Now look, Pokey, you made them niggas day. A happy nigga is a good nigga," Fatboy said.

"Yeah, yeah, I hear all that. But if them niggas keep coming up short they came be taking money but our pockets," Pokey said, "and that shit and gonna keep happening," Pokey said.

"Dog, next time I bet them niggas have the bread right!" Fatboy said, smiling for the first time.

"We'll see, but if they don't, the money coming outta your pockets," Pokey said in an angry tone.

Within the next three and a half hours, things were running smoothly, everything was sold out, but a few sacks of weed! When Shine and Boo Boo finally came back from the sleeping dead, they were surprised to see that most of the products were gone. Looking around and saying, "Damn, y'all niggas been booming hard this morning," Boo Boo said, giving us some dap. Like he really couldn't believe it.

"Yeah, dog, we did our thing today. Gotta make some extra cash to keep my dog tight, in case my nigga gotta do a lil time," Pokey said, with a sad expression. "Look, we 'bout to make a move," Pokey said, "the money in the stash spot, and y'all gotta get in touch with Sterling, a.k.a. Mr. Big, and re-up or close down shop for today and have these fiends lined up at the door, like the government giving out free cheese," Pokey said, laughing.

"I got it, dog, I'mma hit the nigga up," Shine said, giving Fatboy some dap and a hug.

"Good luck, my nigga, appreciate it, 'cause I'mma need it," Fatboy said. "Let's roll, dog, if you coming. It's about that time, and I gotta go change clothes and get cleaned. Gotta make a good impression for the judge," Fatboy said, walking out the door, laughing to himself, with Pokey right behind him, counting money.

Five minutes later, they were walking up the stairs to Fatboy's mom's crib. As he opened the door, he noticed his mother bent over the sofa, on her knees praying.

"Ma, you all right?" Fatboy asked.

"Oh yeah, baby, I'm all right," she said, wiping a falling tear from her cheek as she got up.

"I was just praying, that's all." When she seen Pokey, she looked at him with disgust in her eyes.

"Hey, Mrs. Walls," Pokey said.

"Hi, boy," she said, trying to be polite. "Fatboy, you know you got court in about thirty minutes, so you better hurry up."

"I'm coming, Ma. Just give me a minute," as he ran to his room. He grabbed his shoe box that held all his money and took it and placed it in the top drawer. So his mother would know where to look if she ever needed money, or if they locked him up and he needed money, she would know where to get it from. As he started changing fits, he grabbed his favorite CD, *All Eyes on Me* by Tupac and put it in his back pocket and ran out the door.

"All right, Momma, I'm ready to roll." As they all walked out the door and toward the car, Mrs. Walls stopped dead in her tracks.

"Hold up, where you going?" she asked Pokey.

"I'm rolling with y'all, Mrs. Walls," Pokey said. "That's all right, ain't it?" he said, feeling a lil hurt.

"Momma, why you tripping on my dog?" Fatboy asked.

"'Cuz he might be the reason your ass get locked up today, that's why!"

When Pokey heard that, he began to walk off but turned around and told his friend, "Dog, I'm hoping for the best, and I'll get up with you later. If the worst happen, I'mma write you and shit and hold the fort down," Pokey said, walking off.

"Dang, Momma, that's how you gonna do my friend. Don't you think if he didn't feel bad enough, he woulda never paid you all the money back with extra that you bonded me out with? All he wanna do is ride with us, to make sure I'mma be okay."

As Mrs. Walls heard the sadness in her son's voice, her heart began to break, and she realized that we all make mistakes. "All right, baby, call your friend and tell him come on."

"Thank you, Momma. Hey Pokey, Pokey. Come on, dog."

As Pokey turned 'round and walked back with a smile on his face, Mrs. Walls said, "Boy, I apologize. I'm just frustrated right now."

"I understand that, Mrs. Walls," Pokey said. As they got into the car, Fatboy pulled the CD out his pocket and placed it in the CD player and pushed play, and the song began to play. Fatboy turned around and told his friend, "This one for you." As Tupac began to rap "I Ain't Mad at Cha," he was playing this song for a reason, to let his dog know no matter what happens today in court, I still ain't mad at cha. Fatboy was thinking, "We was once two niggas of the same kind / used to holla at a hoochie with the same line / You were just a little smaller but you still rolled," as they started booping they heads to the beat. Mrs. Walls looked at her son and began to smile. She knew in her heart things would turn out all right as she listened to her son rap along.

"In my cell thinkin hell I know one day I'll be back.

as soon as I touch down. i told my girl I'll be there, so prepare to get fucked down.The homies wanna kick it, but i'm just laughin at cha.cause youse a down ass bitch and I ain't mad at cha.

As the song found its ending, they pulled up in front of the courthouse.

"Before y'all get out," Mrs. Wall asked, "let's say a prayer." As she began, the boys bowed their heads. When she was done, they shouted, "We'll amen to that!" And they hopped out the car, feeling better about the outcome. As they entered the courthouse, they were told to walk through the scanner, to check for any weapons, which no one had. Once past all the bullshit, they proceeded to court room 3A.

About ten minutes later, the judge said, "Gore v. State."

"Well, that's me y'all," Fatboy said as he walked up to the front. Once there a white lady by the name of Mrs. Clark said she was my public defender and said she would be representing me today. "All right, cool," Fatboy said.

"Listen, Mr. Gore, this is your first time in trouble, but you already said it was your gun and not someone else's, right?"

"Yeah, that's right," Fatboy said.

"Well, being that this is your first offense, the judge is willing to give you two years probation, if you plead guilty right now."

"Shit. Oh my bad, I mean shoot. Where do I sign okay?"

"Hold on," the PD said. "Your Honor, my client is willing to plead guilty to the gun charge in exchange for the two years probation."

"Son, is that correct?" the judge asked.

"Yes, sir."

"And you know if you mess up, it's a 99 percent chance you'll be locked up."

"Yes, sir. I understand."

"And you're sure you're willing to plead guilty right now?"

"Yes, sir, I am."

"Son, you do know two years probation is nothing compared to what I could do give you. But I feel in my heart, you made a mistake that you won't make again. Am I right?"

"Yes, sir judge."

"All right. You can go now. You probation officer will let you know what's what," the judge said.

As Fatboy began to walk off, he looked at his mother who was smiling and hoping this would open her son's eyes.

"Baby, you know everything happens for a reason. If you get a chance, take it. If it changes your life, let it. Nobody said it would be easy, they just promised it would be worth it," his mother said holding her tears back.

"Momma, I got you. And trust me, I'mma be all right. Two years on probation ain't nothing, it's like taking candy from a baby," he said, hopping in the car and pushing play on the CD, turning it up to hear Tupac's "Life Goes On," as his mother drove them back to the projects.

"It's always another day but the same ole shit!" Pokey was thinking.

"Damn, now I'm on papers. A nigga can't do shit," Fatboy said. Once his mother was outta sight, "Chill, dog, everything gonna be good," Pokey said.

"Shit, as long as we making this money, all you really gotta do is pay that shit off, and them crackers will take you off that shit. You know they don't want shit, but money from a nigga anyways."

"All right, dog. Whatever," Fatboy said, taking a sit on the steps. As he watched his friend, he realized, "Maybe this ain't the life I wanna live, but knew it was too late 'cause he put his bid in. already, so I'mma ride to the end," he was thinking. "I just hope it's worth it in the end."

"Look, Pok, I'mma go in the crib and chill out a minute. I'll meet you 'round Shine and Boo Boo house in about two hours."

"All right, dog, that's what's up," Pokey said, getting ready to leave.

"Hey, before you go, check this out."

"What's up?" Pokey asked.

"Dog, in a few months it's your B-day, and that's when ya unc is supposed to put you on. Well, if so, let's get all the money we can and fall back from the game," Fatboy said.

"All right, dog. We'll do that," Pokey said, looking at his friend sideways, wondering where all this was coming from. As he turned around and walked off, he had a bad feeling, "Damn, I hope this nigga ain't getting soft on me, 'cause if so, he know the rules to the game. Once you in, it's only two ways to get out, buy out or death," Pokey was thinking. But just as fast he shuck the thought, "Na'll, that's my dog," he said, walking in the house. "He living better than that thug life."

CHAPTER 13

My Day

"DAMN, IT SEEMS like these last few months would never get here," Pokey said, hopping up outta bed, feeling good and fresh. "Damn, something smelling gooder than a motherfucker." As he made his way into the kitchen all he saw was a plate full of pancakes, eggs, and bacon.

"Happy birthday, baby," his mother said, walking up to him and giving him a hug.

"Thanks, Ma, but who all this food for?"

"Baby, it's for you," his mother said. "You finally turned sixteen. And, baby, I wish I had enough money to throw you a party or buy you something, but I don't 'cause I had to pay some bills. I'm sorry," his mother said.

"Momma, you good, it's just another day to me," he said, trying to make his mother feel better. "This good enough. Right here," he said, digging into the food.

"So what do you got planned for the day?" his mother asked.

Knowing 'round five six o'clock tonight, he would have a surprise waiting from Sterling, a.k.a. Mr. Big told her, "Oh, Mom, I'll probably chill with my dogs. Probably hit the mall or something."

"Well, if you do, just be careful, 'cause you been doing good staying outta trouble," his mother said. "Oh, I almost forgot, here you go," she said handing him a enveloped. "This from your sister."

"Who?" Pokey asked.

"Boy, stop acting silly. You ain't got but one sister, and that's Tisha. She told me to make sure you get this. What is it? Open it and see," his mother said. As she watched her son tear open the envelope, she began to smile, knowing the card would make his day. "Pokey, read it out loud," his mother asked.

"Okay. To my only brother, Pokey I just wanna wish you a happy b-day, with many more to come. I want you to know even though sometimes you are a pain in the ass, I still love you, and I want the best for you. You're my only brother. And I know with time it seems as if we grew apart, but lil bro, that's not true, 'cause everywhere I go, you're always there in my heart. Love always, Tisha PS Look on back."

As Pokey turned the card over, he saw a mini picture of his sister taped to a hundred bill. As he began to smile, he looked over at his mother, "Mom, Tisha wrote this?" he asked.

"Yes, she did. I watched her write right there where you read it from yesterday night."

"Mom, if you see her before I do, tell her I say thanks," Pokey said.

"All right, boy, his mother replied."

As Pokey got up and came 'round the table, to his mother's surprise, he bent down and gave her a hug and said, "Ma, I love you, and I don't need this," he said, giving his mother the hundred dollars his sister gave to him to her.

"Baby, that's your money from your sister," his mother said.

"Mom, I know. Somebody gave it to me who loves me, and I'm giving it to somebody I love. Just look at it as Mother's Day," he said smiling, as he watched his mother wipe at a falling tear. "Momma, I'll be back later. I'm going to holla at my dogs," he said racing out the door. As soon as his feet hit pavement, he heard his two friends screaming, "Happy birthday, nigga!" As they made there way up to him, Pokey already knew what time it was.

"What y'all fools smiling and laughing about? What, I look funny or something?" Pokey said, watching Fatboy and Flick rush him, as they began punching him, in the arms, legs, anywhere but the face. "All right, man. Damn, y'all gone kill a nigga," Pokey shouted, laughing at the same time.

"Nigga, you know we gotta get them birthday licks," Flick said, giving Pokey some dap.

"Check it out though, Pokey," Fatboy said. "Walk to the crib with me. We got something for you."

"Look, if it's another ass whooping, y'all can keep it," Pokey said, laughing.

"Nigga, come on," Flick said.

"Hold up, y'all. Let me run upstairs right quick and grab this," Fatboy said.

"Flick, what that nigga going to get?" Pokey asked.

"Man, just chill, you'll know in a minute. Just be patient," Flick said. "Here he come now," Flick told Pokey, as Pokey was looking the other direction.

"Huh, dog, this from me and Flick." As he passed Pokey something wrapped in paper, Pokey began to open it with caution, thinking it might be a joke.

"This aint' no bomb, is it?"

"Man, just open the damn thing!" Pokey's two friends screamed.

"All right all right. Damn, y'all ain't gotta get a attitude about the shit," Pokey said. When he finished tearing the paper off, in his hand was a jewelry box.

"Open it, boy," Flick said.

When he opened the box and seen what was in it, he had a giant smile on his face.

"Damn, this bitch clean." As he took the gold chain out the box, you could see a shiny gold charm with the word "GABOS" on it.

"Yeah, dog, we thought you might like this. It's to remind you what we live by," Fatboy said.

"Man, thanks. Y'all did y'all thing with this. What this shit cost?"

"Nigga, stop worrying about prices. Just know it's paid for!" Flick said.

"All right, now that that's outta the way, what you wanna do today? Everything on us."

"Shit, that's what's up. Y'all know how I get when I'm spending another nigga's cheddar, so I hope you'll got enough cheese to supply a rat, 'cause I got some shit I need," he said laughing, but really playing. 'Cause within this last four and a half months, Mr. Big gave him all he needed. Plus with the money they were now bringing in from Mrs. Jones's house, they were sitting all right for three jits. They just never imagined the table would turn once this birthday party was over, and they would make it to the top. "But how long will they stay there! Shit always seems to go from sugar to shit," Pokey was thinking.

"Damn, nigga, you deaf or something?" Fatboy said. "So what's up? What you wanna do?" 'cause Fatboy and Flick were told by Sico and Mr. Big to get Pokey to go somewhere, "So we can sneak in and set up shop. We gonna surprise him with a birthday party, something he never had nor expected," Sico said, as Mr. Big just listened.

"All right, we got y'all," Fatboy and Flick said.

"Look, 'bout six o' clock, everything should be set up. But y'all gotta keep him gone somewhere until that time."

"We got y'all. We can handle that."

"Huh. Here's a little extra cash," Mr. Big said giving Fatboy and Flick about a grand apiece.

"Bet that up, Mr. Big. Now we can take dog balling."

"All right, y'all, we gone," Sico and Mr. Big said.

"Damn, we talked to them niggas 'round eleven o'clock. It's now 11:45 and we still ain't gone," Fatboy was thinking.

When Pokey said, "Shit, we can either hit the mall or walk over to the park," Pokey said.

"Dog, it's your choice whatever you wanna do, we with cha."

"Hold up," Pokey said, running up the stairs.

"Now where this nigga going?" Flick asked.

"Hey, Ma. You think you can drop us off at the mall, my friends talking about taking me shopping."

"Yeah, I can drop y'all off. But give me 'bout ten minutes. As soon as I finish washing these dishes, I'll take y'all," his mother said.

"All right, Ma, I'll be downstairs with my friends when you ready," Pokey said. Walking out the door, "Well, dog, look like we headed to the mall!" Pokey yelled at his friends. "My momma said she'll drop us off when she finish doing what she doing!"

After about five hours of clowning around in the mall and just having fun talking to the females, the three boys were ready to make tracks back to the projects. On the way home, Pokey said, "Dog, I appreciate all y'all did for me today. Y'all really made something outta nothing. And thanks for these brand-new Jordans, y'all niggaz coped me," he said holding up the Foot Locker bag, feeling good about the way things turned out.

"Yeah, dog, but understand something, the party is just getting started," Fatboy said, as they walked up in the projects, they heard ain't no but a gangsta party. Nothing but a gangsta party.

"Man, what the hell going on out here? This bitch look like the park," Pokey said. And that's when everyone shouted, "Happy birthday, Pokey!"

"Damn, dog, y'all threw a nigga a surprise party," Pokey said.

"Na'll, dog, your Uncle Sico and Mr. Big set this up. We just played our parts, keeping ya ass out the projects all day, that's all," Fatboy said.

"Damn, this bitch on swoll. What, they musta told everybody from the 352 area code to show up," Pokey said.

"Dog, look, I don't know but here come ya uncle, ask him," Flick said.

"Whats up, nephew? Happy birthday!"

"Oh, Unc, what's up! And thanks for the party," Pokey said, looking at his unc like he was looking at a ghost, 'cause his uncle was looking bad and Pokey felt like he was the only one who seen it.

"Nephew, it's your time. Walk with me right quick," as they began the walk to his uncle's car, Pokey wanted to ask him so bad what was wrong with him but decided against it. Just to see what this nigga had in store for him.

"Remember I said I was gonna put you on when you turn sixteen? Well, I'm a man of my word, so I'mma do just that," he said popping the trunk. "Now I'mma put you on, but you gotta do ya own work. I heard how y'all booming over at Mrs. Jones's house, so it shouldn't be no problem to get off these," he said, opening a book bag with three kilos of crack in it.

"Damn, Unc, what I'mma do with all that shit?" Pokey said.

"Boy, what you think? Make money like you supposed to. The only thing is this all your money, feel me? Happy birthday, nigga. When the party over you can come get this, but right now, go have some fun!"

"Hey, Unc."

"What's up, nephew? Man, what's wrong?"

"I mean, good looking out," he almost slipped but caught himself. "I'mma just handled business, and when the time is right, I gotta go head and do, Unc, before the drugs take full effect," Pokey was thinking, as he watched his unc get in the ride and roll up the dark boys. "I bet this nigga finna smoke that shit right now," Pokey was thinking, as he turned around and walked back to the party. With his thoughts still miles away, he tried to enjoy himself, which shouldn't have been hard to do when there were so many hoes walking 'round in nothing, lil skimpy outfits that barely covered anything.

"Damn, these bitches fine," Fatboy and Flick said, walking up to his dog who was in a daze.

"Pok, you all right, dirty?"

"Oh yeah, I'm good. Just checking these chicks out!" he lied.

"Oh, Mr. Big said when you get time, come holler at him," Flick said.

"All right," Pok said.

"He over there talking with ya mom's."

"All right I'll holla at him in a lil."

"You know Amanda here, right?" Fatboy asked Pokey.

"Word, where she at?"

"She chilling with Rosie and Shakia."

"Damn, nigga, ya girl here too?" Pokey asked Fatboy.

"Yeah, her auntie dropped her off! Well, I'm gone," Fatboy said, going to holla at his shortie.

"Me too," Flick said, doing the same.

As they made their way over to their shorties, Amanda was on her way to Pokey.

"What's up, baby?" Amanda said, "and happy birthday," she said, giving him a kiss, as he felt all over her body. "Stop, boy. I'mma give you that later," she said. "Right now, it's too many people here.

"All right, cool!" Pokey said. "Baby, hold up one minute, let me holla at my dogs right quick," he said, walking off. "Yo, Flick, where Fatboy at?"

"Oh, he handling some business."

"Look, dog, since you got ya shortie here, I know you trying to smash, so tell Fatboy y'all can use my room. Since my momma chilling out here," Pokey said.

"Too late, dog. That's where Fatboy and his girl Shakia just headed to get there freak on!"

"That's what's up," Pokey said.

"Yeah, when he done, me and Rosie going up there," Flick said, squeezing Rosie on her ass.

"Well, let me go, 'cause I see you two niggaz already on point," Pokey said, giving his lil dirty some dap, as he made his way back over to Amanda. "Baby, come on," he said, grabbing her by the hand. "Walk with me to holla at this nigga Mr. Big."

"Okay, since you 'bout to snatch my arm off. I might as well come," she said, laughing. When he walked up to Mr. Big, he stopped talking to Mrs. Queen, Pokey's mom, and got up and met Pokey.

"Happy birthday, birthday boy! How you like the party?" Mr. Big asked.

"It's off the chain! Mr. Big, what you and my momma was talking 'bout?"

"Oh, I had to make sure it was cool with her, about what I'm about to give you. She said it's cool so."

"What, you finna give me your kingdom?"

"Come on, Pokey, it's too soon for that," Mr. Big said, laughing. "You gotta lot more work to put in before your ready to take over. Come on," he said. "You can bring ya shortie too," Mr. Big said.

"Come on, Amanda." As they began to follow Mr. Big, they saw Sico.

"Yo Sico!" Mr. Big called, looking at Sico like he knew something was wrong with his lil brother. "Yo tell Trirena to go 'head and bring that.

"All right," Sico stuttered before walking off.

Ten minutes later we heard before we saw the same song "Ain't Nothing But a Gangsta Party" coming from this brand-new box Chevy, painted candy apple red, with bucket seats, being driven by none other than Mr. Big's daughter Trirena. As Trirena pulled up right in front of Pokey, she exited the car with all smiles and said, "Happy birthday, lil nigga," panting at the ride.

"Na'll, man, y'all bullshitten a nigga, right?" Pokey asked, dumping in the driver's seat, while Amanda made her way to the passenger seat.

"Hold up! Before y'all take a spend," Mr. Big said, "Happy birthday again. I got you this ride so you and your friends can get around better. Not to be getting in trouble and shit, all right?" Mr. Big said.

"I got you, Mr. Big," Pokey said, backing the car up.

After about thirty minutes of joy-riding, Pokey pulled up in the park, which was empty, due to most people were at the party.

"Baby, you ready to give me my present now?" Pokey asked Amanda. And she started climbing in the backseat and lay on her back, removing her panties.

"Damn, baby. I guess you ready," Pokey said. Climbing in the back, positioning himself between Amanda's thighs. As they began to kiss and fell all over each other, Amanda began to moan, "Give it to me," and Pokey didn't hesitate. Fifteen minutes later, they where headed back to the projects. Pokey was thinking, "Damn, this day turned out to be good. I got a brand-new ride. My girl gave up the kitty kat, my dogs looked out, and my momma had a smile on her face. Something I usually don't see."

"Well, baby, it's close to midnight. So the party 'bout over. When it's done, I'll take y'all home. So go call ya mom, and tell her you got a ride."

"All right, baby," Amanda said, leaving the car. Two minutes later, his Uncle Sico walks up to the driver's side, looking high as hell.

"What's up, nephew? How you like the ride?"

"It's straight," Pokey said, looking at his uncle sideways.

"Look, this party is about to come to a end. So come get that," Sico said.

"All right, Unc."

"And you right, the party is about to end, with you leaving this earth," Pokey was thinking, as he followed his uncle to his ride, who he knew was high, 'cause he kept talking to himself. Once to the ride, Pokey got what he came for and burned rubber, without so much as a thank you.

"Damn, what's wrong with that ungrateful-ass nigga?" Sico said. Pulling out his pipe, "Fuck 'em!" he said, taking a hit as he watched Pokey walk off.

CHAPTER 14

Making Moves

AFTER THE PARTY was over, everybody called it a night. After dropping Amanda, Rosie, and Shakia off at home, Pokey called it a night also. The next morning, he was awoken, bright and early, by his two friends Fatboy and Flick.

"Pokey, hey Pokey. Boy, get your behind up and see what them boyz want," Mrs. Queen said.

"All right, Ma. Dang, I just fell asleep. Tell them I'll be down in a minute or two," he said, yawning, as he began to get outta bed.

"Y'all need to stop all that yelling, he said he'll be down in a minute or two. So y'all just be patient," Mrs. Queen said, slamming her door and walking back to her room to get some more sleep.

"Damn," Pokey said, walking out the door. "What y'all niggaz want so early in the morning?" Pokey asked, still yawning.

"Damn, dog, it's like that?" Fatboy asked. "Don't tell us you getting brand new on a nigga all of a sudden."

"Na'll, dirty. A nigga just tired, that's all. I been up almost all night, plus you nigga wasn't nowhere around last night when I had to take my girl home and y'alls," Pokey said, looking at his dogs.

"Oh, dog, my momma made me come home right before twelve," Flick said. "But Rosie said her momma was gonna scoop her up, well, she didn't. I took her home."

"And where was you, dog?" Pokey asked Fatboy.

"Dog, I was tired, so I called it a night. But my shortie said her auntie was scooping her, and that she would be all right for twenty more minutes."

"Well, that's not the case. I took her home too, and that shit took like a whole hour to get there and a whole hour to get back," Pokey said.

"Man, who let you drive they car to do all that?" Fatboy asked.

"Look, niggas," Pokey said, smiling and pointing at the brand-new ride. "That's my shit," Pokey said.

"Yeah, right," Flick said, "and I'm Roy Jones."

"Na'll, real shit. Mr. Big brought me this for my birthday. He said so we can get around better. Man, this bitch clean, and this shit sitting on 22 inches with a sound system in it. Guess who drove it here?"

"Who?" Fatboy asked.

"Sterling/Mr. Big's daughter."

"The one who was at his house when we went?"

"Yep, what's her name?"

"Tri, Tir, Trirena."

"Yeah, that's her."

"Anyways, what's up? We setting up trap today or what, 'cause you know them niggas Shine and Boo Boo depending on us to open and close nowadays," Fatboy said.

"Yeah, we gonna stick to the script, but in a minute we gonna change shit up. Check this out. Look what my basing-ass Uncle Sico gave me," he said, going to the back of the trunk and opening it. "Man, y'all niggaz gonna flip when y'all see this shit," Pokey said, unzipping the book bag that was containing the three keys.

"Now expose for us to see. Damn, dog, we can come up big time with all that shit," Flick said.

Eyes wide now seeing the money, "Man, we already doing our lil thing, but with this, we can triple our money in no time," Fatboy said.

"Yeah, dog, we can if shit goes right. But we first gotta find a place to sell all this shit, we can't be cutting into the pie over at Shine's and Boo Boo. Never bite the hands that feed you," Pokey said.

"All right, why not just sell all this shit when they run out?" Flick said.

"'Cause then them niggas will catch on, plus Mr. Big gone wanna know why we ain't asking for more product," Pokey said.

"Yeah, you right about that," Fatboy said.

"So look, let's just get us a spot somewhere else and see what we can do, or we can just sell these shits for the low-low, eighteen to twenty thousand a piece and be done with it. It's not enough money to live good on, but it's enough to get our old girl up out the hood," Pokey said.

"Look, let's just chill. And when the timing is right, we'll think of something to do," Fatboy said.

"All right, we'll do that," Pokey said.

"Come on, let's go 'head and open up shop. What, we just gonna walk 'round there, or you driving the whip?" Flick asked.

"Dog, remember we sticking to the script, so that means we walking," Pokey said. "Let's roll them to their surprise."

Once they reached the spot, it was already jumping.

"Well, I guess them niggaz wasn't depending on us too bad, 'cause shop is up and running."

"Well, that's good. It's about time them niggaz do something 'round this bitch."

"What's up, y'all," Shine said, as Pokey, Fatboy, and Flick stepped inside.

"What's up, nigga? We see y'all up early," Pokey said.

"Yeah, y'all know how its is. The early bird catches the worm," Boo Boo said, coming from the kitchen. "Where y'all niggaz been anyways?"

"Man, you know last night was my birthday! So we chilled out and had a lil fun," Pokey said. "Why you niggaz ain't come?" Pokey asked.

"For what? Niggas ain't worried about no motherfucking birthday party, niggas trying to make this money, so we can party every day, not no motherfucking one time out the year type shit," Shine said. "While you niggas was acting like lil bitches at a party, me and lil bro was making this cheddar."

"First off, nigga, you need to watch your motherfucking mouth, for a nigga get that shit right," Fatboy said.

"Nigga, fuck y'all," Boo Boo said. "My brother said just what he meant. If ya niggas don't like it, do something about it," Boo Boo said, pulling his gat out.

"Nigga, calm down, lil bro, look at these niggaz scared straight," Shine said. "Man, we just playing with y'all, trying to clear the air," hoping they wouldn't tell Mr. Big about this shit.

"Yeah, we scared straight," Pokey said. "But check this out. Since it feels like we ain't wanted here, we gonna holla at y'all." Not knowing in Pokey's mind that he was now ready to move to the next level. "It's only one way we'll survive in this game, and that's by getting rid of all our enemies one by one," he was thinking, as he walked out the door with his dogs behind him.

"Well, fuck y'all niggaz then. Y'all niggas ain't bred for this type of life anyways," Boo Boo said, running to the door and shooting in the air. *Boom, boom, boom, boom,* the gun sounded. Fatboy and Pokey and Flick didn't even flinch; they just kept on walking.

"Remember what Mr. Big told us?" Fatboy asked.

"Yep, don't pull your gun, unless you intend to use it. See how stupid the lil nigga is. Them same four bullets, probably coulda saved his life," Fatboy said, looking at Pokey. As Pokey began to smile, he knew what time it was, and he was proud of his lil homie. "My nigga got heart," Pokey was thinking.

When he heard Flick say, "Them niggas gonna be problems, but before they become a big problem we need to handle our business and solve the problem before it's too late."

"What you mean by that?" Fatboy asked Flick.

"Nigga, stop acting stupid. Y'all know what I mean. Them stupid niggaz pulled a gun like we was gonna run. Sad thing is though, they shoulda use it," Flick said, "'Cause payback is a bitch. Now we just gotta be smart 'bout the whole thing. We gotta make sure whatever we do we don't get caught."

"Word," Fatboy and Pokey said.

"Look, I got a good plan. We just gotta get in touch with the nigga Turtle, and make some type of deal with them nigga," Fatboy said.

"Now you thinking," Pokey said. "We'll let them niggas do the dirty work, and we'll sit back and watch."

"Word. I'm down with that. This what we gonna do," Fatboy said. "Flick, when you go back to school tomorrow, holla at the nigga Turtle and his crew and tell them I got something sweet for them, but it's more like a come-up, 'cause they'll benefit from this lovely if they with this. Tell them to meet us at the auditorium on Martin Luther King Tuesday evening when they got the basketball games. For the jits."

"All right," Flick said. "I'll handle that ASAP tomorrow when I see the nigga. Other than that, what's up? What we 'bout to do?"

"Look," Fatboy said, "we gotta plan this shit right. We got three keys that we can make money off. And the good thing is, if we get Shine and Boo Boo out the way without us being involved, I'm pretty sure Mr. Big will still let us do our thing out that crib."

"Well, I'm in," Flick said.

"Me too," Pokey said. "So when the time comes, we'll set everything up, and afterwards it's on and popping. We'll be selling our own shit. So what we make is all ours, and if we decide to get more, we'll just cope from Mr. Big for the low-low," Pokey said, smiling.

"So now that that's over with, what we gonna do?"

"Shit. Let me take this shit upstairs right quick," Pokey said, popping the trunk and snatching the bag. They held the dope hostage, and throwing the bag over his shoulder, he made his way up the stairs. After hiding the stuff at a safe spot, he left just as quick as he came.

"Come on, y'all. Let's ride around and see what going on in Ocala." As Pokey dumped behind the steering wheel, Fatboy climbed in the passenger seat and Flick hopped in back.

"Let's ride."

As the car started backing up, Pokey hit the play button on the stereo, and all you heard was "Wonder Why They Call You Bitch" by Tupac.

"Damn, nigga. You just like ya Uncle Sico. All you niggaz listen to is some damn Tupac," Flick said.

"Nigga, who better than 2Pac?" Pokey said, turning the shit up "That's what I thought," Pokey said.

"Nigga, you crazy. Biggie Smalls," Flick said.

"He good, but Pac don't see that nigga," Fatboy said, siding with Pokey on 2Pac. "So where we going?"

"Shit, well just ride through the other projects and see what's going on." As they rode around, they came to the projects known as Parkside. As they slowly rode through, they saw three as bad hood chicks.

"Man, look, ain't that Baby Tony? Fine as hell."

"Yeah," Flick said. "And that's her sister Tiffany," Flick said.

"Well, who is the dark skin chick with the fat ass?"

"Oh, that's Nichol Mathis. She ain't doing shit, she fucked up 'bout her baby daddy," Flick said.

"Well, let's see," Fatboy said. Nigga tapped the horn. *Beep, beep.* As the horn sounded, all three girls turned around, trying to figure out who the hell these niggas were.

"Hey, Baby Tony, check this out!" Flick yelled.

"Boy, what's up?" Baby Tony said.

"Nothing, nigga just chilling. Checking your fine ass but that's all. What's up though? What you 'bout to do?" Flick asked.

"Chill with my sister and cousin. Why, what's up?"

"First off, tell ya cousin Nichol, my dog said check this out."

As Baby Tony delivered the message, the girl Nichol made her way to the car.

"What? What y'all want?"

"Damn, it's like that?" Fatboy said. "Nigga just trying to see what's up with you."

"What you want to be up with me?" Nichol asked.

"Hold up," Fatboy said, hopping out the car. "Now let me holla at you in person."

After ten minutes of talking Fatboy got what he wanted, a number and possibly a down-ass chick. Even though in his mind he knew his shortie Shakia would always be number one, it was just something about the way this girl swayed her hips.

"All right, y'all, let's ride." As they left Parkside and went about four blocks over to the projects called Marion Minor, they rode around but wasn't nothing popping, no hoes outside, so we ended up in Buzz B Quarter, where shit always seems to be alive. We rode around, hollered at a few chicks, then left. 'Round 9:45

that night we pulled back up in our projects, K-Mart Projects, feeling good to be home. As all three boys exited the car, they said, “Dog, I’ll see y’all tomorrow.” Before everyone went in for the night, Fatboy told Flick, “Flick, don’t forget to handle that with the nigga Turtle.”

“Y’all, dog, I got you. I ain’t gonna forget. Word. I’m out.”

CHAPTER 15

Two Days Later: The Setup

"DOG, YOU SHOW them niggas said they gonna be here?" Pokey asked Flick.

"Dog, I told you the nigga Turtle said he'll be here 'round 6:30. It's only six o'clock, so if the nigga don't show in thirty minutes, we'll just bounce and do the shit ourselves," Flick said.

"All right, that's what's up," Pokey said, taking a seat on the bleachers, watching the basketball game. "But that lil nigga in number 23 jersey be balling, watch what I tell you. That's lil Jordan, that's what they call him anyways, he from Parkside."

"Man, stop talking so damn much and let us see what the lil nigga 'bout," Fatboy said, as the game started up about fifteen minutes later. Turtle walks in with two other dudes, who we never seen before.

"Hey Turtle, over here," Flick waves, and Turtle and the other two niggas started walking over to us.

Pokey whispered, "Man, what's up with this nigga Turtle? Instead of bringing his crew, he bring two niggas we don't even know, but fuck it," Pokey said.

"What's up, niggas?" Turtle asked. What y'all wanna holla at a nigga 'bout?"

"Remember though if it's not about that paper, we really ain't got no reason rapping."

"We feeling that. But trust us, this 'bout that paper. But first, where your dogs at? And who these niggas is?"

"Man, look, y'all asking a million questions for no reason. When I feel shit might have to get ugly, I leave the crew and ride with family, 'cause we all know blood is thicker than water. This my cousin Lo-P and my other cousin Rim. These two niggas 'bout that wife, and I mean 'bout that life," Turtle said, smiling.

"Well, we'll soon find out. Look, let's bounce. Y'all come take a ride with us. Why we put y'all up on game and how the shit gotta go down," Pokey said, getting up and walking to his ride.

"Look, my cuzzo drove his whip. So we just gonna follow y'a'll, and when we get to where we going, we'll talk then."

"Well, since it's Monday let's hit the park. It won't be but a few people there," Pokey said.

"Man, let's just get this shit over with. Niggas got shit to do," Turtle said, hopping in his cousin's Ford F350D pickup truck that was sitting on gold rims.

"Shit, look like them niggaz already sitting on paper," Pokey said.

"By the shit they driving, man, let's just get this shit over with," Flick said, booping his head to the beat, 'bout twenty-three minutes later as we pulled up in the park.

"Its was a few people here and there, nothing to be suspicious about though," Fatboy was thinking as they parked the ride. With Lo-P and them, pulling up right beside us, hopping out all at the same time.

"Now what's up?" Turtle asked.

"Look, man, chill out and relax. Let's go have a seat at the picnic tables, then we'll get things started," Fatboy said, walking over to the table and having a seat. Him and his two friends on one side, Turtle and his two cousins on the other side.

"All right, look, we got a minor problem. We need handle. We could handle it ourselves, but shit won't look right. We got everything y'all will need."

"What you mean?" Turtle asked.

"If y'all need fire, we can get it, y'all lil homie. I got my own fire," Rim said. Pulling out a chrome .44, placing it on the table. As we looked over at the nigga Lo-P, we seen him pull out the exact same fire. Just a dark black color with a gold grip handle.

"Man, listen. If we doing any shooting, we gonna take our chances with our own shit," Lo-P said, while his lil brother Rim just shook his head.

"All right, that's cool with us," Pokey said.

"But how do we know we ain't being set up?" Turtle asked.

"'Cause, nigga, I ain't no snake," Pokey said.

"That don't mean shit," Turtle said. "Outta the blue you calling on me for help like we dogs or something."

"Look, dog, either you gonna trust me or not," Pokey told Turtle. Looking him dead in his eyes, letting him know he's dead ass.

"All right, what can we make off this lil come-up you got planned?" Turtle asked.

"Being honest 'bout fifteen to twenty grand, with whatever else you find," Pokey said.

"And what is it we gotta do?" Turtle asked.

"Now this the real part. We gotta see if these niggas really 'bout that life. And do they have the heart to murk a nigga?" Pokey was thinking. And he waited 'bout two minutes before saying, "We need y'all to off two niggaz for us."

"Nigga, that's it," Lo-P said, "Man, count us in. We was thinking y'all niggas wanted us to run up on the president or John Gotti himself. But murking two niggas is like clockwork!" Lo-P said, giving his lil brother Rim some dap. "When y'all want this shit to go down?" Lo-P asked.

"Around midnight tonight when shit be moving slow. 'Round this time not too many baser be around," Pokey said.

"Damn, y'all niggaz moving quick. Y'all want the shit done tonight," Rim said.

"Hell yeah," Fatboy said.

"If y'all can't handle business tonight, we'll just do it ourselves," Flick said.

"Na'll, na'll, we got y'all," Turtle said, looking at an easy come-up. "So where this shit popping off at?" Turtle asked.

"Oh, in the projects," Fatboy said.

"Nigga, which projects?" Turtle asked.

"Nigga, our projects, K-Mart Projects. Niggas, y'all in or what?" Fatboy asked.

With the thought of the robbery and possibly murder going down in these niggaz own projects, Turtle kinda had a funny feeling, like they were being set up.

"Look, y'all hold up a minute, let me holla at my cousins right quick. Lo-P, Rim, check this out," Turtle said, walking 'bout twenty-five paces before asking. "Man, how y'all niggas feel 'bout this shit?"

"Turt, you know how we feel. If it's about that paper, we there if them niggaz trying to set us up. Trust this, they going down with us," Rim said. "So fuck that shit, count us in."

"Man, y'all sure?" Turtle asked.

"Dog, count us in, ride or die."

"All right, fuck it," Turtle said. "It's on and popping," he said, making his way back toward Pokey, Fatboy, Flick, who were just waiting, talking amongst themselves. 'Cause whether Turtle them took up the offer or not, the job would get done either by Turtle and his crew or by Pokey and his two dogs who would rather do the shit themselves, 'cause it's better to be safe than sorry.

"Check this out, we gonna handle this shit for y'all," Turtle said.

"That's what's up," Pokey said, smiling. "Check this out though. We gonna be the ones to let y'all in. Na'll change that, huh, here go a key," Pokey said, removing the key from his keychain. "The number 2301 that's downstairs. What we gonna do is when we leave here. we gonna go holla at them niggas, like everything kosha. Help them run shop and shit, let a few familiar faces see we was there. But right around 11:55, we gonna burn up, and on our exit, we'll walk by y'all that will let you know everything is set up," Pokey said.

"All right, we feeling that," Turtle said. "But where the money gonna be at and the drugs you talking about?"

"Look under the kitchen table. It's a rug, lift it up, and you'll see a stash spot, The number to that is 21-33-16, you know how to unlock a lock, right?" Pokey asked.

"Yeah, nigga, I ain't dumb!" Turtle shouted.

"All right, and the dope will be most likely on the table where the stucked, nigga Booboo keep it screaming 'bout. If the fiends can see it, it will make them want more," Pokey said, laughing.

"All right, we got all that. But what if we don't walk by y'all, then what?"

"That just means y'all missed us. But shit still gotta go down," Flick said. "And y'all do know, anybody in the crib dies, right? Man, whoever in the motherfucker, murk them, ask questions later, all right?"

"We got y'all. And we'll be there 'round 11:30, we'll just park somewhere in a dark cut. Then when we see y'all leaving we'll come," Turtle said.

"So everything is set. It's on and popping," Pokey said, getting up.

"Well, let us go handle our part," Fatboy said. "We gotta make these niggas feel unalarmed."

"Man, go do y'all," Rim said.

"We'll be there. Let's bounce," Pokey said.

Being that the park was a walk away, about three minutes later, as we pulled up in front of Mrs. Jones's house, we saw Boo Boo stick his head out the door, wondering who was bumping outside their door. When he seen us exit the car, he ran to the door with his gat in hand.

"Man, what y'all niggaz want?" Boo Boo asked.

"Who that?" Shine asked, coming from the back room with the same chick he slapped a while back. "Take ya ass back in the room," he told the girl.

"It's these niggas," Boo Boo said.

"Well, what the fuck you guarding the door for, like you Rambo? Let the niggas in and see what's up, 'cause as you can see we ain't being selling shit without these lil niggaz," Shine said, looking around at all the dope on the table. "Seems like when these niggaz left, the whole city left with them," Shine was thinking.

When Fatboy said, "What's up, y'all? Everything running smoothly?"

"Nigga, who is you to be asking questions!" Boo Boo yelled, getting mad at how calm these niggaz were.

"Man, chill with the dumb shit, nigga ain't on the bullshit right now. Nigga trying to make some money, 'cause y'all was right about what y'all said. We shoulda been here helping y'all make this money, instead of running to a party like a bunch of jits," Fatboy said, playing on their intelligence. Pokey looked at his dog like he was crazy, until he seen his dog wink his eye, then and only then did Pokey catch on to what Fatboy was doing.

"Make a nigga feel like he right. He'll swear he the man, and you need him," Pokey was thinking.

When Boo Boo yelled, "We told you, niggaz. We don't need y'all, y'all need us!"

"Boo Boo, shut the fuck up!" Shine yelled, becoming angry.

And Boo Boo turned 'round to face him, "Look, nigga, I don't know who you think you be talking to."

"Man, y'all chill out with the bullshit. We got money to make you remember," Flick said, cutting Boo Boo off.

"Yeah, y'all right," Shine said, still easing his lil brother. "Open shop, buck up, lil niggaz, gimma go take a nap before I snap in this bitch," Shine said walking off. As all three boys began to do their thing, it wasn't even twenty minutes and it seems like the baser, fiends, junkies, and crack smokers smell these niggaz and started coming from all angles; shit was booming again.

"What's up, Double D? Long time since I seen ya ass around," Pokey said.

"Shit, I just gotta outta jail, not even twenty-five minutes ago, that why," Double D said, laughing. "Man, look, I'm on my dick 'cause I just got outta jail. Let me get a twenty till later on, I'll bring the money ASAP tonight."

"All right, Double D, don't be playing," Pokey said, giving him the twenty. Even though things seem to be back in place, Boo Boo still had a funny feeling about something, he just couldn't put his hands on what it was. But he had his mind made up. Any wrong move and he would drop all three of these niggaz, he don't care whose son this nigga is.

"I was always told my life is more precious than the next man," he was thinking, as he watched customers come and go, left and right. He also realized something he never seen before. "Maybe these young niggaz was made for this shit, and maybe it was us who wasn't," Boo Boo was thinking when he seen Pokey open the door and in walked his shortie who was carrying his seed. The girl was five months pregnant and finer than Halle Berry.

"Damn, baby, what you doing here? You all right?" Boo Boo asked,

"Yeah, I'm all right. Me and my mom's just got into it, and I'm tired of that shit, so I came over here," the girl named Bre said.

"All right, baby, gone in my room and chill out. If you need anything, just holla."

"All right," the girl said, walking away.

"Boo Boo."

"What?"

"Who that?" Fatboy asked.

"That's my baby momma, why?"

"'Cause, nigga, this a trap house, and anything can happen at any given moment, and you got ya girl up in here."

"Man, fuck that, and fuck y'all. A bitch know better than to run up in here. So why you bitching?"

"All right, nigga, you dead right," Fatboy said, shaking his head. "It's already six o'clock, we got 'bout five hours and forty-five minutes of hearing this nigga's mouth," Fatboy was thinking, as he finished helping his dogs serve up the fiends.

"Well, it's about that time. I'm about to roll," Pokey told Boo Boo who kept a close eye on the niggaz the whole time they where there, but couldn't detect nothing, so he let his guards down.

"What's up y'all closing shop down?"

"Na'll, man, let's just take a break till 1:00 a.m. Fatboy, Flick, come on, let's go get something to eat."

"All right," his two friends said, looking at the clock. It was now 11:53.

"Hold up, where y'all going?" Boo Boo said.

"Shit, probably Krista, since that's the closest," Pokey said.

"All right, huh, bring my brother and girl and me something to eat," Boo Boo said, passing Pokey a fifty-dollar bill.

"I got you, nigga," Pokey said, walking out the door at exactly 11:55. When he hopped in his car, him and his friends and slowly pulled off, he saw Turtle and his two goons creeping up on the house, guns in hands. He flashed his lights twice, letting them know all was good. The thing he didn't notice was Double D was headed to the house at the same exact time as the three goons were to cope and pay him his twenty dollars.

Double D said he had a funny feeling tonight, "It's too quiet and ain't nobody out but me. Oh well," Double D said, as he kept pacing till he got to the door. *Tap, tap.*

"Yeah, who that?" Boo Boo yelled.

"It's me, Double D."

"Oh come on in, old-ass nigga, it's open." As Double D pushed the door open, he felt cold steel to his head.

"Nigga, if you scream, this where you die at," the masked man said with a icy tone. As he pushed Double D in the house, he caught Boo Boo by surprise. When he reached for his gun, the other two goons said, "I wish you would." As Boo Boo put his hands on top of his head, "Man, y'all got that. Whatever y'all want y'all can have," Boo Boo said. "Please, niggaz, just don't hurt my baby mother."

With the thought of somebody else in the house, Turtle told Lo-P, "Man, check the rest of the house out. Anybody you see, smoke them."

"Hold up, man, my nigga, shut up," Rim said, kicking Boo Boo in the mouth.

"Turn that radio on," Turtle told Rim as he watched Boo Boo squirm all over the floor with blood gushing out his mouth. As soon as the radio was full blast all you heard was *boom, boom,* two gunshots rang out. But people woulda thought it was just the music, as Lo-P crept in the back room. He found a nigga having sex with a girl, and without warning, he let his .44 do the talking, putting a whole in back of the nigga Shine's head and blowing a hole through the chick's head, who just stared at him, like she wasn't scared of death. "Look like that nigga had a ride-or-die bitch on his team," Lo-P was thinking.

As he exited the room and entered another one with the gun in front of him, what he seen kinda froze him. The naked girl lying on top of the covers was beautiful and sound asleep, like she didn't even hear the gun go off thirty seconds ago. As Lo-P crept up on the girl, he stuck one finger inside her to find her warm and wet, and she began to moan, thinking it was Boo Boo. She spread her legs wider while keeping her eyes closed. As Lo-P began to stick two fingers in her, he noticed the lil lump. "This bitch pregnant," he was thinking. "I know this pussy good," he began to unbuckle his Guess jeans, when the girl opened her eyes and screamed. "Oh shit," Lo-P said, slapping the girl. "Bitch, if you wanna live, you better shut the fuck up right now," he said while gritting his teeth. As he watched the girl began to shake, he couldn't help but squeeze one of them round pretty titties, as tears started falling from her eyes.

He listened to her, "Please, oh please, don't kill me. Do anything you want to me," she said, playing with herself and sticking her fingers in her own juices. She never knew the thought of death would have her so hot; even though she was scared, she also was turned on. But Lo-P remembered this was a mission, nothing else. He said, "Sorry, baby. I'mma pass this time, but you almost had me slipping," he said, grabbing the chick by her hair.

Snatching her up off the bed, which only turned her on more, as he walked her in to the living room but-ass naked. Rim and Turtle said damn, but still held their gun on the prey.

"Man, let her go!" Boo Boo cried. "She ain't got shit to do with this."

"Man, look, I'll let all y'all go, if y'all give me what I want. I want the money out the stash step that's under the table and all the drugs," Turtle said.

"I knew them niggas was up to something," Boo Boo was thinking. "How else these niggas know 'bout the stash spot, unless somebody told them?"

"All right, man, the drugs are in the duffel bag in that closet," Boo Boo said.

"Check it out, Lo-P." And Lo-P looked in the closet he open the duffel bag, "All here, dog," he said, placing the bag over his shoulder.

"Now the safe, nigga," Turtle said.

"Man, it's under the rug under the table right where you said it would be. The combo number is 21-33-16."

"That's what that nigga told us," Turtle was thinking. "Lo-P, open that shit, get the money, and let's ride," Turtle said.

When Turtle said, "Let's get the money and ride," Boo Boo had a glimmer of hope that he would make it outta this alive. But not Double D, when he heard the nigga slip and say Lo-P, he knew they were gonna die. "Shit, live by, die by. I enjoy my life, so fuck it,"

"I got the money, dog. It's like fifteen thousand. Let's roll."

"All right, go 'head," Turtle said to Lo-P. "Rim, off that nigga," and Rim opened fire on Boo Boo. Blood splashed everywhere. As his girl began to scream, Turtle shot her right in the throat, only to watch her grab her throat like she could stop the blood from pouring out. As he watched Boo Boo and his girl squirm in defeat, Rim walked up to both of them and put a hole in their head. Double D tried to get out the hold Turtle had on him, "But the young buck was to strong," Double D was thinking.

When Turtle said, "Old school, you see anything?"

"Na'll, man, I didn't see shit."

"I know," Rim said, shooting Double D in the eyes. "Let's roll, Turt," Rim said.

"Police will be here in a minute, and this shit's a mess. They said running in the night till they reach they ride. That's what I'm talking about. Y'all niggas did that," Turtle said, pulling off in the truck.

Rim asked Turtle, "Yo, Turtle. You act like you was about to let the old nigga go or something."

"Man, the nigga ain't nothing but a baser," Turtle said.

"Yeah, and that same baser coulda had all our asses sitting in jail or in the dirt one. You know how we get down, Turtle? Leave no witnesses, there is no crime," Lo-P said.

"Word," Turtle said, changing the subject. "Anyway, we hit a pretty good lick, man.

"We'll see when we get to the crib," Rim said. And all three became silent in thought.

CHAPTER 16

No Remorse

"DAMN, MAN, I hope them niggaz ain't mess up," Pokey said aloud to no one really in particular, just speaking his mind. As he drove back to the projects with the car smelling of hamburgers and fries, like they had planned, just in case Turtle and his two goons got scared and called it off. "Well, it's one in the morning, over a hour since we left," Pokey said, pulling up into the projects to see police cars everywhere, lights flashing like crazy.

"I guess them niggas handle they business," Fatboy said, jumping out the car with a Krista bag in hand.

"Just follow my lead," Pokey said, running up to the officer guarding the door.

"You can't come in here, son. This is a crime scene."

"Man, my two lil cousins live here!" Pokey screamed. "What the fuck happen?"

"Well, from the looks of things, it looks like a home invasion 'cause we didn't find any drugs or money, just four, no, five dead bodies. One guy was still alive but died while he was trying to tell us something."

"What guy was that?" Pokey asked, with tears in his eyes, faking the funk.

"Some older guy," the police said. "Look as you live here."

"No, I just told you. I had two cousin living here," Pokey said, as Fatboy and Flick walked up beside him.

"Dog, what happen?" Fatboy said, putting on a show as well.

"They say my cousin got killed and some older dude."

"Who else?" Flick asked, knowing the female was there also.

"I don't know, dog."

"Look," the officer said, "can y'all help us out?"

"Doing what?" Pokey said.

"Well, you said they were ya cousins. So can you ID them for us."

"I should be able to," Pokey said.

"All right, come on it."

When Pokey walked in, all he seen was blood everywhere. But instead of becoming sick, he likes the smell of death as he looked round. He saw all the dead bodies lying, unmoving, as he walked up to what was left of Boo Boo. He told the officer, "This is my lil cousin Boo Boo," and pointed at the naked young girl with the hole in her throat and head and said, "I don't know her name, but this was his baby's mother. Well, she was pregnant with his child."

"Damn, these niggas ruthless," he was thinking. As the officer asked if could he identify this person, he walked over to a person who looked like Double D, and he almost lost his breath.

"So this the nigga that almost told what went down."

"Yeah, man, I mean, Officer. This was a friend of their late mother, who y'all killed a while back. This is Double D," Pokey said, looking at the big asshole that entered his eye socket and I guess found a resting place. Somewhere in his head, as bad as Pokey wanted to feel sorry, for what he planned, he couldn't bring himself to feel any remorse.

"Look, son. We got two more dead bodies. I know you have seen a lot, but it's almost over. Could you please come with me and identify the last two remains?"

"Man, whatever," Pokey said. Walking behind the officer, with a slight smirk on his face, still really not believing he set these niggas up to get murked. As they entered the room, they found Shine still between his girl's legs. With a hole in the back of his head, and his girl's face half blown off. "I hope you got off before the bullet hit cha, nigga," Pokey was thinking.

"Look, Officer, this my oldest cousin Shine. And that's his girl April. Can I please go now? This shit is making me sick," he said, acting as if he was about to throw up. "Uggh."

"Go 'head, son. You can leave now, thanks for the help," the officer said, watching Pokey as he walked away, knowing something wasn't right. "This kid acted like he didn't even see all these dead bodies lying around," the officer was thinking.

When Pokey walked outside, he saw Fatboy and Flick talking to Mr. Big, who had a sad expression on his face. "Damn, here we go with all this crybaby-ass shit again," Pokey was thinking as he walked up to them. "What's up. Y'all all right out here?" Pokey asked.

"Yeah, dog, we good. What it look like in there?"

"Man, it's a mess, whoever did that wasn't even playing, them fools was playing for keeps," Pokey said. "Whoever was in the house at the time got put to rest. Damn, Shine and Boo Boo gone," Pokey said, playing the part in front of Mr. Big.

"You gonna be all right, Pokey?" Mr. Big asked.

"Yeah, I'mma be fine. I just need sometime to think about life, 'cause one minute you here, the next you gone."

"Look, y'all, whoever did this will pay. Life for a life," Mr. Big whispered, with no remorse seen in his eyes.

"You know Double D got murk too. He was in there too, along with Boo Boo's girlfriend. And the sad part is she was pregnant and killed butt-ass naked."

"Yeah, that's fuck up," Mr. Big said. "But I won't rest until I find out who did this, 'cause I got a feeling something ain't right about this. Anyways, it's a good thing y'all wasn't in the house, or y'all probably would be dead too. Why wasn't y'all here anyways?"

"Oh, 'round midnight we closed down shop, like always. And went and grab something to eat from the Krista's up the road."

"And it took y'all a whole hour to get back," Mr. Big cut in.

"Man, we was just having fun, talking to some females that was up off into the place," Fatboy said, defending them. "Why you questioning us like it's our fault? Shit, them niggas coulda rode with us. Before we left we told them will be back in a hour. We can't help somebody spared us and not them," Fatboy said, feeling no remorse for the loss of Mr. Big.

"All right, let's forget all this for right now," Mr. Big said. "Lord, please tell me these kids and my own son ain't have nothing to do with this," Mr. Big asked God in silence, "'Cause something just ain't right. When I look at these kids' eyes, I see no sign of tears, no sign of hurt, no sign of remorse. And that's strange, they been working together for close to seven months now," Mr. Big was thinking, till a voice brought him outta his thinking.

"Mr. Big. Damn, Mr. Big, you deaf? When I walked through the crib, I seems like everything was took. The stash spot was uncovered, and the bag holding the dope was gone," Pokey said.

"Boy, I ain't worried about no money, no dope, nothing but my two lil brothers at this time. I can make plenty money, get plenty dope. But I can't bring back the ones who was lost here tonight," he said, becoming tearful.

"Damn this nigga pie. This nigga always crying," Fatboy was thinking.

"Anyways, I'm closing down shop. Shit's getting too dangerous. And I ain't about to bury y'all too."

"Na'll. Hell na'll, Mr. Big. You can't just close down shop when shit get hot. Shit, for seven months we been doing this shit, and any given day, we coulda met the same fate they met today," Pokey said, becoming angry.

"Look, son. Shit is gonna be hot right now. This the same house somebody got killed in a few months ago."

"Man, we know all about Mrs. Jones. You forgot we went to the funeral!" Pokey screamed.

"Listen, what you saying makes sense, so I'm feeling that," Mr. Big said. "But we still gotta close down shop for at least a month or two."

"Man, you tripping. Then all the customers will go elsewhere."

"Man, stop being stupid. I ain't telling y'all to stop hustling, I'm just saying you can't do it here. This shit's bound to be watched," Mr. Big said.

"Oh, okay, we got you."

"Look, y'all. If there is anything y'all need, I mean anything, let me know," Mr. Big said. "Right now I gotta go. Get everything ready for the upcoming funerals. Damn, this shit crazy, y'all stay outta trouble," Mr. Big said, hopping in his ride and peeling off. "Man, I know this my son and all. But this lil nigga's heart is cold as steel. I got a bad bad feeling about this shit. I just don't believe some niggas walked off in the crib and just murk my brother them. Them niggas always on point. So it had to be a setup," Mr. Big was thinking deep in thought.

"Dog, we the shit," Pokey said, jumping in his ride with his two dogs. "We fooled that nigga. Now he don't suspect shit," Pokey said. But Fatboy and Flick didn't feel so sure. They knew Mr. Big was street-smart so they knew they had to stay on point. And keep this nigga Pokey in check, which won't be easy. Seems like the killings gave him more energy.

"Well, what's up? What y'all wanna do?" Pokey asked.

"Dog, take me to see my girl. I'mma call her from a payphone and let her know I'm on the way," Fatboy said.

"It's been a minute since a nigga had some, a night cool," Pokey said. "But I ain't gonna be waiting all day, while you sneaking in windows and shit."

"Nigga, fuck you," Fatboy said, playing.

"Shit, after that nigga done, take me by Rosie," Flick said. "I ain't gotta call. Her moms work tonight, from 2:30 a.m. till 9:30 in the morning."

"Let's ride, fuck all the talking," Pokey said, turning on the tape player. "Yo live in die in LA, is the place to be, You got to be there to know it," was the last thing Flick heard before he fell asleep.

When he woke up, he was sitting in the car alone with Pokey, who was dead-ass sleep. "Damn, I been sleep a minute," Flick thought. When he seen Fatboy give his girl a kiss as he landed on the ground, from climbing out the window.

"Pokey, let's go," Fatboy said, as he got up and began to scratch.

"All right, dog. Next time, nigga, don't be taking all motherfucking day," Pokey said, looking crazy.

"Nigga, fuck dat," Fatboy said.

"Look, I got something to tell y'all. But I'mma tell y'all later.

"Whatever, nigga. Wake me up when we get to Rosie's," Flick said, lying down in the backseat.

CHAPTER 17

Stopping up Our Game Three Months Later

"DAMN, WE GOT shit on smash with the three keys ya uncle gave you and Shine and Boo Boo out the way, we been seeing major paper. It's a good thing Mr. Big gave us a chance to show him we can handle shit on our own," Flick said.

"Yeah, but we can't forget the first two months was pure hell. So I guess it's true, at the end of every rainbow it's a pot of gold," Fatboy said, looking over at the bundles of money they made in the last three months.

"The sad thing is Mr. Big said this it's he done lost to many friends and family members behind this game. Not that we mad, 'cause we ain't. We still got enough money to cope our own shit and keep business booming. It just won't be as cheap-ass Mr. Big shit, that's all," Pokey said. "So look, we can't be mad. He said as long as we can keep the lil rent up, we can use the lil building all we want."

"Dog, remember when I went to court for the gun charge and said if we ever make enough money to do the shit we want, we would give the game up?" Fatboy was telling Pokey.

"Yeah, I remember that bullshit," Pokey said, "but that's before we started making all this money. It's too late to quit now, people depending on us." Pokey said. "We done came too far to turn back now. Just look around, you got all the clothes, shoes you want. You got your own ride sitting on dubs. You getting ya momma a house build out in the country. What else could you want, nigga?" Pokey said,

"A normal life, nigga, that's what. A nigga get tired of looking over their shoulder every day, worrying about the police, the boys, and whoever else may be plotting on a nigga."

"Nigga, fuck the police, the kack boys, and whoever else think they gonna take a a nigga shit. I'll die before that happens," Pokey said, becoming angry.

"Look, dog, we are living good, but that shit don't last forever. Y'all know the saying us niggas die of three ways. We either get shot, die in prison, or die from AIDS. And I ain't trying to go out either way," Flick said.

"So what y'all saying," Pokey asked, "this it, this where y'all niggas get off the train?" Pokey said, pacing back and forth, looking at his two so-called friends.

"Man, we ain't saying shit. All we saying is let's get out while we still can."

"No!" Pokey screamed. "You niggas know the rules, GABOS. We in this shit till the end," Pokey said, with tears in his eyes.

"Man, you tripping," Fatboy said. "What else can we do?" Fatboy said, looking his dog dead in the eyes.

"Man, we can become the most feared niggas in this city," Pokey said.

"Or the most dead," Fatboy said.

"Pokey, do you honestly believe it's better to be feared than love?" Flick asked his friends, who just look at him like he was crazy.

"Look, Pok. Fuck it, I'mma ride with you to the end. No matter what," Fatboy said.

"I just hope you see the light before it's too late."

"That's what I'm talking about," Pokey said, embracing his dog. "I thought you was getting soft on a nigga," Pokey said. "What about you, Flick?"

"Shit, if Fatboy still in, I'm in," Flick said. "Boy, peer pressure is a motherfucker," Flick was thinking. "Look, y'all know since we cope our rides, I've been going to see my shortie on the low-low, and I was gonna tell y'all the night Pokey took me to see my shortie. But I forgot you talking 'bout the same night I went and saw Rosie," Flick said.

"Yeah, dog, that night. Well, look, my girl Shakia told me she was pregnant, and having a nigga shortie. She's three and a half months or four now. The baby is a girl, we already got a name."

"What is it?" Flick asked.

"Tykia," Fatboy said, smiling.

"Tykia, Tykia. What kind of name is that?" Flick asked.

"Nigga, it's a name."

"But congratulations, nigga. Nigga, this should be the main reason you wanna stay in the game. So you can give ya daughter all we never had," Pokey said.

"Yeah, I'm feeling that. I just don't wanna end up missing out on my first child's life, that's all," Fatboy said. "But I'm in."

"So I'm the goddaddy, right?" Pokey said.

"Yeah, man. Y'all both the goddaddy. So pay up that cash," Fatboy said, "the baby needs Pampers."

"Nigga, the baby ain't here yet."

"Stupid, it's better to be sorry than late," he said, laughing.

"All right, man. Let's do this. We 'bout out of everything, so I'mma get into contact with my Uncle Sico and see what he can do."

"All right, dog. Do that," Fatboy said.

"I guess we ain't gonna stop making money, until these crackers run outta trees!" they said, laughing. As Pokey made his way to call his Uncle Sico, "Hey y'all, go 'head and do y'all while I holla at this nigga right quick," Pokey said, picking up the phone. Five minutes later, there was a knock at the door.

"Hey y'all, cover that money up right quick," Pokey said, while talking to his uncle. "You never know who that is," Pokey screamed.

As Flick went to look out the window to see who that was, the door came crashing in with three niggas in masks yelling, "Nobody move, nobody get hurt!"

"Damn, we got caught slipping," Fatboy said, trying to make a slight move for his piece. But before he could, the tallest of the three masked men put a gun to his face and said, "Nigga, don't be motherfucking superhero, unless you ready to meet the maker," he said, pushing the gun in his face. As he snatched the gun from Fatboy's hip, "Let me get this, you won't need it no time soon," the nigga said and smiled.

"Yo, dog, what you want me to do with this nigga on the phone?"

"Nigga, what you think?" the fat kid said. "Make the nigga get off that bitch."

"The easy way or the hard way? Nigga, hang the motherfucking phone up," the masked man said. As Pokey kept right on talking, the nigga hit him dead in the head with the gun. "Nigga, you think I'm playing? Hang that motherfucker up, or next time it's gonna be the bullet that hits you in the head."

"Pokey, hang the shit up!" Flick said, worried 'bout his friend, as he saw the blood gushing out his head. Pokey looked at Flick and hung the phone up.

"Now check that nigga for a piece, and that one too," the fat nigga said, pointing at Flick. As the masked man searched them both, they found a piece on Flick but none on Pokey.

"All right, dog, find something to tie this niggaz up right quick. And hurry up 'cause you never know who the nigga was talking to over the phone, so we gotta move quick." As one goon ran in the room, he came back ripping up a sheet. With the ripped-up sheets, they tied Pokey, Fatboy, and Flick to three chairs.

"Now listen, we can do this one or two ways. The easy way is y'all tell us where all the money is, and we out. Nobody gets hurt. If you don't, we kill all y'all, and tear this bitch up till we find the money," the masked man yelled.

"Nigga, fuck you," Pokey said, spitting blood and spit at the nigga who made the threat. "Do what you gotta do, but we ain't telling you shit," Pokey said in pain, wondering how them nigga couldn't see all the fucking money covered up under a blanket 'cause they didn't have time to put it in the stash spot.

"Look, let's talk to these nigga before we kill this stupid-ass nigga. Man, I'm pretty sure y'all love ya lil friend over there, but if y'all wanna see him alive, y'all better start talking."

"Nigga, fuck y'all," Fatboy and Flick said. They already knew they would make it outta this alive. "'Cause if these niggas came to kill, we woulda been dead," they were thinking.

"Do what y'all gotta do," Fatboy said.

"Is that so?" the fat kid said, taking his fire and putting it to Pokey's head. "Y'all think this is a motherfucking game, huh? That's what y'all think," the fat kid said, slapping Pokey with the fire, knocking him out cold for just a second. When Fatboy and Flick seen that, they tried to get up outta their seat and help their dog but realized they were tied up.

"Man, chill the fuck out," Flick said, worried 'bout his dog who wasn't moving.

"Let me ask y'all a question, which one more important, life or money?"

Neither Fatboy nor Flick said anything, they just kept their eyes on Pokey who was starting to come through.

"Niggas, I asked y'all a question."

"Yeah, and your answer is money makes the world go round, so without it, nigga, fuck life," Fatboy said.

Then the fat kid rushed Pokey and started hitting him all over the head with his fire, "Niggas, do I look like a nigga who gives a fuck about y'all lil friend?" the fat kid said, breathing hard and heavy. As he eased up on Pokey, his head dropped to his chest, with blood coming from everywhere. "Now look, niggas. This the last time I'mma ask y'all, where the motherfucking money at?" the fat kid said, cocking his gun.

"All right, man, chill, we gonna tell you. Just chill out," Flick said. "Man, the money is –" Just as Flick was about to tell the niggas where the money was, Sico and Mr. Big ran in the house, guns pointed at the two niggaz they see first.

"Nigga, if y'all wanna make it outta here alive, drop that shit," Mr. Big said.

"Yeah and if y'all wanna see this nigga alive again, drop y'all shit," the fat kid said, pointing the pistol at Pokey's head, who was bleeding badly. When Mr. Big saw Pokey tied to a chair and bleeding damn near to death, he blinked out and grabbed the closest nigga to him and put his gun to his head, and Sico did the same.

"Now we got a Mexican standoff. Look y'all got about five second before we turn this bitch into a blood bath," Mr. Big said, knowing the kids were scared.

"Yo, Rico, let's just go, the niggas said they gonna let us live, right?" the tall kid was asking Mr. Big.

"Yeah, I'mma let y'all go."

"Man, nigga, shut yo punk ass up," the fat kid said. "You think these nigga gonna let us live? Nigga, you stupid as fuck!" As the fat kid was talking, he never really noticed Mr. Big ease up closer and closer.

"Nigga, I ain't leaving without the money," Rico said, slubbing at the mouth. "I came for one thing, and I ain't leaving till I get it," Rico said, looking around. "Now where the money at, before I put a bullet in this lil niggaz head," Rico said.

"Man, I got all the money you need," Mr. Big said. "Just let the lil nigga go, so we can get him to a hospital."

"Nigga, fuck this nigga," Rico said, slapping Pokey with the fire once again. As Rico was about to slap Pokey again, Mr. Big removed his fire from the kid he had in front of him and opened fire on Rico, hoping not to hit Pokey. As the gun sounded, Rico slowly grabbed his chest and stuck his finger in the hole, where the bullet opened a hole the size of a golf ball. When Rico realized he wouldn't make it, he tried with all his might to take somebody with him, but he couldn't pick up his pistol. As he realized his body was shutting down, he fell to the ground. With one last try, he tried to raise his pistol, but it was to let Mr. Big step over him and put a bullet in his head.

As Fatboy and Flick watched all that went on, they noticed the one kid Mr. Big let go of reaching for a pistol on the floor, so they yelled out, "Mr. Big, watch out!" But before the kid even got a chance to move, Sico already seen the move and opened up fire, leaving the kid sucking for his last breath. As he watched the kid take his last breath, he turned round and shot the other masked man in the face, watching him fall to the floor.

"Look, we gotta get these niggaz up outta here, and we gotta get Pokey to the hospital," Mr. Big said, untying Pokey and picking him up, placing him in his arms, running out the door to his car.

Back in the house Sico was untying Fatboy and Flick, who couldn't wait to get loose. As they were freed, they both had the same thing on the mind. "Let's see who these niggaz are," Fatboy was thinking as he made his way to the tallest kid and took off his mask. He looked down at a dead man, as Flick looked over at Fatboy, he said, "Dog, I don't know who this is. The face shot fucked him up."

"Whoever it is, we ain't gotta worry about no more though. Look, y'all go ahead to the hospital with my nephew, I'll handle this," Sico said, pulling out his cell phone, and dialing a number.

"You sure, Sico?" Fatboy asked.

"Yeah, lil nigga, I'mma handle the bodies. Now go 'head before Po Po gets here. I promise I'mma handle all this," Sico said, calling a few trusted friends who would get rid of the bodies ASAP. "Damn, I know I shouldn't have put my lil nephew in the game. All this is my fault," he said. "But shit, that's just life. I just hope he be all right, 'cause from the looks of it, he took a beating," Sico was thinking as he hung up the cell phone. "It's a good thing I heard all the bullshit them niggaz said while I was talking to my nephew over the phone. And it's a smart move my lil nephew made to stay on the phone, so I could hear the nigga scream, 'You think I'm playing'," Sico was thinking to himself. "Or my nephew and his two friends probably woulda been dead," he was thinking. As he saw the black van pull up in front of the house, he knew it was his two trusted friends whom he called the body removers.

"I'm glad y'all got here before Po Po," Sico said, watching the two niggaz load the bodies in the van. Without so much as a word, when the last body was loaded in the van, the Mr. T-looking nigga turned around and said," Send the money to the same place," as he jumped in the van and pulled off.

CHAPTER 18

Still Breathing

WHEN FATBOY AND Flick reached the hospital and entered the waiting lobby, they saw Mr. Big and Mrs. Queen sitting by each other, with worry written all over their faces.

"Mr. Big, what's up with Pokey? He gonna be all right, right?" Flick asked.

As Fatboy sat down beside Mrs. Queen, who was crying silently, "Mrs. Queen, what the doctor talking 'bout? What's up with my dog? He gonna be all right or what?" Fatboy asked.

As he waited for Mrs. Queen to say something, she just looked at him and began to cry harder. As he reached over and tried to give her a hug of support, she screamed, "Don't touch me, don't you touch me. If it wasn't for you and him," she screamed, pointing at Flick, "my baby wouldn't be in this damn hospital fighting for his life. Now get out!" Mrs. Queen screamed.

"Look, Mrs. Queen, I know you're upset and worried right now, but I ain't just gonna up and leave my dog. I'mma be by his side all the way through this, 'cause I know if it was me lying in the hospital bed fighting for my life, he would do the same for me," Fatboy said, watching Mrs. Queen get up and walk to the other side and have a seat, looking off into space.

"Damn, Mr. Big, why she tripping on us?" Flick asked.

"Look, y'all, that's her only son and mines too," Mr. Big said. When Mr. Big said his too, Fatboy said, "What you just said, Pokey ya son?"

"Yeah, he is," Mr. Big said. "I was gonna tell him but didn't know how to."

"Well, tell him when he come through," Flick said.

"I will," Mr. Big said, placing his face in his hands, as he started to cry.

"Mr. Big, what's up with Pokey? Damn, y'all ain't gonna tell us shit," Fatboy said, getting angry.

"Listen, y'all, I know that's y'all friend, and y'all worried about him. But that's my son and hers too. Right now shit hard on us."

"Man, fuck that shit you talking. Yeah, he ya son, but he our brother too," Fatboy said. "We bleed the same blood he bleed, what he going through in there we going through in here," Fatboy said, touching his heart. "So will you just tell us is he okay, or do we have to act a fool in this bitch and just rush off in the room to see our dog?" Fatboy said, now walking around in a circle.

"Come on, take a walk with me outside," Mr. Big said. "I wanna show y'all something." As they walked outside, Mr. Big said, "Look at this," pointing at the ground. When Fatboy and Flick looked down at the ground, all they seen was a bunch of red spots, leading from the door to somewhere else.

"So what, what does this have to do with Pokey?" Flick asked.

"Lil nigga, what you looking at is my son's blood. He lost a lot of blood on the way over here. And the doctors say it's not looking good, 'cause we got him here so late. It's a fifty-fifty chance that he'll make it. Look," Mr. Big said, making his way to his car and opening the door. As he opened the door, he said, "Look." When Fatboy and Flick looked inside the car, they saw blood all over the front seat.

"Damn," Fatboy said, and that's when he finally noticed all the blood on Mr. Big's clothes. "I guess that's from him carrying my dog," Fatboy was thinking.

"Look y'all, I'm sorry," Mr. Big said. "I'm pretty sure y'all know and seen whoever did this, didn't make it."

"Yeah, we know, Mr. Big. But it's nothing we can do to help Pokey, is it?" Flick asked.

"Yeah, it is, all you can do is pray and hope for the best. He strong and the doctors said it's really on him. If he fights, like I hope he will, he'll pull through. Right now he's in a light coma. Every now and then he moves his fingers when his mother says she loves him, so I'm praying that's a good sign," Mr. Big said.

"Can we see him?" Flick asked.

"Look, right now they working on him. The nigga that beat him in the head with the gun did a good job. He gotta have stiches, and they said he gone have a scar for life. If he pulls through, as soon as the doctors let us in again, y'all can come with us," Mr. Big said, walking the boys back in the waiting lobby. When they entered the building, they saw Mrs. Queen, holding hands with another woman, eyes closed like they were praying or something.

"Damn, I see every time something bad happens, everybody wanna get all religious, like it's a God out there who really hears prayer. This shit crazy," Fatboy said, taking a seat.

"Look," Mr. Big said, "it's probably gonna be a while before we are allowed in to see Pokey. So if y'all wanna burn up and come back later, y'all can."

"Man, you tripping. We gonna sit right here and wait on our dog to come through," Flick said. He looked over at Fatboy, who was shaking his head up and down, saying, "That's right," without saying a word.

"That's fine with me," Mr. Big said.

"Hey, Mr. Big, can I ask you one question?" Flick said.

"Yeah, what's up?" Mr. Big replied.

"How come you never told Pokey he had a daddy? Maybe if you woulda, he wouldn't be stuck to a hospital bed right now," Flick said.

"Shortie, you got a lot to learn, but I'm pretty sure it's the same question Pokey will ask once I tell him. So I might as well explain myself to his friends as well," Mr. Big said. "Listen, in this life, it's a lotta things we will regret but something you can't help nor change. If I woulda knew Pokey was my son for real, half the shit he went through woulda never happen. Listen, growing up, I was just like y'all, determined. I wanted the whole world in my hands. Me and his momma Mrs. Queen, we used to love one another, but I loved the street life more than I did her, so she up and left. And even though I was told by my lil brother Sico that she was having my baby, I never really paid it any attention, until the time I seen y'all at the park. When I saw this lil nigga, I knew he was my son, so I started doing lil things to help y'all out. But now I realize it wasn't the best thing to do, 'cause it may cost him his life if he don't pull through. That's why I'm getting out the game, 'cause I hope he'll learn from this and give it up too," Mr. Big said, wiping away a tear. "I got enough money for all us to live off of, I just –"

As he was about to say something else, Dr. Van walked into the waiting room and said, "Mr. Haywood, which is Mr. Big and Mrs. Queen?" looking around until Mr. Big and Mrs. Queen were standing next to him. "Mr. Haywood and Mrs. Queen, I've come to inform you of your son's well-being."

"What is it, Doctor? Is he gonna be all right?" Mrs. Queen asked.

"Listen for a moment," Dr. Van said, "your son took a very bad beating to the head. As we speak the other doctors are working to remove the fluid from around his brain, which we already informed you about. If we can remove all the fluid without any problem, he'll have a 75 percent chance of being normal again."

"And if you can't remove the fluid from around his brain, then what?" Mr. Big asked.

"Then his chances of living is none to zero," Dr. Van said, as he watched Mrs. Queen fall to the floor and start crying.

"Doctor, please help my baby, please!" she yelled.

"Ma'am, I assure you we are doing all we can to save this young man's life," Dr. Van said.

"When can we see him again?" Mr. Big asked.

"Right now, he is still in a coma. He lost a lot of blood, but he's a fighter. Many others woulda been gave up if they would have took a beating and lost as much blood as he did. But I can promise you as soon as he's outta harm's way and we got all the fluid removed from his brain, I'll call y'all, in to see him. But I want you to remember, he doesn't look good, due to there's a lot of swelling on his face. But if he pulls through, all that will go down," Dr. Van said, looking at both parents and feeling sorry for them both. "Well, let me get back in here and do my job," Dr. Van said, walking off, listening to a mother's cry and remembering a father's sad look that touched his heart.

Five and a half hours later, Dr. Van came back out with a lil smile on his face.

"Mr. and Mrs. Haywood, I have some good news and some bad news."

"What is it?" Mrs. Queen asked.

"Well, we got all the fluid from around his brain," Dr. Van said.

"So that's the good news," Mr. Big said, feeling some relief. "But what's the bad news?"

"Well, the bad news is he's still in a coma, but I'm pretty sure with the fluid from around his brain, he will wake up soon. I have no timetable to when, everything is now on him. We sewed up the hole in his head, and already some of the swelling is about to go down."

"Well, when can we see him?" Mrs. Queen asked.

"Oh, you can go see him in about twenty minutes. They are removing him from the operating room as we speak," Dr. Van said.

"Thank you, Doctor. Will it be okay if his two friends come along? They were there when things went down, and they're really worried about him," Mr. Big said.

"It's okay with me," Dr. Van said.

"Okay, let me go tend to another needed patient," the doctor said, walking off.

"Fatboy, Flick, come here," Mr. Big said. "Look, the doctor just gave us some good news and some bad."

"What is it, Mr. Big," Flick asked.

"Well, they removed all the fluid from around his brain, that's the good thing, so he's outta harm's way."

"And the bad news?" Fatboy asked.

"Well, he's still in a coma," Mr. Big said. "And the doctor said he has no timetable how long he'll be like that."

"But he straight, right?" Fatboy asked.

"Look, all I know is the worst part is over," Mr. Big said. "Now it's on him, how long he wanna sleep," Mr. Big said, taking a seat, saying a silent prayer to himself.

Then Mrs. Queen called Fatboy over. "Fatboy, listen, I just wanna say I'm sorry for yelling at you earlier. I was just under a lot of stress with my baby boy being like he was," Mrs. Queen said.

"That's all right, Mrs. Queen, I understand," Fatboy said, giving her a hug.

"Let's pray," Mrs. Queen said to everyone. As she started her prayer, she was interrupted by Dr. Van, who called out Mr. and Mrs. Haywood.

"Y'all are allowed to see y'all son now. He's in room B23."

"Okay, Doc, thanks," she said, walking off, with Mr. Big, Fatboy, and Flick on her heels. When she opened the door, she seen her baby lying in the bed, still as a dead body, with wraps around his head. He didn't even look the same. In a few short hours, it seems like Pokey done lost 'bout fifty pounds, it broke her heart to see him like that. As she made her way to his bedside, she began to let the tears fall freely. "Oh baby, I'm so sorry this had to happen to you, I love you so much." Each and every time she said I love you, Fatboy notices his dog's finger move just a little bit. As they all walked to his bedside and took a look at Pokey, they all thought it would be best to leave a mother with her son. As they started walking out the door, Mrs. Queen said, "Look, I know y'all wanna talk to him too, so I won't be long," she said. As she watched them all exit the room and close the door, she began to talk. "Pokey, I'm sorry I lied to you about your father. I just didn't wanna lose you like I lost him by you following in his footsteps. I don't know what I'll do if I lose you. So, baby, fight, fight for me, fight for your friends, fight for life. I love you, baby," she said. As she got up from his bedside, she never noticed his fingers moved. As she made her way to the door, she stopped to look at her son one last time, before walking out the door.

As she came out, Mr. Big came in, walking with his head down. As he sat next to his bedside, he grabbed Pokey's hand and placed it in his. As he began to talk, a tear escaped his eye. As he let it fall, he said, "Pokey, I know I haven't been in your life long, but its seems when I come in your life, shit like this happen. If you can hear me, I want you to know the life you was living before this happen, you don't have to live no more. If you want, you can come live with me, and I promise shit will be gravvy." As Mr. Big was about to say something, he felt Pokey's fingers move inside his hand. But when he picked his hand up that was holding Pokey's hand, it stopped. So he thought it was just his imagination. Then he got up and said, "I'll see you tomorrow, and hopefully you'll be awake," Mr. Big said, walking out the door to see Fatboy and Flick standing against the wall.

"Y'all can go on in. I think y'all got 'bout fifteen minutes before visiting hours over. I'mma go ahead and head home, go get cleaned up, then I'll be back," Mr. Big said, walking off.

As Fatboy and Flick entered the room, they both grabbed a chair and sat on opposite sides.

"Pok, I know you can hear us, so listen up, hardhead nigga. We started all this shit together, so you need to wake up so we can finish building this empire we started as a team together. I'm sorry, dog, we got caught slipping the way we did. If we was on point none of this shit woulda happen. So I hope when you pull through this, you ain't mad at us. I just want you to know the niggaz that did this to you are no longer breathing. So, my nigga, best believe you in a better state than they are," Flick said, catching himself before he started shedding tears. "Fatboy, I'mma wait on you outside in the car," Flick said.

"All right, dirty, I'll be there in a minute." As he watched Flick walk out the door, he turned back toward his friend. "Pok, nigga you need to stop bullshitting and come outta dreamland. You know a nigga need you out here with us. I understand you wanna take a break," Fatboy said, smiling to himself, "but you the one said you'll sleep when you die, and you got a lot of living to do. So what's up with all this sleeping? Really though, dog, I'm sorry. I've sat out in the waiting area, wondering why it had to be you and not me. Dog, if I could change places with you, I would in a heartbeat, but then I know if the shoe was on the other foot, you'll be telling me this same shit. Listen, dog, when I come back up here, you better be awoke, 'cause we got things to do," Fatboy said, getting up, squeezing his dog's hand. As he felt his dog try to squeeze back, he knew in his heart his dog heard everything he just said, he knew he would pull through. As he let go off his hand and looked down at his dog, he whispered, "Much love, my nigga," before walking out the door.

CHAPTER 19

Danger Zone

AFTER LEAVING THE hospital and feeling better about Pokey's outcome, everything seemed to be going good. As they headed back to the projects to freshen up, they never noticed the all-black Regal with tinted windows following close behind them. As Fatboy and Flick were caught up in a small conversation, they stopped at a red light, and that's when Flick looked over and saw the black Regal pull up alongside them. As the back window and driver side window came down, all he saw was two barrels pointed in his direction. Fearing for his life, he screamed.

"Fatboy, go, nigga, go. It's a hit," as Fatboy just hit the gas, he heard the guns go off. *Boom, boom, tat, tat,* missing them only by inches. As the back window exploded, Flick came up shooting, boom, boom, but missing.

"Go, dog, them niggaz on our ass," Flick said, watching Fatboy weave in and outta traffic thinking, "Damn, if these niggaz don't kill us, this nigga gonna kill us by running into another car," he was thinking when he heard police sirens in the distance. "Slow down, dog, them niggaz done turned around," Flick said. "Damn, dog, that was close."

"Yeah, a brush with death," Fatboy said, laughing at his friend of how scared he looked.

"Man, that shit ain't funny," Flick said.

"Nigga, them niggaz was trying to take us out this world. I wonder who that was," Fatboy said.

"Dog, I ain't too sure. But the nigga in the back look like the nigga Rachet," Flick said, feeling angry.

"Well, one way or another, we'll find out," Fatboy said, turning into their projects. As they pulled up in front of their building, Fatboy jumped out the car and checked to see how bad the damage was to his ride. As he walked around his ride, all he noticed was the back window was gone, and one tail light was busted. Other than that all was good. "Nigga, get out the car with your scary ass!" Fatboy said, yelling at Flick, who was deep in thought. As he hopped out the car, he told his friend, "Yo, dog, this shit getting crazy. First a nigga rob us, or try to rob us, fuck our dog up in the process. Now niggas trying to take us out the world all behind this," Flick said, pulling out a knot with fifties and hundreds. "Dog, you know what they say, so why you tripping money is the root of all evil," Fatboy said.

"Yeah, I understand that," Flick said. "But a nigga ain't trying to lose his life for no fucking green paper!" Flick yelled.

"Man, look, this what will do. When Pokey pulls through, we'll tell him we through with the game. That's what you want, lil dog?" Fatboy asked, as he looked at Flick, who said, "Dog, the money is good, but I got so much shit I wanna do in life."

"Yeah, and all that shit you wanna do, you can't do it without this paper," Fatboy said.

"Man, it's more ways than one to make butter I can go off to college somewhere."

"Yeah, you right," Fatboy said. "You can, but me and Pokey can't. So God whatever you decide to do, go 'head, we with cha." As he was about to say something else, they saw Sico pulling up and parking right beside them. As Sico jumped out the car, looking like he been on Jenny Craig for years, he screamed, "What the hell happen to you? Shit," he asked Fatboy.

"Oh, some niggas just tried to take our heads off, not even ten minutes ago," Fatboy said.

"Y'all know who they was?" Sico asked.

"Na'll, we don't," Fatboy said. "Even if we did, we wouldn't tell him, 'cause we can handle our own business," Fatboy was thinking.

"So what's up with my nephew?" Sico asked.

"He doing better," Flick said.

"Nigga, why you want go and see?" Fatboy said.

"'Cause, nigga, I got money to make, that's why," Sico said.

"Damn, money more important to this nigga than his own nephew. No wonder Pokey wanna kill this nigga," Fatboy was thinking.

"Look, if y'all need me, y'all know how to reach me," Sico said, getting in his ride. "Oh by the way, tell Pokey come holla at me when he get out the hospital," Sico said, pulling off.

"Man, that nigga out there real bad," Flick said. "That nigga smaller than a motherfucker."

"Hey man, it's his life. He gonna do what he want with it, right?" Fatboy said.

"You right, dog," Flick said, "but what we gonna do about these niggaz who tried to take us out?"

"Look, we gonna handle business on that. But first let's go freshen up and get back to the hospital with Pokey," Fatboy said. "And you driving, lil nigga," Fatboy said.

"No problem," Flick said. "I'll be back around in 'bout thirty minutes."

"Word!" Fatboy said, walking up the stairs and inside the crib.

CHAPTER 20

Rude Awakening

"DAMN, WHERE AM I?" Pokey said, looking at this bright light that was before his eyes. Trying to pick his hand up to block the light but realized he was too weak, when he started hearing voices.

"Pokey, Pokey, nigga, say something. Damn, you got them big-ass eyes open, but you ain't saying shit." He heard the voice again, this time trying his hardest to remember where he was and say something. But all that came to mind were the years he spent in prison, fighting for his life, 'cause this nigga and that nigga was hating on him. One memory in particular stayed on his mind. The night before he was to go home, a couple niggas tried to stop that from happening. He could see it clearly now, three niggas running off in his cell. While he was lying down reading a book called the *Jux*, his roommate Old School was asleep, or so he thought, when outta nowhere, one kid pulls something that looks like a knife but was a prison shank, just as deadly as a knife.

"Yeah, nigga, I know you thought we was gonna forget how you did our boy. I told you, I promise I'mma get you before you make it home," the kid said, making his way closer to the bunk, when outta nowhere, Old School jumped up with a shank as long as a sword.

"Look, lil niggas, if y'all wanna make it home alive, y'all better get the fuck up outta here, 'cause whether y'all like it or not, this kid right here will see the streets tomorrow." As the kid with the shank started to say something, Old School said, "Man, y'all got 'bout ten second before I start using this bitch."

As Pokey watched the three dudes leave, he said, "Thanks, Old School. I guess them niggaz didn't wanna see a nigga make it home."

"Look, Pokey, I know you got the heart of a lion, but tomorrow you going back to the free world. Get out there and do something with your life, 'cause a lotta people ain't lucky to leave and make it outta prison in one piece. So be thankful and always remember what I told you, life is precious, don't fuck it up being stupid."

"I got you, Old School." Pokey remembers saying watching the light go dim, when he heard, "Pokey, dog, real shit, we need you out here. If you can hear me, dog, it's been three weeks, and you still ain't saying shit," Fatboy said, watching his dog move his hand then his head. As Mrs. Queen and Mr. Big walked in, Pokey blinked his eyes, "I know you heard me, nigga," Fatboy said, looking at his dog, who looked confused as hell.

"Man, what happen? Where am I?" As he tried to sit up, he couldn't, so he looked over at his mother who had her mouth covered with her hands and tears falling from her eyes. "Momma, what's up? Where am I, and what happen?" he asked his mother, with a weak voice.

As his mother came to his bedside, "Baby, I'mma let ya lil friends tell you what happen, 'cause they no better than me. All I can tell you is that you're in the hospital, you been in a coma for three weeks now. And I'm just grateful you came out of it," she said, letting the tears fall.

"In a coma?" Pokey asked, trying to sit up.

"Yeah, dog, in a coma," Flick cut in.

"Nigga, how you feeling?" Flick asked Pokey.

"Other than weak, I just got this big-ass headache," Pokey said, trying to smile for his friend. "So what happen, 'cause I can't remember how or why I got here," Pokey said,

"Look, dog," Fatboy said, "let me see if I can refresh ya memory. Three weeks ago, you remember we was chilling at the house when you was about to call yo Uncle Sico for some help when it was a knock on the door, but before we could do anything, three dudes kicked the door in, catching us by surprise. You wouldn't get off the phone, you acted like the niggaz wasn't even there, so one kept hitting you over the head with the gun. Good thing you stayed on the phone though, 'cause ya Uncle Sico and Mr. Big came rushing in just in time. I guess really with you being hardheaded and staying on the phone, you saved all our byes. You remember any of this?" Fatboy asked.

"Yeah, dog, it's coming back to me, slowly but showly now. So what happen to the –" As he was about to ask what happened to the three dudes, the doctor walked in.

"Well, I see you finally decided to wake up," Dr. Van said. "I'm just gonna check your vitals right quick and make sure everything is normal. And if so, within two to three days, you should be able to walk outta here with a little help."

"Hold up, doc," Pokey said, "what you mean with a little help?"

"Oh, no, it's nothing bad. It's just that you have been in this bed for three weeks, plus you lost a lot of blood, so you will be a little weak, until you start using your legs again, that's all," Dr. Van said.

"Oh, cool, I thought I was paralyzed or something," Pokey said, feeling the relief come over his body.

"Well, everything seems to be going good," Dr. Van said. "So I'mma leave y'all alone, y'all have a nice time," the doctor said, walking out the door.

"Baby, listen, I hope you learn from this, and whatever it is y'all was doing, I hope y'all will leave it alone," his mother said. "But right now I gotta go back to work. As soon as I get off, I'll be back," she said, bending over and kissing him on his cheek.

"All right, Mom," Pokey said, feeling better already.

"Look, Pokey, now that Mrs. Queen is gone, I want you to know the three niggaz that did this to you are dead and stinkin'. Ya old. I mean Mr. Big, didn't even play with them," Fatboy said.

"So what happen to all our money?"

"Dog, to be real with you, we wasn't even worried about no money. All we was worried about was you. When ya Uncle Sico untied us, he told us to get up outta there, that he would handle everything. So we left the place and came straight to the hospital. But as soon as we leave, I'll go by there and scoop the money up."

"All right," Pokey said, not liking the fact Sico was left alone with their money, hoping everything was how it is supposed to be. If not, somebody would pay.

"Anyways, dog, we just glad you decided to bounce back. Money we can make again, but a life once it's gone, ain't no coming back," Flick said.

"Anyways, dog, we gonna go check on that right now," Fatboy said. "'Cause I'm pretty sure Mr. Big wanna holla at you for a minute," Fatboy said, looking Mr. Big square in the eyes. "Before we go, we did see ya Uncle Sico 'bout two weeks ago. He said holla at him when you can."

As Fatboy and Flick left the hospital, they were thinking the same shit, "We ain't see this nigga Sico since the last time he rode up on us in the projects when them niggas tried to take us out the world. The nigga ain't been to see his own nephew, not one time."

"Man, something ain't right with that nigga Sico," Fatboy said aloud.

"Yeah, I feel that. I was thinking the same shit," Flick said, having another bad feeling about something. "Dog, while I drive, keep ya eyes open for us. Don't want to get caught slipping again," Flick said, heading back toward the project.

Back at the hospital, Pokey was looking at Mr. Big all crazy and shit, 'cause Mr. Big was just looking at him but not saying shit.

"Mr. Big, man, what's up with you? Why you acting all funny and shit?" Pokey asked.

"Look, Pokey, it's something important I got to tell you," Mr. Big said, "but I don't know how."

"Is it something bad? Something wrong with me, I'm missing a leg or something?" Pokey said, feeling for his leg.

"No, no, nothing like that. I just, I just thought you should know the life you living, you don't have to no more. I'mma make sure you straight," Mr. Big said.

"And why would you wanna do all that?" Pokey said.

"'Cause I'm your," Mr. Big couldn't say the words.

"You're my what?" Pokey said, trying to sit up. "You're my what? Man, what the hell is going on with you? First, you looking at a nigga all crazy, then you start to tell me something then just stop. It's that bad you can't even tell a nigga what's on your chest, but you always spitting that bullshit 'bout my word is everything. Well, tell a nigga what's on your chest. What, you don't wanna fuck with us no more? No big deal, nigga, we can handle our own," Pokey took off. Trying to figure out what it was this nigga had to say, until Mr. Big cut him off.

"I'm your father. There, I said it. I'm your father."

"You my what? Nigga, you tripping! My father died when I was a baby, that's what my momma told me. Now you saying you a nigga father. Man, I ain't trying to hear that," Pokey said.

"Look, you need to calm your ass down with all that yelling," Mr. Big said, "and just shut up and listen. Look, back in the days me and your momma used to mess around. Actually I was in love with her and vice versa, but it was one thing I loved the most."

"And what was that?" Pokey asked.

"The call of the streets," Mr. Big said. "She gave me a choice, said I could either choose her or lose her. I guess you know what happen."

"Yeah," Pokey said, "you lost her, 'cause you wanted to run the streets with ya thug and thought she would be waiting for you."

"Yeah, Tupac, you can say that," Mr. Big said. "But I'm thinking the reason she told you your daddy was dead was because I was dead to her, and she didn't want you following in my footsteps, which is understandable if you ask me," Mr. Big said.

"So you really a nigga father," Pokey asked.

"Yeah, I am. That's why you so much like me, 'cause my blood runs through your veins."

"Is that right," Pokey said. "Well, look, just like you dead to my momma, you dead to me. You aint' been there in the beginning, ain't no need in trying to be here now. I mean you still cool, Mr. Big, but you could never be my father. It's too late for that, I'm a grown man. And everything I learned, I learned from the streets."

"So you willing to die in the streets?" Mr. Big asked.

"If you didn't stop them nigga from killing me, I woulda showed you I'mma die for mines," Pokey said, dead-ass serious.

"So you still gonna try to run the streets after almost dying?" Mr. Big asked.

"I'mma run the streets till I get what I want, or the streets stop me by killing me."

"And ya friends, you gonna take them with you?"

"Mr. Big, maybe you don't get it. We, that means, me, my dog Fatboy, and Flick, bleed the same blood, we in it to win it."

"And what if ya friends tell you they through with this life then what?"

"You nosie ass fuck," Pokey said. "But they know the rules, death before dishonor. And if they choose to back out, then I guess they know GABOS."

"Is that so? So you'll take your own friends' life?" Mr. Big asked.

"Look, Mr. Big, if you try to stop what I'm doing, or them, I'll try to take your life. Just as well as theirs, if they get in the way. I guess you can call me coldhearted, but maybe if I woulda had a father around, shit wouldn't be like it is now. So blame nobody but ya self," Pokey said.

"Yeah, you dead right," Mr. Big said. "I'mma holla at you later."

"Cool," Pokey said with a crazy looking grin on his face. "Fuck you, nigga, and fuck my friends if they rolling with you," Pokey was thinking, as the meds kicked in and he dozed off.

Fatboy and Flick got out the car and walked up to the project building. As they got closer to the door, they realized the door was ajar just a lil.

"Man, be careful," Flick said, pulling out his pistol.

"All right, dog," Fatboy said, pushing the door open to nothing but an empty crib. Everything was gone, wasn't nothing left in this bitch, not even a blood spot.

"Man, go see if the nigga Sico put the money in the stash spot," Fatboy told Flick. As Flick moved the rug, he noticed there was no lock for the stash spot, so he just pulled the lid up and looked inside.

"Na'll, dog, ain't shit in here. This bitch clean as a motherfucker."

"Yeah, dog, I checked the rooms, and them shits clean too," Fatboy said.

"So what the fuck happen to all the shit? Our money is gone, the lil dope we had is gone."

"Only one way to find out, Sico," they said at the same time.

"But how we gonna get in touch with the nigga?" Flick asked.

"Man, your guess is as good as mines, but the way things looking we gonna just have to get the number from Pokey and let him know what's up."

"Dog, something just ain't feeling right 'bout this shit. First we get robbed, then a nigga try to take us out. Now this shit," Fatboy said, looking 'round the empty house. "Something just ain't right. I feel like we being set up, but by who and why?" Fatboy said.

"Dog, it is what it is. We just gotta stay on our p's and q's till we get to the bottom of this. That's what's up," Flick said. "Let's head back to the hospital and check on Pokey right quick," Flick said, hopping behind the wheel, as he watched his dog climb in beside him.

Now on the other side of town, Sico was doing his thing with the money he robbed his nephew and friends, for he was balling outta control. He had his own money, but he called this free money. And with free money, a nigga could splurge, and that's what he was doing. Smoking as much crack as he could, but at this particular time, he was chilling with another baser by the name of Kela in her run-down apartment. As he watched Kela take a hit off the pipe, she began to take off all her clothes. And even though she was a baser, she still had a banging body, standing at 6'1", brown skin, nice round titties, and a fat ass to go with the fattest pussy you ever seen. She began to stick finger after finger in her soaking wet pussy. As she began to moan, Sico instructed her to come to him, which she did. As she began to unbuckle his pants, he stuck two fingers in her pussy and said, "Damn, this pussy wet." As she turned around and sat on his lap, watching her ride him up and down, he forgot all about the fact people told him she had AIDS. As she began to go faster and faster, Sico grabbed her hips and began pulling her down as hard as he could on top of him to hear the sounds of *swssh swssh.*

"Damn, this pussy wet," he said. As she looked back at him and smiled, screaming, "Get this pussy!" As he watched her body began to shake, she cried out, "I'm cumming, I'm cumming, faster, faster!" As Sico felt himself begin to explode, he closed his eyes and enjoyed the moment, not realizing what he did, until it was too late. As he pushed Kela off of him, he zipped up his pants, and just walked out the door. As he started walking down the stairs, Kela, buck-ass naked, ran behind him, "Oh, that's how it is, you just gonna fuck a bitch than leave? Nigga, you ain't shit, basing-ass nigga!"

"Look, bitch," Sico said, stopping in his tracks. "I ain't ya NIGGA. But to shut you up, here you go," he said, giving the girl fifty dollars and a fifty piece of rock, which she gladly took.

"Thank you. When I'mma see you again?" she asked.

"I'll be around," he said, walking off. When he made it to his car, he had a strange feeling come over him, like something bad was about to happen, but shook the feeling, jumped in his ride, pulled out his pipe, placed the crack on it, and took another hit. As he was pulling, his cell phone began to ring. On the second ring he answered, "Yeah, who this?"

"Nigga, this your brother Sterling."

"Yeah, what's up?"

"Look, I just left the hospital with Pokey. I told him I was his father, and the nigga said in his eyes I was dead. So when he come home don't help him do shit, since he think he can do it on his own. I'mma show him without me, he ain't shit," Mr. Big said, hanging the phone up. Knowing now where the feeling came from, fuck it, he said, taking another hit.

"Shit, like nephew say, GABOS, so it is what it is. He shoulda learned never bite the hands that feed you." As he was about to take another hit, he heard, *tap, tap,* on his window, which scared the shit outta him. Rolling the window down, looking in the face of Kela, the bitch he just got done fucking.

"Man, what's up? Why the fuck you beating on a nigga window, like you the police or something."

"Nigga, I was just bringing your ass this dingy-ass bag you left in my house," Kela said, handing Sico the book bag that belonged to his nephew. As she passed him the bag, she stuck her head in the window, sniffing the air. "Damn, nigga, thas how it is, you smoking solo now."

"Bitch, if you don't get ya crabbing ass on somewhere. I just broke bread with you, now you want the whole hog," Sico said, rolling the window back up, resuming what he was doing before he was interrupted, taking the last hit, pulling off from the curve.

Back at the hospital, Pokey was just telling his homeboys how he told Mr. Big he was dead in his eyes, and he never had a father, so he don't need one now, so he could get the hell on.

"Damn, dog, we coulda just used the nigga," Flick said, "'Cause now we ain't got shit but the clothes on our back and the rides we purchase. Other than that and the lil money we got put up, we back to ground zero," Flick said.

"Nigga, what you mean, we strapped? Or you forgot about all the money we left at the crib?" Pokey said.

"That's just it, dog," Fatboy said, "when we went to check on shit, everything was gone, money an' all. The place was spotless."

"So y'all telling me the money we risked our life for is gone?" Pokey said, sitting up in the bed.

"Yeah, dog, unless ya Uncle Sico got it. Remember I told you he said holla at him when you jumped."

"I'mma do just that. And if the nigga ain't got our money, somebody besides me will be lying in this hospital bed, that's on everything," Pokey said.

"I'm feeling that, dog. Also on our way home earlier, some niggaz creeped up on us and started busting. Lucky for us all the bullets missed," Flick said.

"Yeah, but it fucked my window up," Fatboy said.

"So some niggaz tried to get at y'all?" Pokey asked really to himself. "Something ain't adding up. First we get robbed, all our money is gone, now y'all telling me some niggas tried to take y'all out."

"Yeah, that its," Flick said. "So the thing is, we gotta stay under the radar, or stay alert at all times." As Pokey was 'bout to say something to his friends, his mom walked into his room unsuspecting.

"I'mma holla at y'all later. I gotta holla at Mom's right quick. When y'all leave, make sure y'all stay outta trouble. I should be up out this bitch tomorrow or the day after," Pokey said, thinking about the dirt he would do to whoever crossed him. "Payback is a bitch," was his last thought, as he watched his friends walked out the door.

"How you feeling, baby?"

"Oh, I'm feeling fine, nice of you to ask," Pokey said. "Mom, look, I'mma get straight to the point. Why you lied to me all these years, telling me my daddy was dead? Now all of a sudden, this nigga pops up talking 'bout he a nigga daddy. That's messed up. So let me ask you a honest question, when does a heart stop bleeding? 'Cause nothing to the point has been able to stop the constant stream, the hole you made in my heart is too big. You plunged your knife into it that day you lied to me about not having a father. 'Cause all I went through could have be avoided probably when I woke up wondering what had happen, what I done. This nobody nigga I met at the park is in here, telling me he's my father. Why couldn't you tell me, why not you? I thought me and you had a bond that couldn't be broken, but I guess I was wrong."

"Baby, we do have a bond," Mrs. Queen said, letting her tears soak the floor. "I lied to you 'cause I didn't want my only son following in the wrong person footsteps. But I guess it was something I couldn't change nor stop, 'cause you falling right into the same life he trapped in. So yes, I lied, I had to lie to keep him out our life. I loved that man with everything I had, and he choose the street life over me, over us," she cried. "I'm sorry, yes, I'm sorry that he found away into your life. I'm sorry you had to learn about this, this way, but some things I can't change."

"I know," Pokey said.

"Baby, I'm just glad you're okay, that's all. And I hope that all you went through will open your eyes and help you enjoy life more, 'cause we only get one chance at it," she said.

As Pokey began to talk again, "Mom, what if I woulda died, I woulda went to my grave believing my father was dead. Now how can a son forgive his own mother for her disloyalty? I didn't ask him to be my father, you did, 'cause that's who you loved at one time."

"Look, Pokey, all I can say is I'm sorry, and if I'm wrong for wanting the best for you, then so be it. But you gotta learn in life, without adversity you have no character, without character you have no hope. Always keep in mind, never lose hope, 'cause I never lost hope in you. I love you," his mom said. As she turned around and headed for the door, reaching out her hand to turn the knob, Pokey called out.

"Hey Mom, all is good. I forgive you, and I love you too. It's him I refuse to forgive." As Pokey said those words, Mrs. Queen turned around and walked back to his bedside and kissed him on his forehead.

"Thank you, baby. But now that your father is in your life, don't you want him to stay?"

"No, I'm good. I never had a father growing up, I can do without now," Pokey said, watching Mrs. Queen lower her head.

"Baby, look, I'mma head home and cook. Hopefully you'll be outta here tomorrow."

"Okay, Mom, I'll see you later." As his thoughts kept drifting to how he was gonna get the man they called his father. "One or the other would be king, and I never knew two kings who ruled the same palace," he was thinking. "So one of us gotta die," he mumbled as he watched his mother close the door. To leave him alone with his own thoughts, which was a deadly combination.

CHAPTER 21

'Bout Time

THREE MONTHS AFTER everything that happened, with the robbery to Pokey being placed in a coma, you woulda thought that woulda opened a few eyes, but it didn't. All it did was make us more heartless, 'cause at the same time, we had a place to be and a world to take over. So the heavens was the limits and any way possible.

"Yo, Pokey, you still ain't get in touch with ya Uncle Sico yet?" Fatboy asked.

"Na'll, dirty. I been trying to get in touch with that nigga since I been out the hospital. You know I need that cheddar that nigga took from us. Real shit though, it's like this nigga just disappeared off the face of the earth," Pokey said.

"That's the way it seems. Shit, if I woulda ghosted a nigga for his loot. I wouldn't answer the phone or come 'round either," Flick said.

"Yeah, but that's a dead giveaway. I know Unc ain't that damn stupid," Pokey said.

"Nigga probably somewhere, getting high or dead one," Flick put in.

"Y'all no, what else is funny though," Pokey said.

"What's that?" Fatboy asked.

"I haven't heard or seen the nigga Mr. Big since the last time he left the hospital and told him he was dead in my eyes," Pokey said.

"Shit, you can't even be mad 'bout that!" Flick screamed. "That's the same nigga who saved our life, then kept it real with you and told you he was your daddy . . . and you straight up dissed the nigga."

"Shit, I wouldn't holla at ya grimy ass either if I was that man," Fatboy said, meaning every word.

"Man, fuck that nigga and Sico too!" Pokey screamed. "Y'all either with me or against me. The way I see it, is, if them niggas wanna play the game dirty, than we can play by the same rules. Nobody ever said in this games there is ties. So somebody gotta win, and somebody gotta lose. See, he slipped when he showed us where he lay his head. You know niggas get caught slipping when dealing with emotions. When the nigga momma died, he was so caught up in his feelings, he lead us right to his spot. So now we got the upper hand, so it's his downfall, and our come-up," Pokey said, throwing our come-up out there to see what kind of response he would get from his two homies. As he watched their expression go from one of doubt to one of greed, he knew these niggas was on the paper chase and would be down to rob Mr. Big, and if he forced their hands, add some hollow points to his body, if the need arose.

"So, my niggas Fatboy and Flick, y'all ready to run these streets or what?"

"Dog, if the paper worth the chance, count me in. But at the same time, we gonna need a lil backup when dealing with a nigga like Mr. Big."

"Why you say that?" Pokey asked, becoming angry.

"'Cause he hated breaking bread with outsiders, but he listened anyways. First, dog, we really don't know the layout of the nigga crib like that, we only been there once."

"Yeah," Pokey said, "go on."

"And that time, it wasn't nobody there, but his fine-ass wife and his daughter Trirena. But who knows what type of shit this nigga got rigged up for shit like we planning."

"All right, dog." Pokey said. "I hear you, so let me here the plan. Listen, I'mma get in touch with Turtle and his two cousins, and see if they down to ride. And if so, then we gotta get in touch with somebody who holding and selling some fire, just in case we gotta bust our guns."

"In case the nigga wanna fight for what's no longer his?" Fatboy said. "'Cause to be honest with you, a nigga need all the butter he can get, especially when they 'bout to bring a seed in this world, and I can't help if I'm broke," Fatboy said flipping, his pockets inside out, showing he wasn't just talking.

"Damn, nigga, what happen to all the money you was supposed to save up?" Flick questioned.

"Come on, dog, you don't think I'm stupid. I got my momma a house being built, somewhere way out in the boondocks. In two mo' months, my people will have they own shit, courtesy of us and the street life," Fatboy said, smiling, remembering the smile he put on his mother's face when he gave her the keys to her own crib. As bad as she wanted to ask how, she kept her mouth closed and said, "Thank you, baby," knowing in two months, she'll be out the projects. That alone was enough to keep her worries in check!

"It's a good thing what you did for your old girl. I know she was happy," Pokey said. "Yeah, and it's a good thing we all getting our people up out the hood, 'cause after this shit go down, what we about to pull, it's gonna be hot 'round here. So being in the country want be too bad," Pokey said, shooting the breeze.

"Check it though, we on a time frame. We gotta try and have everything planned, right before our peoples move up outta here."

"Damn, nigga, why we 'bout to wait so long?" Pokey asked his friend, ready to smoke a nigga for the paper.

"Chill, dog, this ain't no game. We ain't gonna rush this, 'cause for one, we ain't talking 'bout hitting no small time-ass nigga. We talking 'bout a nigga that's clocking real figures, plus I still got a lil money put up for hard times like these, so chill," Fatboy said. "And just be patient."

"So when we gonna holla at the niggaz Turtle and them?"

"ASAP. As a matter of fact, I'mma see if I can get in touch with the nigga now," Fatboy said, flipping open his cell phone.

"Hold up, dog. First, how you know if we can even trust these dudes?" Pokey asked.

"The same way we trusted them to off Boo Boo, and Shine, that's how," Fatboy said back.

"All right, dog. It's your call," Pokey told Fatboy, staring him down. As Fatboy dialed the number, "Ain't nobody answering," Fatboy said. "Hold up, I'mma try again. Nope, this time the shit went straight to voice mail."

"So that kills that," Pokey said. "Since the nigga ain't picking up, check it though, let's roll. Let's ride around and see what we can get into," Pokey said.

"Let's ride," Flick said, opening his car door.

"Damn, I almost forgot," Pokey screamed. "Y'all hold up, let me go handle something right quick," he said, running up the stairs and inside the crib. As he ran to his room, he heard his momma scream out.

"Boy, you knew ya ass ain't supposed to be doing shit. Ain't that what that doctor told ya hardheaded ass!"

Yelling back, Pokey said, "Momma, I'm straight, that cracker don't know what he talking about!" he screamed while removing the shoebox from under his bed. This where he kept extra cash for times like these. As he pulled all the money out the shoebox, he stuffed the dead faces in his pockets and ran the same way he came. Before he reached the door, he heard his mother voice again saying, "Baby, be careful."

As he closed the door behind him and hit the steps two at a time, till he met up with pavement. Now walking over to the waiting car, he saw his two friends in a deep convo. "What's up? Y'all good or what?" Pokey asked.

"Oh yeah. Yeah, we good, dog," Fatboy said, bringing the convo to a close.

"Y'all ready to roll?" Pokey asked, jumping in the backseat.

"Yeah, let's burn up," Flick said, backing out. As they listened to Trick Daddy, "you don't know na nigga," blaring from the speakers, each person was in their own world, booping to the beat, when Pokey screamed, "Dog, turn that shit down right quick. That shit giving me a headache," Pokey said, grabbing his head, feeling the pain from his latest injury.

"You okay, dirty?" Fatboy asked.

"Yeah, I'm okay, just a slight headache from all this damn bumping Flick got in this motherfucker, that's all, but it's gravvy now," Pokey said, digging in his pocket and removing the dead mans he had saved up from out his pockets. As he began to count the money, he said to himself, "Damn, I gotta break bread with my niggas, 'cause we in this shit together."

"Well, y'all!" Pokey screamed. And Fatboy turned around in his seat, "What's up, dog?"

"What they do. Look," Pokey said, "I got 3,521 dollars in my name, so I'mma shoot y'all a grand a piece, and that should hold y'all fools a minute, at least until we catch up with my Uncle Sico and get our loot back."

"Man, you still stuck on that bullshit?" Flick said. "That nigga Sico probably in Canada some motherfucking where, balling outta control!" Pokey heard Flick scream, and they all laughed.

"Fuck that nigga. Here you go, Fatboy, and huh, nigga," Pokey said, slapping Flick upside the head. "That's for being funny."

"Oh, word," both his friends said.

"This what's up! Look, Flick. Dog, stop at the store right quick, so I can grab me a Tylenol or something, 'cause a nigga head pounding."

"All right, dirty, I got cha," Flick said, pulling up at the 7-Eleven, watching as Pokey exit the backseat. "Hurry up, nigga," Fatboy said to Pokey. "Fatboy, now that the nigga gone, remember what I was telling you before we left projects."

"Yeah, Flick, I remember. After this lick we do with Pokey, that's it, word," Flick said, "'Cause I'm trying to go to college and get paid the right way," Flick said.

"Man, we gonna see how this shit turn out. I hope it's enough cheddar to pull us away for good," Fatboy said.

Back inside the store Pokey felt like his head was about to bust, but realized it was a good thing he caught a headache, 'cause now he was inside the store with Turtle and some female.

"Yo, Turtle, what's up! What's good, man? I've been trying to get at cha today, but your cell kept going to voice mail," Pokey said.

"Yeah, dog, I told my shortie today it would be me and her, that's why I ain't answer. You know I ain't got nothing but my word, feel me?" Turtle said.

"Yeah, I feel you, dog. But what I need to holla at you about is some important shit. So listen, not to fuck up you and your lady's time, but tonight meet me at the underground club around eight tonight."

"All right, dog, I'll be there," Turtle said.

"One more thing," Pokey said, "bring ya cousins Rim and Lo-P."

"All right," Turtle said, smiling, knowing what time it was now. As Turtle and he chick left the store, Pokey walked up to the cash register and paid the chick for the Tylenol he just purchased and walked out the store, with a smile on his face. Making his way back to the car, he had a funny feeling about his two friends but couldn't put two and two together, so he left it at that and hopped in the backseat.

"Listen, I just holla at Turtle in the store. I told him to meet us at the underground club tonight at eight, so we can discuss business. He said he'll be there."

"Word," Fatboy said.

"That's what's up," Flick said, looking in the mirror at Pokey.

"So what we gonna do till then? We got plenty of time left to kill," Pokey said, looking at his watch, while saying under his breath, "By that time, shit should be on and poppin," just loud enough for his friends can hear. While driving around for 'bout two to three hours, they decided to make their way back to the PJ's to talk about how they were going to set things up. Entering the dark cloudy projects about twenty minutes later, they were reminded why this lick meant so much. As they exited the ride, they started making their way to Pokey's crib.

Fatboy and Flick screamed, "Man, I hope Mrs. Queen cooked, 'cause a nigga hungry as fuck!"

"But let's handle business first," Pokey said, looking at his two friends and asking them, "Man, y'all sure y'all ready to take this shit to the next level and run these streets?"

Fatboy said, "Dog, I'm ready."

And Flick said, "Count me in."

As Pokey looked at his two friends for any signs of weakness, after seeing none, he said, "All right, let's go ahead and get ready to wreck havoc, we only got a hour left, to be at the club. So check it, y'all go grab something to eat and then get dress, so we can burn up."

"All right," they both said, walking out the door, heading to their crib. As Pokey hopped in the shower, all he could think about was the come-up they would make, if everything went as planned. Ten minutes later he was getting out the shower, drying off, and throwing on a fresh fit with a fresh pair of Jordans. He picked up the phone and called Fatboy up. After the third ring, he heard Fatboy's voice.

"Yeah, what's up, dog?"

"Y'all niggaz ready to burn up or what?" Pokey asked.

"Yeah, dog, we ready. Flick on his way over now."

"All right, I'm leaving now," Pokey said.

"One," Fatboy replied. As he looked over himself in the mirror, liking the way his fresh white-and-blue Polo fit looked on him, with the fresh white-and-blue Air Force 1s, "Damn, I'm fresh," he said to himself. As he walked out the door to meet his friends, "Come on, nigga," he heard Pokey yell as soon as he stepped out the door, walking over to Flick's ride. He liked the fits his dogs were rocking, Flick was rocking a brand-new Jordan outfit, with the same color Jordan shoes, with a Philly cap and two gold chains around his neck. My dog Pokey had on some brand-new Nautica fit with a fresh pair of Jordans on, a simple chain, with a fat-ass watch. Anyway we were all clean and ready to act an ass if the need came, pulling off from the curb, listening to that (cash money) lights out bobbing our heads to the beats. 'Bout fifteen minutes later, we pulling up in front of the club.

"Damn, this bitch pack. It's a line damn near a mile long. Man, this shit gonna be off the chain tonight, they got some fine-ass bitches up in here tonight," Pokey said, looking around. Then Flick turned the music down.

"Let's find a parking space," Fatboy said.

"Nigga, what you think I'm looking for?" Flick said. After fifteen minutes of riding 'round, we finally found a parking space. As we exited the ride, we see three of the baddest females by the names of Peaches, Pumkin, and Coca. Everybody knew these chicks, call they were 'bout their issue, and making money wasn't a problem. Finally entering the club, we headed straight to VIP to wait on Turtle and his cousins. After waiting 'bout ten to fifteen minutes, Flick looked up from talking to this red chick that was all on his dick and let us know. Lo-P and Rim just entered the building, but no sign of Turtle. 'Bout two minutes later, Turtle came strolling through the doors, they he went right there, he walking over to Lo-P and Rim now. As all three niggas began walking toward VIP like they were dons, Fatboy and his dogs couldn't do nothing but laugh.

"Look at these niggas, they walking in this bitch like they own the shit, not even realizing this could be a trap and the end for them. Shh, here they come," Pokey said.

"What's up, y'all," Turtle and his crew said, entering the VIP room.

"Nothing, dog, just chilling, waiting on y'all," Pokey said, standing up, giving the niggaz some dap. Before they decided to take their seats, "Look, let's get straight to business," Pokey said. "I need y'all help again," Pokey said.

"Is it money involved," Lo-P asked.

"Always," Fatboy replied. "If its ain't 'bout money we wouldn't need y'all, believe dat!"

"I feel that," Lo-P said.

"So what's up?" Turtle said.

"Look, we got a big lick that can put us on top of the game, but first we need some fire power."

Turtle just laughed.

"Nigga, what's so funny?" Pokey asked.

"Oh, nothing," Turtle said. "The shit you just asked ain't no problem though," Turtle shot back. "Just let me holla at this nigga I know right quick. He got everything a army will need."

"Well, ain't no need beating 'round the bush. Go handle ya business," Pokey told Turtle.

"Chill, nigga. The nigga always come through here on Friday nights, so just be patient. Speaking of the devil, the nigga just walked in. See the nigga with the MIA Jersey on?" Turtle said.

"Who that tall black-ass nigga?" Flick said.

"Yeah him, that's my dog Black," Turtle said. "Let me go holla at him right quick," Turtle said, leaving the VIP room. After about ten minutes of talking back and forth, we see the nigga Black looked up here, and Turtle smiled and gave us the thumbs up sign.

"I guess all is good," Pokey said, watching Turtle and Black walk up the stairs to VIP. As Turtle walked in followed by Black, Black was the first to introduce himself.

"What's up, y'all? My name Black, and I heard y'all looking for the good goods, and I got what y'all need."

"Word," everybody said

As Pokey got up and walked toward Black with his hand extended, "What's up, you ready to talk business?" Pokey yelled over the loud music.

"Look, I really don't know you that good, but my dog Turtle told me y'all good people, so I'mma take his word on that and go against my better judgment and tell ya to follow me to one of my cribs, and we'll discuss business, as you point out what you like," Black said.

"That's what's up," Pokey said. "Let's roll, Yo, Fatboy and Flick, let's roll."

"Look," Black said, "we all know bullshit stanks and money talks, so let's make shit happen." As they started walking down the stairs, in Black's mind he knew he was dealing with so lames, or so he thought. So in his mind, all he could do was count the dollars he knew he would make off these niggas. "Another sweet come-up," he said to himself, as he hopped in an all-black two-door BMW.

"Y'all just follow me," Black said. As he watched the three youngins hop in a four-door box Chevy sitting on dubs, he smiled to himself. How sweet money always came his way so easily. 'Bout twenty-five minutes later, they pulled up to this big-ass house that was surrounded by other nice-ass houses.

"Damn," they all said, "this bitch here bigger than a bitch," they said, getting out the car. As they watched Black punch in a code, the door popped open.

"Damn, nigga, you living good," Pokey said.

As they entered the crib and looked around, they noticed how nice the bitch was in the inside, from the all-white fur rug, to the big-ass screen TV, to the sound sytem that goes through out the whole house.

"Damn, you got this bitch laid out," Flick said.

"Come on, I know y'all done seen better," Black said, being cocky. "Follow me, so we can handle business," Black said, leading them downstairs to a basement that was pitch-black, until Black hit a light switch somewhere that damn near blinded all us.

"Damn, nigga, what's up with this bright-ass light," Flick hollered.

"Oh, it's nothing. I put that shit in here, so you niggas can get a good look at all the shit I'm working with," Black said with pride.

"That's what's up? But next time warn a nigga 'bout that bright-ass light," Fatboy said, watching Black pull out all types of trunks from under this long-ass black table.

"So I guess this way they call you Black also, 'cause everything in this bitch black," Pokey said.

"Yeah, you can say that," Black said, pulling out gats from the trunks and laying them down upon the black table. As Black pulled out an AK-47, Pokey walked up to him, grabbed the AK, and asked, "Man, what you want for this piece right here?"

"Oh that, give me four grand and I'll throw in two clips," Black stated. And Pokey looked at this nigga like he done lost his mind.

"Damn, nigga, you trying to tax a nigga, like you the IRS or something? Or you must trying to get off on a nigga, thinking we lame and dumb, huh?" Fatboy said, removing the Glock 9 he had tucked in his back jeans.

"Hold up, man," Black started pleading. "Don't kill me, y'all can have all this shit," Black said, inching slowly backward, wishing he woulda never let these niggaz in his shit. But now was too late to act like a bitch, he was thinking, when he heard Pokey and Flick scream, "Man, fuck this nigga, GABOS," they said, as they watched with excitement as Fatboy pulled the trigger, emptying the clip in Black's face and chest. The first bullet entered his brain and killed him before he knew what hit him. The rest of the bullets found their resting place inside his body, as he lay prone on the floor with blood coming from everywhere.

"Tighten up!" Fatboy heard Pokey scream, which snapped him outta dreamland. "Hurry up, let's find something to put these gun in and burn up," as they all looked 'round the basement for something to put the guns in. Over in the corner Flick found two large gym bags. As he rushed to retrieve the bags, he came back to the table and watched as his friends loaded gun after gun in the bag.

"Look, if you touch it, take it with you," Fatboy said. "That way we leave no fingerprints."

"Word," they all said, as they began to make their exit, the thought of missing out on something good entered Pokey's mind.

"Hold up, y'all. Before we bounce, this nigga sitting too pretty not to have nothing in here, so let see what's up," Pokey said. "Fatboy, hit the upstairs rooms, Flick, hit all the closets, and I'mma check everything else. Make it quick, five minutes we out, with or without."

"Word," they all said, running in different directions. As Fatboy hit the third room, he came across a briefcase, throwing the briefcase on the bed, and popping the latches, he opened it to find stack upon stack. Closing the briefcase up with a big smile upon his face, he proceeded to run back downstairs. When he sees he's the lone ranger in the living room, he calls out, "Dog, y'all let's ride, we straight, I got what we need." As Pokey comes out the kitchen, he looks at the briefcase in Fatboy's hand and just smiles. "Jackpot," Pokey said.

And Fatboy said, "End of the rainbow."

"Flick, let's ride!" Pokey screamed.

"Hold up, I'm coming right now!" Flick screams, walking out the closet, holding what looks like four keys of dope.

"Nigga, what that is?" Fatboy asked.

"Nigga, what it look like, that good white them pigeons. Nigga, four of them thangs."

"Word," Pokey says. "Now let get all this shit up outta here." As Pokey grabs one duffel bag and Flick grabs the other fill with the guns and start walking out the door, they turn around just in time to see Fatboy sat the briefcase down, and the four keys on top of it, grab a lighter that's on the table on the living room table, walk over to the curtains, and set the bitches on fire. Placing the lighter in his pocket, he walks calmly back over to the briefcase and four keys, picks them up, and steps out the burning house, feeling like a rich man. Now that they came upon a good lick, they rush back to the car and pop the trunk.

"Nigga," Pokey tells Flick, as they load the goods in the trunk and hop in the ride. The only thing they hope for now is to make it back to the projects without being stopped by the police on the ride back. Everyone is quiet, deep in thought. As they pull up in the projects, they all began to smile, and that's when the talking began.

"Boy, we did that," Pokey said.

"Fatboy, you crazy-ass fuck," Flick said.

"Yeah, I know. Now tell me something I don't know!" Fatboy said, laughing.

"All right, y'all, enough of the bullshit. Let's get this shit upstairs and see what we working with!" Pokey said, all smiles. "Damn, we straight. What's that, Flick ask. Four keys and seventy thousand dollars.Pokey answer That's twenty-five grand apiece,Fatboy added fast. plus the money we'll make off selling these four birds. But in all reality, this ain't shit compared to the lick that's at hand when we rob that nigga Mr. Big Pokey said thinking out load. We should be on the young, rich, and famous." Fatboy said look at his friends. They all laughed, until they heard Mrs. Queen yelling.

"If y'all don't stop all that goddamn yelling in my house while I'm trying to sleep, I know something."

"Oh shit, my bad, Momma," Pokey said.

"I know it's your bad. Next time it's your ass," she said, and his two friends covered their mouths to keep from laughing at Pokey.

"Y'all let's burn up. We can talk outside somewhere."

"Word," they said.

"Before Mrs. Queen beat your ass," Fatboy said, running out the door, with Pokey and Flick on his heels. All three boys were feeling good with the come-up they just made. They just hoped in the back of their minds they would come out alive when they robbed Mr. Big, like they did on this lick. It's only so many chances a nigga gonna get in life. And they all sat around trying to figure out the next best move.

CHAPTER 22

Three and a Half Months Later

THIS SATURDAY NIGHT was the night they been waiting on. It's been three and a half months since they killed and robbed Black. They made sixty-eight thousand off the four keys, selling them at seventeen apiece. But this is the one lick Fatboy and Flick hoped would get them out the game for good, so they can enjoy the fruits of their labor. As Fatboy, Flick, and Pokey sat inside the baser all-black Chevy with tinted window, they saw Turtle, Lo-P, and Rim pull up in another all-black Chevy that they had the same baser rent in his name. So if anything went wrong, the cars wouldn't come back in their names. As Pokey pulled off, Turtle followed suit by following right behind them off to the journey at hand. The only difference was inside the ride that carried Fatboy and his to friends to their destination, it was quiet, the only sounds could be heard was the low sound of Tupac playing on the radio, "All I need in this life of sin, is me and my girlfriend, down the blocks to the bloody end, just me and my girlfriend." 'cause all three boys were deep in thought, thinking about the outcome. If things didn't go right, they knew it was a fifty-fifty chance they would either come out on top or be thrown to the bottom. Either way it was a chance they were willing to take. In the car following was Turtle and his two cousins, talking shit and loading every gun they brought with them.

In their minds, it's already said, "We'll rather be carried by six, then judge by twelve so everyone knew how they was going out. "Hold courts in the streets, thus style, back up front in the first tide."

Fatboy finally broke the silence, "Dog, what's up? Y'all good, 'cause y'all extra quiet tonight," Fatboy said, looking at his two friends, he hoped not for the last time.

"Na'll, dog, I'm cool, just mentally preparing myself for the battle at hand," Pokey said.

"And I'm okay," Flick said. "I'm just thinking 'bout my momma, and how she would go crazy if something happens to me. That's why we gotta be on point," Flick said.

"No fuckups. We feel you, lil dirty," Pokey said. "But chill, we 'bout to pull up close to this nigga's place of rest, so get yaself together," Pokey advised his friends who started pulling on the ski masks and black gloves to go along with the black dickey outfit they were rocking just for this night.

"That's what I'm talking 'bout," Pokey said, watching his two friends go to work, pulling their masks over their face. "Y'all niggas act like y'all ready for war."

"Ready for war, or ready to start a war?" Fatboy said.

"Dog, we ready for whatever," Flick said. But if the truth was told, his heart was ready to jump out his chest and run back to the projects, but somehow he kept it in check.

"Look, we gonna be in and be out, unless it's some problems," Pokey said. "Listen, we gonna walk through these woods, it's a path that leads to his house," Pokey said, turning the car off, getting out. As he watched Turtle pull up alongside him, "What's up? Y'all ready to set this bitch off like Jada?" Turtle said with a slight laugh, looking over, watching Rim and Lo-P pass the fire to Flick and Fatboy. As they were doing that, Pokey reached back inside the car and came back out, holding a baby Uzi.

"Damn, y'all niggas act like we 'bout to off the president, or rob the Twin Towers with all this fire we got," Rim said.

"Damn, I thought the war was in Israel, not Ocala," Lo-P said. And everyone laughed, trying to loosen up.

"Real shit though, it's better to be safe than sorry," Pokey said. "This a real live street nigga we dealing with, and nine times outta ten, the nigga ain't going down without a fight," Pokey said.

"Man, fuck that nigga, and fuck all this stalling. What's the plan?" Turtle asked, while mean mugging.

"Check it," Pokey said. "I know ain't no dogs or video cameras, 'cause don't nobody know this where the famous Mr. Big rest his head at. So shit should be gravvy getting in the house, as long as we go unnoticed, that is, I've been watching this nigga every move for the last three and a half months, and I never saw anyone come or go besides his wife and daughter." With that being said, Pokey began to think, "It will be fucked up if I let something happen to Trirena who's supposed to be my lil sister. Listen y'all, when we kick the door in, don't nobody open fire, unless a bitch bust on us first. If it's more than one person in the house, don't kill nobody without asking me," Pokey said.

"Man, you tripping," Lo-P said, sliding the hammer back on the ark.

"Look, nigga, either you gonna follow our lead, or you can burn up now and go on 'bout your business," Pokey said, angry. "Your choice."

"Man, y'all niggas on some sucker shit, a nigga supposed to shoot first, ask questions last," Lo-P said. "But this once, I'mma follow y'all lead, but the first sign of trouble, I'm doing me," Lo-P said, looking Pokey square in the eyes.

"All right, no more said," Pokey said, pulling the ski mask down over his face, as Turtle followed suit. "The plan is get in, get out, with as much as we can get from this nigga, y'all got that?" Pokey asked. As everyone was locked in on the house up ahead and as they creeped up on the house, it began to rain.

"Look at this. Luck must be rolling with us tonight. Now with the rain, it will drown out some of the noise we may have to make." As they started toward the door, they saw a light go out, then another one. "Well, we know somebody home," Pokey said.

"Now what?" Fatboy asked.

"We wait 'bout ten minutes, give or take, to give whoever that is, time to relax and get comfortable." Ten minutes later, Pokey said, "Let's do this," watching everyone get up off the ground, fire in hand.

"Lo-P, you and Rim, sneak up to the door, and on the count of 3, kick the door in, and we gonna run in and catch whoever off guard," Pokey said. "Y'all ready, 1, 2, 3!" Boom, the door flew off the hinges, as Pokey, Fats, Turtle, and Flick ran inside the house with gats out, screaming, "One wrong move, bitch, you die," as Rim and Lo-P came in right after them.

"Damn, this easy," Pokey was thinking. "Caught the nigga slipping, here it is. This nigga 'bout to get robbed, and we catch him lying on the sofa with his wife."

"How sweet, look like y'all was about to enjoy a nice movie," Turtle said, looking at the woman on screen eat another woman's pussy. "Damn, y'all freaky."

"Nigga, get ya bitch ass us. And if you wanna live, you better not try shit!" Pokey screamed, sticking the fire in Mr. Big's face. As Mr. Big sat up, he looked at the masked man and asked Pokey, "So this how you repay a nigga that fed your ass, huh?"

Caught off guard by the question, Pokey became heated and screamed, "Bitch nigga, what you just said, nigga? What you just said, don't sweat it jitterbug." Never knowing Mr. Big said what he said, testing the nigga reaction, 'cause everything about the masked man made him feel like this was his own son. And if his gut reaction told him right, he already knew if he made it out of this alive, he would kill his own son.

"Nigga, oh, you wanna play deaf?" Pokey said, slapping Mr. Big in the face with the pistol in his hand, which made a crushing sound, as blood poured from his nose. The force of the hit brought Mr. Big outta his thinking, "Look, nigga, we can do this two ways, the easy way or the hard way, it's your choice. So I'mma be nice and give you thirty seconds to decide, what you wanna do?" Pokey said, counting out loud, as Mr. Big just looked on in defeat.

"Listen, tie that bitch up to a chair or something, just in case she wanna be superwoman," Pokey screamed. As he stopped counting as he watched Fatboy place the gun to the woman's head and politely say, "Get your ass up, and, bitch, you better not scream or say shit, unless you want to leave this earth with a hole in your head." As the woman got up, she was shaking so bad, her blouse came open, revealing a perfect body with a fat pussy and nice-size titties. As everybody stared at the nude lady, she pulled her blouse together and tried to cover herself the best way she could. But Lo-P snatched the whole blouse off, leaving her standing there naked and shaking.

"Bitch, sit down," Lo-P said, and the woman slowly walked to the chair and sat down, with tears in her eyes.

"Nigga, your thirty seconds is up, what you choose?" Pokey asked Mr. Big.

"Nigga, I ain't got shit here, and she ain't got nothing to do with this," Mr. Big said in a calm voice, not blinking, just staring through the ski mask Pokey wore.

"Look, y'all two," Pokey said, pointing at Fatboy and Flick, "go check every room in this bitch, and make sure nobody else is here."

"Nigga, ain't nobody here, you ain't got to worry. It's nobody here but y'all and us," Mr. Big said, nodding his head toward his wife.

"Fuck, nigga, ain't nobody ask you shit," Pokey said. Pointing to Turtle, "Dog, roll with them, I got them two," he said, pointing at Lo-P and Tim. As he kept his gun to Mr. Big's head, he watched as his three friends went in different directions, trying to find more prey. "Now, listen, if you wanna make it through this, all I wanna know is where is all the money."

"Nigga, I told you I don't keep nothing here," Mr. Big said.

"Nigga!" Bam, bam Pokey slapped Mr. Big with the gun. "Who the fuck you yelling at? You think a nigga playing with your bitch ass, that's what you think. You think this a game, nigga?"

"No, all I see is history repeating itself, Pokey," Mr. Big said.

"What, damn, this nigga know it's me," Pokey was thinking. "Well, looks like you want live after all," Pokey said, snatching the mask off, revealing his identity. "'Cause you can call it history repeating itself, the difference is, it won't be nobody coming to your rescue. So like I said, you can make it easy or hard."

"Nigga, fuck you!" Mr. Big yelled. "Suck my dick, lil punk-ass nigga. I'm the same nigga who put ya punk ass on, now you on some cutthroat shit!" Mr. Big kept yelling till he heard Pokey said, "GABOS, game ain't based on sympathy, nigga. The whole time I've been plotting on your ass. See, sometimes you gotta play up under a nigga to get what you really want."

"Is that so," Mr. Big said, trying to get out the chair, but it was no use. Pokey hit him with the gun again, damn near knocking him out cold. As blood oozed down his face, he felt himself being tied up to the chair that was holding him up. As he lifted his head, he looked Pokey dead in the eyes and said, "Lil nigga, you better make sure you kill me."

"Oh, don't worry about that, it's taken care of," Pokey said, patting Mr. Big on the head. Just as Pokey took a step back, Mr. Big spat a glob of blood at him, missing by a feet.

"Oh, you wanna play tough guys. Look, bitch, if you wanna see this nigga alive again or yourself, you better tell him, to come up off that paper."

"Look, please, please, I'll take you to the bank in the morning and give you all the money you want," the woman begged. "Please don't kill us."

"Bitch, shut your stupid ass up. Do I look stupid or something? If I don't get that money tonight, somebody gonna meet the maker." As Pokey finished what he was saying, in came Fatboy, Flick, and Turtle, shaking their heads.

"All is good, ain't nobody here but them two, like the nigga said," Fatboy said, looking at Mr. Big to find him knocked out.

"Look, I got a trick for this nigga ass," Pokey said. "Look, Flick, go grab a pot of water out that kitchen right quick." As Flick came back carrying a cold pot of water, he watched as Pokey took the pot from him and threw the ice cold water on Mr. Big, bringing him outta his sleep.

"What, what the fuck," Mr. Big mumbled, looking up in the eyes of Pokey.

"Yeah, nigga, get your bitch ass up, it's party time. Since you wanna play so tough, I'mma see just how tough you really is. If you don't hand over that loot I know you sitting on."

"Nigga, like I said before fuck you, do what you gonna do."

"All right, Rim, Lo-P, and y'all, this nigga still wanna play Superman, but y'all know they say, a way to a man's money is through his heart. So I'mma see which one means the most, his money or his bitch," Pokey said, walking over to the beautiful naked woman, with tears streaming down her face. As she turned and looked at Mr. Big, he mouth the words, "I love you," but she knew in her heart, he wouldn't let nothing happen to her. As she heard Pokey say, "What's it gonna be, the money or your ride-or-die bitch?"

"Nigga, fuck you," Mr. Big spat, this time reaching his target. As Pokey wiped the spit from his face, he looked at Mr. Big and said, "No, nigga, fuck you." As he walked up to the woman, he forcibly pushed open the woman's legs to expose her nude pussy. He then rammed three fingers inside her. As she tried to close her legs and scoot out the chair, to no avail, the rags that tied her down were too tight. All she could do was shed tears and hope her silent pleas would make this nigga stop, but it didn't. As she looked at her husband for some help, with tears falling faster, he dropped his head in defeat, only picking it back up when he heard Pokey say, "Man, y'all untie this bitch, I got a trick for her ass. Since she seem to like this so much, she gonna love what I'm about to do to her."

As Fatboy started to stop Pokey from doing what he knew was wrong, he heard Mr. Big say, "You niggas gone die," and said, "Fuck it, GABOS." As Pokey started feeling on her nice firm titties, while still playing in her pussy with the other hand, she begged him to stop.

"Please stop, I'll tell you where the money at."

"Bitch, shut up. If that's the case you wouldn't let shit get this far," Pokey said, stopping what he was doing to say what he said. "You know what? Man, fuck this shit, y'all untie this bitch." As Rim and Lo P untied the woman, Fatboy and Flick looked at each other, shaking their heads, 'cause they knew this wasn't in the plan. But what could they do now? As the woman fell limp in Lo-P and Rim's arms, she collapsed to the floor. "Man, pick that bitch up and put her on the couch. No, hold up, as a matter of fact, throw her over the arm of the couch ass out, so Mr. Tough Guy can see me fucking her from the back," Pokey smiled. "Yo, Mr. Big, get a good look at this," Pokey said, spreading the woman's pussy lips open. As he unzipped his pants, he spat on his hand and wiped the spit between the woman's nice-size ass cheeks, then he rammed his dick inside the woman, blood raw, and the woman screamed out in pain, "Stop, stop! Please, please!" As she tried with all the strength she had to get away, she couldn't and realized she was in a no-win situation, with the two niggas who untied her now holding her down. All she could do was cry out in pain and hope this would all come to an end. She knew it wasn't a dream, 'cause she woulda been woke up, so she knew this was really happening to her. As the man she loved watched, suddenly the nigga behind her, who was trying to rip her guts out stopped, and she knew it could only be God who heard her. As she heard her husband say stop.

"Oh, now you wanna talk? You ain't so tough now," Pokey told Mr. Big as he stayed inside the woman.

"No, nigga, I just want you to know the same way you did her, I promise I'mma do you," Mr. Big said and laughed, "Ha, ha, ha, ha!"

"Oh nigga, you think this a joke? You find something funny?" Pokey said, pounding the woman again. With all he had watching blood ooze down the woman's asshole, as Pokey was on the verge of cumming, he stopped and pulled out. "Never leave no DNA," he said, stepping back, looking at the mess he made. "Damn," he was saying in his mind, "I'm tripping, but fuck it."

"Who's next?" As he looked at Fatboy and Flick, they just shook their heads no.

"I'm good," Fatboy said.

"Me too," Flick followed suit.

"Shit, hold up, don't speak for me," Rim said. "I got this," roughly flipping the woman on her back, grabbing both legs, and bending them over her head, ramming inside the woman's bare back. As she lay motionless, Rim looked over at Mr. Big and seen tears in his eyes.

"Yeah, nigga, this what happens when a nigga wanna be tough. Nigga, take your cheddar and fuck your rat, now you crying like a bitch while fucking his wife."

"All I can tell you," Mr. Big said, "is get all you can while you can, 'cause if I ever catch you in this life or in hell, I'mma fuck you up. That's my word. So just know and realize y'all are dead men walking," Mr. Big said, watching his wife go in and out of consciousness.

As she looked over at Mr. Big for the last time before blacking out, she said, "This nigga would rather die than tell these niggaz where the money at. If I knew I woulda been told," she said, blacking out.

As Rim busted a nut inside the woman, he got up, zipped his pants up, and started telling his friends, "Man, y'all go head, the hoe got some fire-ass pussy."

"Na'll, that's enough of that fuck shit, we came here for one thing. Now one thing done led to another. Let's get this paper and bounce," Fatboy said, looking at the bloody woman, covered in her own blood, remembering how kind the woman was to them complete strangers. "And she treated us like kings. She didn't deserve this." But he would never tell them that, 'cause he knew all they would scream was GABOS.

"Look, just tie the hoe back up!" Pokey screamed.

"Na'll, ain't no need for that, she out," Fatboy said, watching as the blood still poured out from her ass.

"Look, man, let's kill this nigga and burn up," Flick said. "It's obvious he ain't gonna tell us where the money at, so we wasting our time."

"No, fuck that," Pokey said, walking around the room. "We ain't come here for nothing."

"We see that," Fatboy said, looking at the woman, as he bent down and picked up the ripped robe and placed it over the woman's naked, battered body.

"We came for that loot, and we ain't leaving till we get it," Pokey said, looking at his dog sideways. "These niggas aint made for this," Pokey was thinking, as something came to his mind. "I got something that will make this nigga talk, as he walked back toward Mr. Big and pulled his head up, so he could look him in the eyes. "I told you before in my eyes you are dead. Look like I was right, wouldn't you say so," Pokey said, slapping Mr. Big in the face with three light touches. "If your look was a bullet, I'll be dead," Pokey said. "Look, somebody go grab me a knife from the kitchen right quick, see if a lil saying will work, a nigga will save his own life if you touch his skin. So let's see, how true the words of Satan's are."

"Man, you might as well kill me, 'cause I ain't telling your punk-ass shit," Mr. Big said out his mouth. But in his heart he knew he shoulda told the niggaz where the money was. But after what they did to his wife, he said, fuck it, he was thinking. As he felt a sharp point touch his neck, "You still don't wanna talk?"

"Man, fuck you," was the only words he got out, as the knife sliced through his thigh, Mr. Big tried to scream out in pain. But before he could, someone covered his mouth to bring the yell to just a mumble. As the woman slowly opened her eyes again, she looked over to see her husband bleeding from the head, now the leg. She tried to say something, but her words went unheard, as she started to say wait . . . , but the pain she felt inside her heart from her husband choosing money over love and her husband just watching her be raped was too much, and she passed back out. As Mr. Big tried to free himself, he saw his wife trying to say something, which brought joy to his heart, to know she was still alive. But before she got her words out, she blacked out again.

"Nigga, you ain't getting up outta that chair, so you can stop trying," Pokey said, watching Mr. Big struggle to free himself. "So you ready to talk or what?" And once again, he heard Mr. Big shout, "Nigga, fuck you!" And Pokey sliced him again, this time on the other leg, then in the chest. As blood gushed out from the open wounds, Mr. Big said, "Stop, I'mma tell you, but you gotta take me with you, 'cause you'll never find it solo."

"Is that so?" Pokey asked, knowing it could be a trap, but he had to take his chances while the nigga wanted to talk. "Okay, where the money at?"

"Then I just tell your lil punk ass. I can give you direction, but you'll never find it."

"All right, nigga, but if you on the bullshit, your wife will be the first to receive a one-way ticket to hell, and you'll catch her with the next bullet train through ya head. Look, Lo-P, Rim, y'all gonna ride with me. Turtle, Fats, and Flick will stay here and guard this bitch," Pokey said walking over to the lady, removing the robe and feeling her titties one last time before looking at Mr. Big to let him know he was dead ass for real. "Listen, untie this nigga, and if he try anything, kill him," Pokey told Rim and Lo-P, who were nodding in the affirmative, looking 'round the house. Pokey noticed a cell phone sitting on the charger. Walking over to retrieve it, he took his own cell phone off and threw it to Fatboy.

"Look every twenty minute, I'mma hit you up to let you know all is good. If I don't call, you know something with wrong. That means kill the bitch and burn up, okay?"

"I got you, nigga." Just as Pokey and Fats got through talking, Turtle came out one of the other rooms, holding a fresh round of duct tape.

"That's what's up, Turtle. You always on point, now let's tape this nigga up, like a Christmas present. First let's tape the nigga's feet. Now that that's done taped his hands."

"What about his mouth?" Rim asked, always asking a million questions.

"No, stupid-ass nigga. How we gonna get the direction if he can't talk."

"Oh yeah, you right," Rim said, looking silly.

"All right, we got the nigga taped up. Now let's load this nigga in the backseat," Pokey said, watching Rim and Lo-P carry the nigga to the car. As Pokey was about to exit the door, he stopped. "Yo, Fatboy, you got this right?"

"Yeah, nigga, I got this," Fatboy fired back, getting tired of this nigga thinking everybody was soft but him. "All right, I'll hit you every twenty minutes, word!"

"Word, nigga," Fatboy said, as he saw Pokey looking him dead in the eyes. "I guess the nigga trying to see fear but ain't none," Fatboy said. As Pokey closed the door behind him, jogging to catch up with Rim and Lo-P. As they made their way back through the woods to reach their ride, "Damn, nigga, what took you so long?" Lo-P turned around, asking Pokey as he jogged up to them.

"Oh, I had to make sure, shit was solid with them niggaz back there. We done did enough slipping already," Pokey said. As he walked behind Rim, carrying Mr. Big on his shoulder, while Lo-P kept the Glock 40's trained on his skull. Once they reached their destination, Pokey hopped up front, with Rim and Lo-P jumping in the back, with Mr. Big between them.

"Hold up, Lo-P, this shit gotta look right, just in case Po Po jump behind us. Shit, gonna look suspect with me driving, and three niggas coped up in the back. So Lo-P slide up front with me, Rim –"

"I know," Rim said, cutting him off. "Stay in back with this nigga, and if he try anything, bust his fuck ass, no more said."

"You on point, young nigga," Pokey replied to Rim.

As they pulled off, "Listen, if we get stopped by the police, I'm letting y'all know I'm holding court in the streets," Pokey said, "'Cause I ain't going back to prison, not with no kidnapping charge and possibly rape. Them crackers will fry our black asses."

"We with you, dog. Anywayz, you ain't have to warn us, 'cause we live by the code of the streets, live by, die by," Lo-P said, dapping Pokey.

"All right, nigga, we on the highway. Where to now?"

"Get on 1-95, when you reach the exit up ahead, bend a left," Mr. Big said, showing signs of pain from the beating.

"All right, we did all that. Now where to?"

"Make a left up besides the McDonald's up ahead." As Pokey was making the left turn, he snatched up the celly and called Fatboy.

"Yeah," Fatboy said on the first ring.

"All is good," responded Pokey.

"All right one, one," Fatboy said, passing the woman something cold to drink.

"Can I ask you a question?" the woman asked.

"Yeah, go 'head."

"Why y'all doing this to us?"

"To be honest with you, it's something personal. Not with you but your husband. I guess you can say, with you, wrong place at the wrong time." As they watched tears slowly fall down the woman's face, she asked, "Are y'all gonna kill us?"

"I wish I could tell you yes or no, but I can't. Only time will tell," Fatboy said.

As the woman started crying harder, "Listen, you gonna have to chill with all that fucking crying," Turtle said. "That shit getting on my nerves. We already slipping by letting you get comfortable, so unless you wanna get tied back up, I'll suggest you kill the crying."

"Okay," she said, dropping her head to her chest.

Twenty minutes later, Pokey found them pulling up to what looked like an abandoned building, but it was more like a warehouse when you got closer to it.

"All right, y'all, we here. So be on point, for any flaw shit." As Pokey climbed out the car, he grabbed his AK-47 and slipped the chamber back, ready to blast anyone, and anything if he had to. "Y'all get out and grab this nigga."

"Man, fuck carrying this heavy-ass nigga!" Rim screamed, bending down and unwrapping the tape from around his ankles. "This bitch can walk on his own two feet."

"You right, dog. Just keep ya eye on the nigga," Lo-P said, placing the same two Glock 40's in Mr. Big's face. "Try anything, nigga, and I promise these bullets will open your head like a melon. As they started walking toward the building, Mr. Big stops.

"Look, once y'all get what y'all came for, I'm free to go right, yeah, you free to go," Pokey said, looking at Mr. Big. And Lo-P and Rim stared in dumbfounded amazement.

"Remember a man ain't shit without his word," Mr. Big said.

As Pokey pushed him forward, "Man, shut your talking ass up and let's get this bread." Once they reached the door, they noticed the bitch had a lock on it. "Nigga, what's the combo number?" As Mr. Big stepped forward, he turned the lock this way and that way, but realized he couldn't open it with his hands taped, so he stepped back and screamed out the number: 26-17-17-10. As he watched Pokey turn this way, then that way, he heard the slight click of the lock popping open. As all four men walked in the building, looking for a light switch, Pokey put the AK to Mr. Big's head and said through gritted teeth, "Nigga, turn on the fucking lights." As Mr. Big did what he was told, the lights came on, momentarily blinding everyone. As Pokey screamed, "Damn, these some bright-ass light!" As their vision slowly came back, in front of them was a big-ass oak table that had twelve chairs and a big ass sixty-inch flat screen TV hanging on the wall. In the far left corner was a pool table, but what stood out the most was all the expensive paintings hanging on the wall.

"All right, nigga, where the money?"

"Nigga, look behind the third pictures on your right. The number is 17-23-10, the money is in there," he said, nodding his head in the direction he just told them, 'cause he couldn't open it himself 'cause his hand was taped together. "These niggaz so stupid, they don't even see the video recording all this shit," as Mr. Big fell into thought, "he said one thing for sure, if these niggaz off me, they got the same thing coming, so it's a rude awakening."

"Nigga, this better not be no trap either. Nigga, open the safe."

"The money in there," Mr. Big said, spitting blood out his mouth. As he saw Pokey open the safe and remove a bagful of money and screamed jackpot, reaching he hands inside the bag, feeling the Benjamins. "This what I'm talking 'bout!" Pokey screamed. Now what was so hard 'bout this? See, all this shit that went down could have been avoided, but na'll you wanna play big man. Now look, we still got the money."

"Yeah, you got the money, now what?" Mr. Big said.

"Hey, Rim, Lo-P, y'all check behind the rest of these pictures, and make sure this nigga ain't holding out."

"Man, you got what you came for, and that's it," Mr. Big said. "That's close to a mil right there, nigga. Come on, I know you got more than this, you sitting too pretty, just to be sitting on close to a mil."

"You gonna believe what you want, so fuck it, once they finished looking behind the pictures," Pokey told them to take the bag and wait on him at the car, he gotta have a word solo with Mr. Big. As he watched his two friends leave, he told Mr. Big to have a seat, pulling the chair out for him. Mr. Big limped over and took a seat as instructed. Once seated, he kept his eyes glued to Pokey as he walked around the table and sat in a chair of his own.

"So Mr. Big, a.k.a. Sterling, Pops, Dad, let me ask you a simple question, how does it feel to fall victim to your own flesh and blood? Not so good, huh?"

"Nigga, fuck you!" Mr. Big shouted. "I know that's how you feel, so you ain't gotta keep stressing the issue."

"I never was shit to you, that's why you was never around, huh?"

"Listen."

"No, you listen!" Pokey screamed, cutting Mr. Big off. "Just know it's a thin line between love and hate. See, I never told no one this, but while I was in prison, 'cause I tried to feed my family. A old school nigga told me he knew Uncle Sico, and that you was his older brother, and was supposed to have a son name Pokey. So I put two and two together and realized why Sico told me to call him Unc, and now why momma hated him, it's because of you. But what made mad sense was when he said the woman he had a son by was name Queen. Right then I knew it was me, and still to this day I never told a soul 'bout this but you. I knew one day I would find you and repay you for shitting on me and my momma."

"Boy, I didn't even know you existed!" Mr. Big yelled.

"I know, maybe if you woulda choose us over the street life, things wouldn't be like this, but karma always comes back around and kicks you in the ass. Good thing I'm on her side," Pokey said, pulling a Glock 40 from behind his back and pointing it at Mr. Big. As he was 'bout to pull the trigger, he stopped. "Damn, I gotta call Fatboy," he said, dialing the number. On the first ring Fatboy answered. "Yeah."

"All is good with me," Pokey said.

"Damn, nigga, one second later we was gonna off this bitch and burn up."

"Dog, we should be back in thirty minutes, so sit tight," Pokey said.

"Um, Pok, before you go, I want you to know we got somebody else tied up, but I promise we ain't gonna do shit till you get here."

"All right, as long as you got shit under control, I'm cool," Pokey said, hanging up. While Pokey was locked in on the phone, Mr. Big got up and slowly made his way up to Pokey. When Pokey finally noticed, Mr. Big was trying to pry the gun away from him, but he was too weak from the blood he done lost.

As Pokey pushed him down, Mr. Big started pleading, "Look, I swear I didn't know you was my son. Anyways, y'all got what y'all came for, so let bygone be bygone."

"Come on, old man, do I look stupid to you? I know if I let you live, you coming for me, and I can't take that chance. These streets will now belong to me," Pokey said.

"Man, I promise I won't fuck with you, that's my word."

"Yeah, and promises are made to be broken, right?" As he watched his own son raise the gun, he heard the words. "You showed no love, you will receive none."

"Wait, wait," Mr. Big said, stalling for time. "I'll make you a deal, you already have, you just don't know it. I win, you lose. I'm your blood, you just gonna off your own father over money," he cried.

"Na'll, this ain't really about money, this is something personal, between me and you. You was never around, so why try to be now?" Pokey said, letting a lone tear slip down his cheek. As he raised the pistol again, this time not to be sidetracked with all the talking, he lowered the gun from his face and shot him in the chest three times. *Boom, boom, boom*, the Glock 40 sang out in frustration. As Mr. Big felt the bullets enter his body, he said a quick prayer, "God, help me please." As he watched his own son leave him to die, as he struggled to breath, he had one thing on his mind, "If I can only make it to the phone, sitting on the table, I'll probably make it," he said, trying to pull himself up as he struggled to breathe. It was hard, but through all the pain, he reached the phone and dial a number. On the first ring Sico picked up, knowing the number by heart.

"Yeah, what's up?" Sico asked.

"Sico, Sico, I need help," Mr. Big pleaded in pain, while coughing up blood.

At the sound of his brother's voice, Sico's highness went away ASAP.

"What's wrong? I'm at the warehouse, and I've been shot. Call the ambulance," was the last thing Sico heard before Mr. Big passed out. Calling the ambulance then grabbing his keys to rush to his brother's aid. About ten minutes later, Sico pulled up to see police cars and an ambulance. Rushing out his car, he saw his brother being carried away in a stretcher.

"Hold up, sir, you can't."

"I'm his brother," Sico said.

"Well, he's been shot, but he's fighting. We have to rush him to the hospital before it's too late," they said, loading his brother in the waiting ambulance. As soon as they put him in the van, they took off. On the way to the hospital, the nurses went to work, trying to keep him alive. Three minutes later, they heard *bppppppppppp* as Mr. Big stopped breathing. The nurses went even harder trying to bring him back to life. "On the count of three, one, two, three," the nurse screamed, as she hit Mr. Big with the iron shocker three more times. As they were about to give up, they heard *beep, beep, beep*.

"He's breathing but barely. Hold on, sir, we're pulling up now." As they pulled up in shade emergency room, more doctors rushed out to save a life. As Sico pulled up in the parking lot, he grabbed his cell phone and dialed his brother's cell phone, hoping his wife had his phone. On the first ring a voice said, "Yeah, what's up?"

"Um, where Chris at? It's important."

When Fatboy heard the familiar voice, he hung up, thinking it was Pokey. "Damn, I hope my nigga good," he was thinking. When the cell phone rang again, "Yeah, what's up? Everything good?" Pokey asked.

"Yeah, dog, everything good, I was kinda scared for a minute."

"Why, dog?"

"Na'll, we just got a unexpected phone call from, oh, Sico. I hung up though."

"Well, listen, we'll be there in a minute, so just chill."

As Sico looked at his phone like it was crazy, in his heart he knew he heard that voice before, he just couldn't put a face with the voice at this time, but it will come to mind. "Plus I'll swing by there when I check on big bro," Sico was thinking, and he exited his car and ran inside the hospital.

"Sir, how may I help you?" a female said on the other side of the glass. As Sico started talking all fast, "Sir, you gonna have to calm down, so I can understand you," the woman said.

"Bitch, look, my brother just got shot, Lord knows how many times, and you telling me to calm down."

"Sir, it's the only way I can help you," not being fazed by the word bitch. In the hood, she knew she coulda been called worst, so she brushed the dirt of her shoulder and kept it moving. "Sir, what is his name?"

"Man, what type of shit is this? I just told you, my brother just got shot a million times, and you wanna know his name."

"Well, sir, for you information your brother ain't and will never be the only one getting bullets in his ass," she said, showing she could let her ghetto side show.

"My bad, you right, his name is Sterling Haywood."

"Damn, was that so hard. Now hold on a minute while I type in his name." As she finished typing, she paused, looked at Sico, and said, "Sorry, sir, but your brother is in the operating room as we speak, and no one is allowed in until the doctors are done."

"And how long will that be?"

"Sir, I can't tell you all that. All I can tell you is have a seat, and as soon as the doctors are finish, they'll tell you what's up. As a matter of fact I'll let them know you're his next of kin, that's all I can do," the woman said, closing her window.

"Fuck you too," Sico said under his breath, as he took a seat, he pulled out his cell phone, and dialed his brother's house. After five rings and no answer, he hung up. "Man, what the fuck is going on?" he said, standing up, josing for a hit.

When Fatboy and his friends heard the phone ring, they grabbed their guns they had close at hand, 'cause the sound of the phone ringing scared them to death.

"Chill out, dog, before y'all kill somebody," Flick said. "It's just the phone ringing." As he looked over at Trirena, Mr. Big's daughter, who was silently crying, she looked at her mother, who was in a bad state. "Damn," Trirena was thinking, "why did I have to come home to this? I knew something wasn't right, as soon as I got out the car, and I still came in here." As she heard her mother moan. "Why, y'all won't let us go?" Trirena asked, startling everyone in the house, and Turtle jumped up, looking like he was ready to slap Trirena. "Dog, if you wanna live past tonight, don't do it," Fatboy said, watching Turtle sit back down. Trirena finished what she was saying. "Why y'all doing this? Y'all already got my daddy, and y'all just gonna let my momma die," Trirena said, crying, knowing the whole time who two of the masked man were. It was the dark-skinned one who acted like he was gonna hit her that she didn't know.

"Look," Fatboy said, breaking her train of thought, "y'all gonna be all right."

"Yeah, ain't shit going to happen to y'all," Flick said, forgetting to disguise his voice. Not that it matter anyways, the lil lady sitting in front of them already knew their identity. "Listen, as soon as our boy come, we up outta here, and you can get some help for your old girl," Flick said, pausing 'cause he thought he heard something. "Chill, y'all, somebody coming," Flick said. "Be quiet." As they listened to the sounds of footsteps, all three boys had their guns cocked and loaded, ready to burn whoever walked through the door. *Knock, knock.*

"It's us!" Pokey screamed, walking into the house, with Rim and Lo-P behind him, all three rocking the ski masks again.

"Damn, y'all scared the shit outta a nigga," Flick said, coming from behind the sofa. As Pokey was about to say something, he froze in his tracks when he saw Trirena tied up to a chair, with tears streaming down her face.

"What the fuck," Pokey was thinking. "If it's not one thing, it's another."

"Yo, Rim, clean this shit up so we can bounce, and don't touch the girl."

"Hold up," Fatboy said, knowing what the lick was. As he walked over to Trirena, he whispered, "Look, I'm sorry about this, but some things I can't help." As soon as she heard the words, tears started falling one after another. As she felt her hands being untied from the chair, she knew someone was helping her out the chair, but the state of mind she was in had her elsewhere.

"Unplug every phone in this bitch. Make sure she can't call nobody, at least till we're good and gone. Flick, go outside and cut or slash hole in each car tires." As Pokey watched Fatboy take his sister to the game room, about twenty seconds later, he followed behind them. Standing in the doorway, he watched as Fatboy made her sit in another chair and tied her hands back up but not too tight. He turned around and walked off. As soon as he bent the corner, he heard *blaka, blaka.* And what followed hurt him to his heart, as he heard his sister's piercing scream. "No, please, God, no!" knowing in her heart that the sound she heard was two bullets going into her momma. As that thought came to her mind, she cried harder than she ever did in life. "No, please, please, God, not my momma." As she remembered the words her momma and daddy used to tell her: "Baby, ain't no rules in this game. Sometimes it costs to live this life, so always be prepared for the worst." As she looked up, she locked eyes with Fatboy for only a moment. As he dropped his head and walked away, Trirena began to think, the same rules they live by, GABOS, would also apply to them. She was already plotting revenge for the death of her momma, and she already knew she would go to any length to do it. As she dried her tears, she started wondering what's the fate of her father, 'cause she knew the outcome of her mother, and in her heart, she wouldn't stop seeking revenge until everyone involved was six feet deep or their body was floating in the ocean. It was now her business to find all the souls that played a part in taking her mother away from her. As she shed her last tear, she knew in order to win this game she had to turn her heart cold.

"They showed no mercy, they will receive none," she was thinking. As she heard the door slam, only then did she try to free herself. As she struggled with the ropes, they finally gave way. As she slid one hand after the other out the ropes, she got up, cracked the door open, and peeped round the corner, walking like a m into the living room. She dreaded what she knew she would see. Holding back a scream that wanted to escape her throat, she looked over at her mother's bloody body for what she knew was the very last time. As she cradled her mother's body in her arms, she saw firsthand how wrong they did her mother. As the blood poured down from the gunshot wounds, she made a promise to her mother. "I'mma get the people who took you away from me, Momma. I promise you," she said, rocking back and forth. With her mother still in her arms, as she looked down, she hoped her mother was now in peace, 'cause Triena knew she wouldn't have none "till the job was complete!"

"Waiting inside the hospital for over two hours, the doctors finally came out to speak with me," Sico was thinking. As the doctor walked up to him and asked him to walk with him a moment, he looked at the nigga like he was crazy, 'cause there ain't too many black doctors, but this nigga was black and his name tag read, "Dr. Van."

"Listen, Dr. Van, we two big boys, so just tell me what the fuck is going on with my brother!" Sico yelled, scaring the doctor.

"Sir, please calm down. I assure you we're doing all we can to help your brother. Right now he's on life support, he's lost a lotta blood, got shot in the chest three times. The good thing is none of the bullets hit major organs. We removed two of the bullets. The third one is still lodged over his heart. We stopped the bleeding, but to remove the bullet so close to his heart is dangerous, so we need your permission to move it, or let it stay. After a while it will heal on its own, and possibly with time, it will move up away from the heart. Then we can go in and remove it. That's the worst of his problems, like I said. The major problem is the amount of blood he's lost. He's still in the operating room, 'cause whoever did this tried to torture him, 'cause he had three bad knife cuts, one on the upper chest, two on his legs." As the doctor was about to say something else, Sico remembered the stranger answering his brother's phone and took off running, leaving the doctor standing there, looking flabbergasted.

"Damn, I'm really slipping," Sico said, hopping in his ride. "I gotta leave this crack shit alone," he said, punching the steering wheel, as he headed to his brother's crib.

On the way back to the projects, Pokey was deep in thought, along with Fatboy and Flick. Finally, Fatboy broke the silence, "What's up? Y'all two niggas good?"

"Yeah, dog, I'm good," Pokey lied. This was followed by, "I'm straight. I'm just thinking, that's all."

Flick said, "I just don't understand why y'all let that nigga off the woman. She was already outta there nine times outta ten. She wouldn't remember shit that happen."

"Yeah, I feel that, but it's a chance I couldn't take, 'cause you never know."

"So why keep Trirena alive? Why not off her too? What if she knew it was us," Flick asked.

"Dog, I doubt that. But if she did, they gotta prove it in the court of law."

"Nigga, y'all must forgot, y'all raped the woman," Flick said.

"Man, listen, fuck all that. If she knew, she ain't show it. And if she did and put the crackers on us, we all know ain't no such thing as justice in a white man's world. So I'm holding court in the streets."

"So what's up with Mr. Big?" Flick asked.

"Let's just say he took a nice, unwanted vacation, a long one. He won't be back no time soon. *Blaka, blaka!*" Pokey screamed, letting his friends know he handled business by offing Mr. Big. Once they pulled up in the projects, all six boys jumped out the ride, ready to see the profits of a hard day at work. "Y'all listen right quick," Pokey said. "If the police ever come around asking questions and shit, y'all don't know nothing."

"We cool on that, 'cause we know loose lips, sinks ships."

"Listen to this, the nigga said it's close to a mil in this bag. We gone split it evenly. Then everybody go their way, till tomorrow, and we'll hook up. That's cool?" Pokey asked.

"Yeah, nigga, cool," Lo-P said.

"Now let's count this money, so we can see what we working with. All right be quiet, 'cause I ain't trying to hear my momma talking shit," Pokey said, walking into the house with all of the rest following him. "Good, we made it without being seen. Now let's count this money," Pokey said, dumping the money out the bag.

"Goddamn, we rich!" Flick screamed.

"Nigga, shut up," Pokey said, punching Flick in the chest.

"Damn, nigga, my bad," Flick said.

"Well, it's gonna be easy to count this, being that they in stacks. Stacks of what though?" Fatboy asked.

"We just gotta find out," Pokey said, grabbing a stack and counting it. "Damn, they in five-thousand-dollar stacks, so let's count them by five." Ten minutes later, they were done counting the money.

"What we got, man?"

"We got seven hundred thousand dollars."

"Damn," Rim said, "we get what?"

"A hundred grand apiece, plus some change."

"Sweet lick, man. Just give us a hundred grand apiece," Turtle said, "so we can bounce."

"All right, huh," Pokey said, giving Rim, Turtle, and Lo-P the money.

"Nice doing business with y'all," Turtle said.

"Word," Pokey said. "Remember we gonna get up with y'all tomorrow."

"Word," Lo-P said, walking out the house with a bagful of money.

"Damn, dog, we hit the jackpot!" Pokey yelled.

"Nigga, calm down," Fatboy said.

"Look, y'all go get y'all book bags to put y'all cash in. We get 100,330 apiece. We rich, boy," Pokey said, watching his two friends shake their heads.

"We rich, but in the end what will it cost us?" Fatboy said, walking out the room, with Flick on his heels.

"These niggaz tripping," Pokey was thinking as they left.

"Seems like I been driving for hours," Sico was thinking as he pulled up in his brother's driveway. Looking at the house, he noticed all the lights were out. Getting out the car, walking toward the house, as he looked around, he saw all the cars sitting on flats. Now kinda scared, he ran back to his car, opened the glove box, and pulled out his 9mm. Sliding the chamber back, he rushed up to the house, hoping for the best. But seeing the worst as a picture of his brother's bloody body flashed before his eyes. Ringing the doorbell, he got no answer, so he tried the knob to find it unlocked. Hitting a light switch so he can see what happened. As the lights came on, reality came with it. What he saw broke his heart, as he saw his niece on the floor, holding her dead momma in her lap. As he walked toward her, she looked up with so much hurt and pain in her eyes that Sico couldn't hold back his tears. As she whispered the words, "She's gone, she's gone, it's too late." Trirena repeated this over and over until she felt her uncle removing her mother from her and placing her dead body on the couch.

"Trirena, I'm sorry, baby, we gotta go," Sico said in a sad voice.

"No, I'mma stay here with my momma, she needs me!" Trirena screamed.

"Tri, listen to me, please. It's nothing we can do for her. I wish it was, but it's nothing we can do. Baby, I know this is hard on you, but your father needs you. He's fighting for his life as we speak."

At the mention of her father, she spoke up. "What you just said, Uncle Sico?"

"I said your father needs you. He's in Shane Hospital, fighting for his life. I just left there, and they still operating on him. He was shot three times in the chest. Whoever did this tried to kill him, but somehow he's still fighting. I think it will help if he can hear your voice."

"Okay, I'mma go, but I gotta get these clothes off," Trirena said, looking at the clothes that her mother's blood now lived in.

"Baby, do what you gotta do. Just hurry up."

"Uncle Sico, listen, please don't call the police. I promised Momma I would handle this, and I gotta keep my promise to her or I couldn't live with myself," she said, walking toward the shower.

As he watched his niece head in another direction, he wondered if she knew something he didn't, but he decided he would ask her when she got her mind clear. Ten minutes later, Trirena walked into the front room, fully dressed, rocking a Polo shirt and a Polo skirt, with a pair of all-white Air Force 1s. As she looked over at her mom, she blew her a kiss, then started walking toward the door. Turning the knob, she stopped and remembered.

"Uncle Sico, I gotta use your car. I remember them saying slash all the tires and unplug the phones." As she said that, Sico said, "That's why I couldn't get through." Digging in his pants' pockets to get the keys, he said, "You right, all the cars sitting on flats," tossing her his keys. "I'mma handle this," he said. As she closed the door, he removed his cell from his belt loop and dialed a number. On the first ring, a voice said, "Talk to me."

"Look, this Sico. I need y'all again, come to big Sterling crib ASAP."

"We on our way right now," the raspy voice said, hanging up.

"Well, that's done," Sico said, thinking of his niece. He knew his niece was a sweet girl, but if and when she felt crossed, he knew she would become coldhearted like her daddy. "I guess she had the streets running in her veins," he was thinking. He got up and turned the lights back off, now wondering who coulda did this. "I know now I gotta go holla at his son Pokey, but I'll wait a few days to find out how my brother is doing before I step to him. Just in case my bro wanna keep the attempted murder on his life a secret. He just might know who did this and want whoever did this to believe he's dead. If he pulls through this, which I know he will," Sico was thinking, when he saw lights through the window. "Well, that was quick," he said as he opened the door and showed the two black men the body they would be removing. Without questions, they loaded the body in a bag and walked to the van. Coming back after they put the body in the van, they walked up to Sico and said, "You know where to send the money!"

"I got y'all," Sico said, closing the door and walking back inside the house.

CHAPTER 23

Ruthless

AFTER TWO HOURS of waiting, Trirena was finally able to go see her father. As she entered the room that held her father's life in its hands, she mentally prepared herself for the worst. As she listened to the sounds of all the machines, she saw her father hooked up too. She almost shed a tear at the sight of her father lying helpless in the hospital bed. Making her way closer to his side, inch by inch, she looked around the room, hoping that all this was a dream. But the image of her dead mother is what made her realize this is all reality. As she held her father's hand, she listened to his labored breathing, looking at her father like this made her question God. And she whispered, "Why, God? Why my mother had to get killed? Now you got my daddy fighting for his life." As she rose up above her father and kissed him on his forehead, she said, "Daddy, I need you just like you need me. I lost my mother. Please don't make me lose you too. Fight, Daddy, please. I know it's more peaceful in the world you're in now, but we got revenge to pay to what those niggaz did to Momma and you. I know you're not going to let it go down this way," she said, hoping to hear an answer from her daddy. But receiving none in return, the only answer she received was the sound of the machines and the heart monitor going *beep, beep, beep*. As of right now, that was all the hope she had and needed.

As she prepared herself for the fight that's about to go down, taking her seat beside her father and grabbing his hand again, she wanted to let him know it was time, time for her to step up. She will always be his little girl, but things were about to change in Ocala, all because they killed her mother, who was innocent in her eyes. "Fuck the rules of the game," she said aloud. "As of now, I make my own rules," she said, shaking her head at the sight of her father. "Daddy, you always told me to be prepared to take care of myself, if something every happen to you or Momma. Well, Momma's gone, and them same niggaz got you on life support fighting for your life. So as I speak, it's me against the world. I'm sorry this had to happen, I know you never wanted me to get involved in the game, but when you're forced to do something, it's nothing you can do about it but go with the flow," she said, rising from her chair. Looking down at her father, who looked so helpless, she kissed him on the cheek.

As she made her exit, a major change took over. The once-sweet girl was now ready to get back. As she calculated her next move, she stopped at the nurse's station. "Please don't let nobody in his room, 'cause I don't know who did this, or if they'll come back to finish him off," she told the nurse.

The nurse replied, "I can do that, but what about the man who was here three hours ago, Mr. Sico?"

"Listen, ma'am," Trirena said in a nice voice. "If it's not me or the doctors, I don't want nobody in his room," she said, walking off, but stopped and turned around to add emphasis. "Listen, if anything happens to my father, I'm coming for you. I promise you that," she said, smiling politely, like they were the best of friends. And she made her exit, promising not to return until her father was doing better or she had to prepare for his arrangement to go to heaven. Either way, it was the only time she would step foot back in this hospital, 'cause she couldn't stand the sight of how fragile her father looked. And she hopped in her ride with one thing on her mind, "Time to play the game." As she heard the words play over in her mind that her daddy used to tell her: "Baby, life is not always a matter of holding good cards but sometimes playing a poor hand well." As she prepared herself to face the ones who killed her mother, she knew she had to play this off to a T. She was thinking as she jumped on Highway 200, heading back home, 'cause tomorrow she would head to the projects to see her brother. Thirty minutes later, she was home, and as soon as she walked into the house, all the memories of her and her mother and father came back all at once, making her break down to her knees, but she stilled herself to get up and not shed a single tear. As she looked around the house, she noticed it was clean. Just like nothing happened. Looking at her uncle, who was asleep on the sofa, she wondered, "How could he sleep at a time like this?" Walking over to the sofa and tapping his foot, she whispered, "Uncle Sico, Uncle Sico, I'm back."

As her uncle opened one eye, then the next, slowly sitting up, he asked, "How you doing, baby girl?"

"What kinda stupid-ass question is that to ask?" she was thinking, but she answered anyways. "I'm holding up."

"So how's my brother?" Sico said.

"Really, he's still on life support, but he'll bounce back," she said. "He's a fighter, it's just a matter of time," she said, sitting on the sofa beside her uncle.

"So you took care of my mother's body."

"Yes, I did, but why you didn't wanna have her a funeral or something?"

"'Cause that's a giveaway. I want whoever did this to feel like we just gonna let the shit blow over. That way they won't be asking questions about my father," she said.

"I understand," Sico said, thinking, "Smart move." And he looked at his niece again. "Baby, you sure you all right?"

"Yeah, I'm fine," she said, reaching for the picture on the table that was of her and her mother smiling together at the zoo. "Life is crazy. One minute shit is going good, next it's falling apart," she was thinking.

"Trirena, if you need me, I'm here," he said, giving his niece a hug. "I got all the tires fixed on the rides, so you can get around."

"Okay, thanks," she said, as Sico got up to leave. When he reached the door, she called out, "Uncle Sico!"

"Yeah, sweetheart, what's up?"

"Tomorrow morning I'm going to tell Pokey his father got killed and that they killed my momm."

"And why you gonna do that?" Sico said, looking at his niece like she done lost her mind, 'cause her daddy ain't dead.

"'Cause I want everybody to believe he is," she said.

"And what if he asks about the funeral?"

"I'll tell him you got rid off the bodies, till we find out who did this," she said, slamming the picture down, watching glass fly everywhere as the pain flowed through her heart.

Sico asked, "Baby, you sure you gonna be okay?"

"I'm straight, Uncle Sico. Please go 'head and do what you gonna do. I'mma be all right. I'm just trying to put this broken puzzle in my head together, about who could have done this and why?" she lied to her uncle, knowing the whole time who did this. She just felt she had to throw her uncle off beat, 'cause she knew if he knew who did this, he wouldn't hesitate to kill whoever did this. But her plan was to make whoever did this suffer a slow and painful death, like her mother did. She was in deep thought, when she heard the door slowly being closed, and that's when she got up, plugged the phone back in, and made a few phone calls to a few trusted friends. Picking up the phone and calling her cousins, she knew they would be down with the plan. After three rings, a female voice said, "Hello, what's up?"

Trirena asked, "Bre, where Blessing and Tahshama at?"

"They right here, why?" Bre asked.

"Look, I need y'all help. Something just went down, but I'll explain it to y'all, when I come scoop y'all up, just be ready," Trirena said.

“All right, Cuzzo, you know we with cha, no matter what it is. Do we need to bring our girlie-girlie stuff?” Bre asked.

“Yeah, do that,” Trirena said. “Look, be ready in about one and a half hour and dress to kill, and be ready to play a little cat and mouse game.”

“Word,” Bre said, hanging up the phone.

She almost felt bad about bringing her cousins in on this, but she remembered GABOS.

As she took a shower and relaxed for a moment, she was thinking of a master plan! One, they would sidetrack her brother and his friends to make them believe she didn’t know it was them.

CHAPTER 24

Thrown but not fazed

As TRIRENA JUMPED out the shower, she grabbed a towel and dried off. Once she finished drying off, she looked in the mirror and said, "Damn, I look a mess." She began to apply makeup to her face from the many forms she had on; she applied this and that. And when she was done, she complimented herself and said, "I wouldn't say so bad myself," smiling for the first time. As she walked out the bathroom and into her room, going toward the walk-in closet, opening the door, she stared at the many outfits she could choose from, walking in, picking this outfit and that outfit. She stopped when she came upon an all-pink Baby Phat short skirt set. "This should do the trick," she said, looking down and grabbing a pair of white-and-pink Air Forces from out the box that held them hostage. "I knew y'all would come in use," she said, looking down at the brand-new shoes. As she laid the outfit on the bed, she began to get dressed. Once dressed, she put her shoes on. Looking around the room, she ran over to her dresser. Looking at about ten different purses, she grabbed an all-white Gucci purse and walked out her room. Once in the hallway, it dawned on her, "Damn, I need some fire." Running to her mom and dad's room, she hesitated as she opened the door. Looking inside the room, memories came flooding her mind. As she shook the thoughts, she stepped in the room and walked over to her father's dresser. As she reached the dresser, she stopped when she saw a picture of her mother and father holding hands, smiling. Picking the picture up, she looked at it and smiled. As she said, "I love y'all," she put the picture back in its rightful place.

Opening the top drawer, she moved a few clothes around, until she came upon a black 9mm. Moving some more clothes around, she found a box with bullets in it. Picking the gun and the bullets up, she tossed it on the bed. As she closed the dresser drawer back, she walked over to the bed, sat down, and bullet by bullet she loaded the gun. Putting one in the chamber, she hit the safety button before dropping the gun in her Gucci purse. Before walking out the door, she looked over at the key rack, walking over toward it. She reached up and grabbed the keys for the BMW. She knew this would get her brother's quick attention. As she exited the house, she was now headed to pick up her cousins.

Back at the projects, Fatboy, Pokey, and Flick were sitting outside on the hood of Flick's ride, waiting on Turtle and Lo-P, as well as Rim, to show up. As they were waiting, Pokey was still trying to get in touch with his uncle. "Man, I done called this nigga five times already, and this nigga still ain't answer the damn phone," Pokey said in an angry tone.

As Fatboy said, "Man, just chill, the nigga will surface soon. It's just a matter of time, that's all. And when he do, we'll be waiting," sliding off the hood of the car to stand up and stretch.

"Damn, these niggas taking forever," Flick said.

"Call them niggas and see where they at," Pokey said, passing Flick the celly. As Flick dialed the number, he was thinking, "This nigga act like he got a do boy," Flick was thinking, when he heard a voice say, "Yeah, what's up?" Turtle said.

"Nigga, where y'all at?" Flick asked.

"Oh, we had to make a lil stop," Turtle said, "but we on our way now. Give us 'bout twenty-five more minutes."

"All right, Flick said, if y'all ain't here in twenty-five, we out."

"Word," Turtle said. About twenty minutes later, a BMW pulls up in the projects, scaring the shit outta Pokey and his friends. They thought they were seeing a ghost, till outta the car stepped Trirena and her three cousins.

"What's up, lil bro!" Trirena yells.

"Oh nothing, what's up, and where Mr. Big at?" Pokey asked, trying to find something out.

"To be honest, we ain't seen him or Uncle Sico. But my reason for coming 'round is to tell you I think something bad done happen," Trirena said, faking tears.

"Why you say that?" Pokey asked.

"'Cause, 'cause last night, they broke in our house and killed my momma."

"Who is they?" Pokey asked, looking crazy.

"I don't know who they were!" Trirena screamed. "But they killed my momma, and I don't know where my daddy at."

"Tri, just chill, I'mma see what I can find out. You gonna be okay."

"I guess I am," Trirena said.

"Look, I'm about to burn up when my dogs get here, and I'mma swing by the house later."

"Another dead giveaway," Trirena was thinking. "This nigga ain't show no emotions, so he know what's up! But it's all good. I got a trick for his ass."

"Look, when y'all come, bring your friends over, my cousin gonna be chilling with me till I feel better, all right?"

"Bet," Pokey said, "I'll swing through 'round 1:00 a.m."

"Okay," Trirena said, walking back toward the car.

"Damn, I thought that nigga came back from the dead," Pokey said to his friends, as Trirena pulled off.

"I told y'all she don't know shit, that's good," Flick said.

"So what's up, what we gonna do?"

"Well, shit, here go Turtle them now, and being that we all young and rich, we might as well spend a lil cheese before we hit the club."

"I'm feeling that, Fatboy," hopping in the rid but feeling kinda strange with the way Trirena was acting, but he kept his thoughts to himself, as he looked out the window and at his friends smiling and laughing. In his heart, he knew this wasn't the end; he just prayed that what he was feeling was just a mind thing. "Shit, I'm young and rich, why am I tripping?" he said to himself. As he watched his dogs hop in the ride and pull out behind Turtle and his cousins, the last thing that came to mind was something his mother used to always tell him before they turned the music up, blasting Rick Ross, warning before destruction! Warning before destruction was the last thing that crossed his mind, as he began to bop to the beat.

Part 2 coming soon!

CPSIA information can be obtained
at www.ICGtesting.com
Printed in the USA
BVOW04s1312150517
484183BV00001B/11/P

9 781483 640945